Lucy's whole body began to tremble as his lips descended to hers, and she sought to forestall what her heart knew was inevitable by reasoning with him.

'This isn't what we planned,' she whispered, shuddering as his lips trailed a hot path across her cheek to seek her ear. 'You promised...'

He smothered what she had been about to say with his mouth, kissing her long and deep until Lucy shivered with the waves of tension shooting through her. The instant he felt her trembling response his arm tightened, supporting her.

'Don't worry, Lucy,' he murmured huskily. 'I'll stop whenever you tell me to.'

Imprisoned by his protective embrace, reassured by his promise and seduced by his mouth and caressing hands, which had found their way under her shirt to bare flesh, Lucy clung to him, sliding slowly into a dark abyss of desire.

Author Note

I read numerous books across all genres. I write Historical Romance and I am never not writing.

Lucy Lane and the Lieutenant is set in the Regency period, a time when people lived through one of the most romantic and turbulent ages of British history. Of course you can't write about the Regency period without the Peninsular campaign popping up somewhere. When I began writing this book I knew very little about it, but what I did know was that novels about that time must have conflict. I wanted to write a story that touched on the campaign but without the battles, for the conflict to be between my two main characters, Lucy and Nathan. It was for this reason that I chose Portugal as a backdrop, when the country was relatively quiet and the battles were being fought over the border in Spain.

Portugal is a world away from Lucy's life as an actress on the London stage, but when her old love, Nathan Rochefort, a spy in the British intelligence, reappears in her life and asks her to accompany him on an assignment—to rescue a woman and her child being held for ransom by rebels in the mountains in Portugal—being hounded by creditors and tempted by the money Nathan is offering, Lucy agrees to go with him. It's a rocky road they travel as they make their way into the Sierras, but then the road to true love is never easy.

LUCY LANE AND THE LIEUTENANT

Helen Dickson

® and TM are trademarks owned and used by the trademark owner
and/or its licensee. Trademarks marked with ® are registered with the
United Kingdom Patent Office and/or the Office for Harmonisation in
the Internal Market and in other countries.

First published in Great Britain 2015
by Mills & Boon, an imprint of Harlequin (UK) Limited,
Large Print edition 2015
Harlequin (UK) Limited, Eton House, 18-24 Paradise Road,
Richmond, Surrey TW9 1SR

© 2015 Helen Dickson

ISBN: 978-0-263-25566-9

Harlequin (UK) Limited's policy is to use papers that are natural,
renewable and recyclable products and made from wood grown in
sustainable forests. The logging and manufacturing processes conform
to the legal environmental regulations of the country of origin.

Printed and bound in Great Britain
by CPI Antony Rowe, Chippenham, Wiltshire

Items on Loan

Library name: Ballyclare Library
User name: Mrs Barbara Todd

Author: Dickson, Helen,
Title: Lucy Lane and the lieutenant
Item ID: C901393256
Date due: 6/7/2018,23:59
Date charged: 15/6/2018, 10:38

Helen Dickson was born and still lives in South Yorkshire, with her retired farm manager husband. Having moved out of the busy farmhouse where she raised their two sons, she has more time to indulge in her favourite pastimes. She enjoys being outdoors, travelling, reading and music. An incurable romantic, she writes for pleasure. It was a love of history that drove her to writing historical fiction.

Chapter One

1812

The elegant, dignified creature who made her way down the stairs was the very epitome of poise and grace, beautiful and refined. Her gown was magnificent, creamy pale gold satin with tight elbow-length sleeves and a low heart-shaped bodice adorned with delicate golden-white lace. Her maid Polly—a nineteen-year-old redhead who fussed over her like a mother hen, seeing that she got the proper rest, the proper food and all the services suitable to a lady of the theatre— had stacked her hair on top of her head in glossy chestnut curls, leaving three long fat ringlets to dangle down between her shoulder blades.

As she reached the bottom of the stairs Jack was there to take her hand. 'Happy birthday,

Lucy. You look adorable,' he said, raising her fingers to his lips.

The startling green eyes sprinkled with gold that glinted from under black eyelashes sparkled and the lovely mouth curled with the suggestion of a smile. 'Thank you, Jack,' she answered coolly, wishing she didn't have to attend this party being held in her own house, a small but charming establishment in Leicester Fields. 'I can't help thinking all this is a little over the top and premature. I'm beginning to think it would have been more appropriate to celebrate my gaining the part to play Portia when they see how well I perform the role. The cost of all this has practically ruined me.'

'It isn't just about that. It *is* your birthday, darling,' Jack purred, 'though how you can be twenty-four when you look much younger defies logic.'

'And you always were a wretched liar,' Lucy remarked, laughing softly.

'You are growing older and wiser, Lucy, I grant you—and more beautiful. Maturity becomes you. Now come along,' he said, drawing her hand through the crook of his arm. 'Everyone is waiting for you.'

There was a rousing burst of applause as they entered the tastefully furnished drawing room. Although the house was small, the drawing room was large and airy with windows looking out over a small flower-filled garden. Decorated in shades of white, pale green and gold, with a lovely pearl-grey carpet on the floor, it was an ideal place for entertaining and roomy enough to accommodate several people. A buffet table had been set up, offering a lavish array of food.

They were immediately surrounded and separated, and Lucy found herself being ever so vivacious and charming to a host of actors, writers, poets, romantics and wistful dreamers and a pack of persistent journalists from Fleet Street who bombarded her with questions and compliments. The company would no doubt become rowdier as the evening wore on and more liquor was consumed.

Lucy was one of those lucky people who was hopelessly in love with the very activity from which she made her living and, since her aunt Dora's savings were now depleted, enabled her to keep the elderly lady in her small but comfortable accommodation. But not for much longer if her finances didn't improve.

In the theatre nothing was certain and the thought that she might sink into penury was a constant worry for her. The past few years had been a struggle as she sought to achieve some success in the world of theatre—a success that would mean relief from the crushing weight of bills that hounded her daily. Aunt Dora had suggested that she give up her rented house and move in with her, halving the bills, and Lucy knew the day was fast approaching when she might have no alternative. But she had lived with her aunt for most of her life and her independence, which she cherished, had been hard won.

At four and twenty and unmarried, Lucy had been employed as an actress since she was fourteen. Almost a lifetime ago, she reflected somewhat ironically. To play Portia in Shakespeare's *The Merchant of Venice* would be her crowning glory. It was a dream she'd nursed since embarking on her career. Opening night was four weeks away. She was terribly excited, but she had much to do before the production took to the stage.

Jack handed her a glass of much-needed champagne. Looking handsome in black-and-white evening attire with an ivory-silk waistcoat, eyelids drooping lethargically over his sleepy brown eyes, his light brown hair neatly brushed, he looked particularly attractive.

'Thank you for rescuing me, Jack. Those journalists certainly want their pound of flesh—if you'll pardon the pun,' she jokingly remarked with reference to Shylock in *The Merchant of Venice*.

Jack cast a casual eye about the crowded room. 'Nevertheless, those chaps from Fleet Street will grow to adore you. They'll soon be writing about you, about the most beloved and talented actress that ever graced the London stage—unaffected, a woman who doesn't give herself airs and graces. Make the most of it while you can.'

Lucy gave him a wry look. 'They will continue to write about me while my popularity lasts, Jack, but I'm a realist. An actress is only as good as the part she plays. The minute the cream roles begin to dwindle and someone else comes along, prettier and more talented, she will disappear into obscurity. It happens all the time.'

Jack gave her a look of reproach. 'You are too cynical for your own good, Lucy. Enjoy your fame. It will last, I am sure of it.'

'You flatter me. Had I been blessed with the talents of Sarah Siddons I could understand it.

As it is I am just one of many actresses trying to earn an honest crust.'

'You wouldn't starve if you married me,' he uttered softly. Lifting a glass of port from a tray on the table, Jack studied her décolletage with an appreciative eye.

Taking a sip of champagne, Lucy smiled tightly. 'Please, Jack, don't look at me like that. I've asked you not to and I've given you my answer. I don't want to marry you. I don't want to marry anyone just now. But thank you for the flowers you sent. They are lovely, but I do wish you wouldn't buy me gifts all the time.'

'Why not? Nothing is too good for my favourite girl. You're not objecting, I hope.'

'No, of course I'm not,' she answered. 'They are lovely.'

She'd been on the back foot when Jack had asked her to marry him. His proposal had been totally unexpected. From the beginning she had told herself she wouldn't refuse his friendship, but anything else was out of the question. He was the youngest son of a peer of the realm, an aristocrat. She was an actress and quite beyond the pale in the upper echelons of society. Men like Jack made women like her their mistresses, they did not marry them—and she couldn't be sure that Jack would honour his promise, once he had got her into bed. He did have one asset to his credit—he possessed a sizeable fortune. But to marry a man for his wealth alone was distasteful to her.

Since they had met one year ago at the theatre she felt as if her life had been taken hostage. Had she given serious thought to the consequences of yielding to his attentions in the beginning, she'd have turned him away right then and there, refusing his gifts of flowers and a book of sonnets. Yet she had been reluctant to be so harsh, for it had been painfully obvious that he was feeling out of kilter since being wounded out of the army. His first visit had led to another and he was soon squiring her about town on a regular basis. Jack was a ladies' man and popular in any company. He was also fun and delightful to be with, but she was always careful to keep him at arm's length and out of her bed.

The truth was that his kisses reached no deeper than her lips and the closeness of his body lit no fires inside her. Some other man had already claimed that privilege by touching his spark to all her deepest and most secret passions. With a kiss that had barely brushed her lips he had breathed his life into her and with his touch as light as a sigh he had marked her as his own.

For a moment she was transported back in time into the arms of her handsome lover, so tall and powerfully built, with eyes as warm as the sun and a smile that melted her senses with wicked pleasure. But that was a long time ago. She had moved on since then. Nothing was to be gained by looking back. She had been bitten once and was determined not to let it happen again. She tried not to think of that time—of the man who had broken her heart—but would find her thoughts turning to him of their own volition. And then she would thrust them away, not wanting the spectre of him to spoil what she had now.

At that moment Lucy's closest friend, Coral Gibbons, a saucy but talented young actress in a fetching low-cut salmon-pink gown, arrived with her latest beau in tow. Jamie Shepherd with his dark blond hair charmingly tousled was a budding young playwright. Coral gave her an affectionate hug, her hazel eyes sparkling and her wide mouth curled with the suggestion of her pixie smile.

'You'll be marvellous as Portia,' she exclaimed.

'Although I must tell you that I fancied the part myself. Are you excited?'

'Of course, Coral. What actress wouldn't be? It's a role I've always wanted to play and I'm so grateful to Mr Portas for offering me the part.'

'The great theatrical manager knows a good thing when he sees it. You'll be an enormous success, I just know it. Your last play was brilliant. You deserve all the acclaim you've received.'

Lucy laughed. 'It's nice of you to say so, Coral, and though I welcome such praise you do have a habit of exaggerating.'

'Nonsense! You'll soon have every theatre manager in London wanting you. You've worked hard and you deserve it, love. But don't work too hard and do think about coming to Ranelagh on Saturday night. You'll love the Rotunda and the pavilion, and the gardens by moonlight are so romantic. Jamie will be our escort and we'll have a marvellous time. Bring Jack along if you like. The two of you seem to be getting closer. It's not gone unnoticed that he hardly lets you out of his sight.'

Coral's remark brought a disgruntled frown to Lucy's brow. 'He is attentive, I agree—so attentive that I'm in danger of suffocating.'

'I don't mind telling you, love, that I worry about you. I really do. A woman as lovely as you should have a dozen beaux, should be going out often. I know you had a very unpleasant experience with that man in the past you told me about—the one you were going to marry and then dropped because you found out he'd been unfaithful, but not all men are like that.'

'No?'

'Well…' Coral hesitated. 'There are a few good ones out there, I feel sure of it. Still, I don't mind telling you that if I didn't have Jamie on tap I'd give you some strong competition for Jack.'

'Be my guest, Coral. I've told him I will not marry him, but he's the persistent type—at least where getting me into his bed is concerned. I'm no naïve, gullible green girl. I don't believe for one minute that he's serious about marrying me.'

'Neither of us is getting any younger, love. My advice to you is to grab him while you can. As his wife or mistress he would be useful. He's rich and titled to boot—the answer to all your money troubles. Men like that are few and far between.'

'You've noticed,' Lucy said.

'Don't be modest. A woman is always flattered to learn a man finds her attractive.'

'As you will know,' Lucy said laughingly. 'It's evident Jamie is head over heels in love with you.' She glanced at Jamie talking animatedly and loudly to Mr Portas.

Coral looked over at her beau thoughtfully. 'Jamie's had far too much to drink already and was vociferously declaring himself the greatest English playwright since Shakespeare as we walked along the street. He's just finished writing his new play and is testing the great man out to see if he might be interested in reading it, but I don't hold out much hope. Mr Portas doesn't like new productions.'

'That's because they're expensive, risky and time-consuming. We both know they can be damned into oblivion by the audience on the first night. The cost of new scenes, costumes and music often make it ineligible to a director of a theatre to accept a new play, especially when it's considered that the reviving of a good play would answer his end of profit and reputation.'

Coral sighed. 'Unfortunately I think you're right. Mr Portas always favours a good old English drama. Duels, brooding heroes and doxies, bloodshed and battles, that's what the public want. I don't think Mr Portas will give Jamie a moment of his time, but he lives in hope. I'd best go and rescue him, although I have a favour of my own to ask the great man.' Leaving Lucy to talk to a cheeky reporter, Coral sidled over to ask Mr Portas, a portly, much-liked dramatist—volatile and mercurial when things weren't going his way—in a slightly rumpled blue suit, if he would consider her for a walk-on part in *The Merchant of Venice*.

It was close on midnight when the guests began to depart—some to stagger out in jovial good humour. Lucy was about to say goodnight to Jack when Polly came to her. The girl looked agitated, for she kept wringing her hands.

'Polly? Whatever is the matter?' Lucy enquired.

'There's a gentleman to see you,' Polly said hurriedly. 'He's in the parlour.'

Lucy looked at her with a measure of amusement. 'The parlour? Why on earth didn't he join us?'

'He said it's a private matter, Miss Lane. He seemed very anxious to see you, but said he'd wait until your guests had gone.'

Momentarily surprised and curious as to who

this visitor could be to call on her at this time of night, Lucy stared at the closed parlour door.

On the point of leaving, Jack came to stand beside her. 'I think I'd better stay.'

Lucy started to speak, but before she could do so, the parlour door was flung open and a man strode out. He was so tall that the top of his head nearly grazed the door frame under which he instinctively ducked. He wore a black military-style coat with brass buttons and a white linen shirt and neckcloth. His narrow hips and muscular thighs were encased in black breeches and his gleaming black boots came to his knees. His unfashionably long hair was drawn back to the nape and secured. It was as black as his coat. His eyes were as cold as Antarctic ice floes, and gave his face with its high planed cheekbones a harsh expression. His mouth was wide and full, the lower lip with that cruel curve she remembered. A thin scar ran down his left cheek in a tanned face harder than iron and a gaze that could only be described as impudent. The scar only served to add a touch of glamour to the nobility of his perfect features.

Lucy caught her breath in her throat and for a moment the world seemed to stand on its end.

Although she had not set eyes on this man for four years, she recognised at once that proud and arrogant form. There could be no mistake.

It was Nathan Rochefort, the man whom she had almost married four years ago, the man she loved—had loved—with all her heart and soul, and now he was the man she most hated in all the world.

The blood drained from her face as she stared at him, unable to comprehend that he was here, in her house. Her heart pounded and her knees grew weak. She steadied herself, willed herself to hold the hysterics at bay. She was paralysed, unable to speak for the moment. The reality didn't frighten her at all. She was shaken, yes, alarmed, too, and she was mad as hell, but she wasn't at all frightened as she stared at Nathan. She drew air in her lungs and calmed her trembling body, eyeing him surreptitiously.

There was a health and vitality about him that was almost mesmerising. In all, he was even more handsome than she remembered. It unnerved her, especially when those thoroughly light blue eyes locked on her and slowly raked her. She had forgotten how brilliant and clear they were. In some magical way they seemed capable of stripping the deceit from whatever had passed between them before. It was all she could do to face his unspoken challenge and not order him out of her house.

In that moment the locked chamber in her mind burst wide open against her will and the memories came flooding back, bringing with them all the pain and anguish she had suffered four years ago. As she looked at him, at his fine strong body, she could almost feel again his hands cupping her breasts and a mouth, hot and sweet, caressing the softness of them, kisses bruising her lips and searing down the length of her throat, strong arms crushing her against a hard body, and the bold thrust of this man between her thighs. She blushed profusely at her own musings and immediately banished the memory, stiffening her spine as she recollected herself.

After a courtship of considerable length and a date set for their wedding, without warning to anyone, overwhelmed with anger, humiliation and a deep sense of betrayal when she had discovered his affair with her closest friend, Lucy had broken off their engagement and disappeared from his life.

And now here he was, as large as life, about to insinuate himself into her world once more.

'I would appreciate a moment of your time,' he said in low, clipped tones.

'Indeed! You have no right to come to my home unannounced,' Lucy said coldly.

'That is a social nicety I chose to waive. The nature of my visit cannot wait.' His glance flicked to Jack, who was unable to conceal his astonishment. 'Please excuse us. What I have to discuss with Miss Lane is of the utmost importance.' Without more ado he strode to the door which led on to the street and held it open.

Jack looked at Lucy. 'What the devil is this about, Lucy,' he demanded. 'Who is this fellow? I'm damned if I'll leave you alone with him.'

Lucy knew she had to reassure Jack. He clearly feared for her. What did he expect? What did *she* expect? 'It's all right, Jack. Please don't worry. This gentleman means me no harm.'

'You know this man?'

'Yes. This is…' She faltered, not knowing how he should be addressed after all this time.

'Lieutenant Colonel Nathan Rochefort,' he provided sharply.

His voice had the same rich timbre and Lucy began to wonder if he had any flaw she could touch upon and draw some strength from. 'Lieutenant Colonel Rochefort and I are acquainted. Don't worry. Please go, Jack. I'll speak to you tomorrow at the theatre.'

'Very well.' His voice sounded mulish. Turning, he strode in the direction of the stern-looking stranger holding the door open with an impatience that he was clearly finding hard to control. Jack paused, looking into a face a foot above his own. 'If you touch her, I'll…'

'You'll what?' Nathan's lips curled with mild contempt. 'Goodnight.' Without more ado he closed the door almost before Jack had time to pass through.

'You must also leave,' Lucy said, her tone brisk.

Nathan's eyes slid towards her and trapped her in their burning gaze. 'Not yet. We have to talk— if you please—'

'I do not please,' Lucy cut him short disdainfully. 'If you have anything to say to me, you may write to my aunt Dora, who deals with most of my correspondence and engagements. She will tell you if I am able to receive you—if I want to.'

'I haven't time for that—although I do intend calling on your delightful aunt. She will not turn me away.'

He was right. Aunt Dora had a soft spot for

Nathan Rochefort—always had. He could wind her round his little finger. As handsome as he was, she could imagine that he had grown quite adept at swaying besotted women of all ages to do his bidding. He did seem to have a way about him and she could not fault any woman for falling under his spell, for she found to her amazement that her heart was not so distantly detached as she might have imagined it to be. Even his deep mellow voice seemed like a warm caress stroking over her senses.

Shaking off the effects of what his presence was doing to her, Lucy took herself mentally in hand and reminded herself of all she had suffered at his hands. Better to remain aloof and save her pride.

'You may be right. Aunt Dora is easily taken in, but my own nature is less trusting.'

He looked at her hard. 'Then it's up to me to make you change your mind. We have to talk.'

'We don't *have* to do anything. We have nothing to talk about.' Considering the turmoil within her, her voice was curiously calm. Her proud, disdainful green eyes met and held his without flinching. For a moment she studied this man, whom she had once loved to distraction. She had believed in him as a god, would have gladly promised to love, honour and obey him had they made it to the altar. So many things had changed after that. As a soldier, when the war with France had broken out, he had left for the Continent. She had got on with her life.

'You cannot be aware of the impropriety of such a visit at this hour, or you would scarcely have ventured to knock on my door. What you have to say must be very grave indeed to justify such behaviour.'

'Hospitality would not seem to be your strong point,' he stated coldly. 'However, what I have to say to you will take a little time—besides being a somewhat delicate matter.'

Striding to her and taking her arm, he led her into the parlour and banged the door shut with his foot on a stupefied Polly, who remained staring at the closed door for several moments before turning away and setting her mind to tidying up after the guests.

In the parlour, Lucy regained her composure and glared at the intruder, and when she spoke her voice was filled with barely suppressed fury. 'I really did not think I would see you again. I confess I am astonished at your impudence! We have been apart four years and then you suddenly appear and demand to see me as though nothing had occurred.'

'It was you who ended the relationship, not me.'

As he spoke, Lucy sensed that he was struggling to contain his anger and decided to speak boldly. 'Yes, I did. It was my decision.'

'And like a fool I awaited your explanation— if you had one to offer—of your astounding conduct. Your explanation and your apology. It would appear that you were suddenly bereft of your senses and of the most elementary notions of respect towards me.'

Lucy stared at him, astounded that he should turn the blame for ending their relationship on her. 'Apology?' she said clearly. 'I think it is not I who should apologise.'

He looked at her, his eyes alight with anger. 'What did you say?'

'That if anyone has been insulted, it is I! What I did was for the sake of my own dignity. I thank God that before it was too late my eyes were opened and I saw that it would be folly for us to marry. But enough of this,' she said, having no intention of humiliating herself by raking over old coals that had long since burnt out. 'I do not have to explain myself and I have no intention of doing so.'

'I do not ask you to.'

'Then why are you here? To see whether I should recognise you? To see if you were still at all like my memory of you? After four years, how would I know?' And she didn't know, for he was changed. Where she had known him as light-hearted with many pleasant sides to his character, she now perceived an air of seriousness about him. He displayed nothing of the easy, fun-loving man she had once known. Perhaps the hardships and tribulations of the war had stripped all humour from him.

'I find you greatly altered, Lucy,' he remarked in a matter-of-fact way. 'Not to your advantage.'

The brutality of his remark, his look of almost elementary politeness, did not impress Lucy in the least. He had long ago lost the power to intimidate her—even assuming he ever had. On the contrary—his rudeness helped to affirm her self-control and she permitted herself a sly smile.

'I doubt you have come here to ask me to do duty for a mirror. These past years have not been easy for me, not even profitable, but I don't see that my private affairs concern you.'

'I was not referring to your looks, but to what is inside you—and no one asked you to suffer.'

'No, I know that and I am still here, carrying on, doing what I like doing best. Please say what you have to say,' Lucy said irately. 'I have no wish to prolong this interview.'

He smiled crookedly at her under drooping eyelids. 'No? Surely this is a most affecting moment,' he stated with heavy irony. 'Two people once betrothed to each other, together again after such a long absence—especially after believing themselves parted for ever. My dear Lucy, you should be glad to be reunited with the man you loved—for you did love me, my dear. You were quite devoted to me as I recall.'

Lucy had had enough. 'That will do,' she retorted sharply. 'You are amazingly impertinent.' She was not going to remind him how he had trampled on that innocent love in the bed of her closest friend. 'You have the audacity to talk about what was between us as if it were merely another of those delightful escapades you men discuss over your brandy.'

Nathan shrugged, but his eyes shifted to avoid Lucy's sparkling gaze. 'It was you who, for some reason, turned it into a huge tragedy. From what

I understand, I was not the only one to be ostracised by you.'

Lucy's head came up sharply. 'Please explain what you mean by that remark? Who are you talking about?'

'Katherine.'

The name fell on Lucy like a hammer blow. Her eyes flew to his, anger, hot and fierce, in their depths. 'Please do not mention her name to me. I will not speak of her. If you insist on doing so, then I will order you to leave my house this instant.'

Nathan held up both his hands, palms outward, a warning bell ringing in his mind telling him not to pursue this. But whatever it was that had gone wrong between Lucy and Katherine was raw. That was clear. Knowing this, there was need for caution.

'I see you haven't changed, Nathan. Still stuffed with the same arrogance and conceit, which I must confess were two of the attributes I most despised in you.'

He appeared totally unfazed by her stinging barb, which angered her further. 'Indeed? You should have told me how you felt when we were together.'

'I doubt it would have made any difference.'

'It might. Speaking of arrogance and conceit, I see you are closely acquainted with Lambert.'

She glanced at him pointedly. 'You know Jack? How?'

He shrugged. 'I have no interest in Lambert. He's well connected. Unfortunately he wasn't thought clever enough for anything except the army. After spending a couple of years in the military where he had a tendency to search out opportunities to benefit himself—where he got too comfortable with the camp-followers—the female kind, I might add,' he said, raising a well-defined brow, 'I doubt his habits have changed and he continues to dally here and there at his leisure. I'm sure you know the type.'

'Yes, actually I'm afraid I do,' Lucy replied, gritting out the words. It nettled her sorely that he should seek to besmirch Jack's character when his own reputation was far from exemplary.

'What do you want?' she demanded. 'What is the reason for this rude intrusion into my home? You have not sought me out to ask about my health or to discuss the weather.' He seemed solemn, earnest. She stared into the frank light blue eyes and something fluttered inside her. 'I have had a long day and I am tired and wish to go to bed, so please get on with it. Say what you have to say and make an end. What do you want?'

He cocked a brow. 'If I were not a gentleman, I ought to answer you. But however delectable you are, Lucy, that is not why I am here. No. For the present my wants are more practical.' His lips curved into what could almost be described as a smile, but it did not reach his eyes. He went and sat down in a large tapestry-covered armchair that stood by the fire, stretched out his long booted legs comfortably and looked up at her.

Lucy stood several feet away from him, her arms crossed over her breasts, visibly struggling against a growing anger which made her eyes gleam like two hard green stones. Even now, after four long years—a lifetime, it seemed—he was still the most handsome man she had ever known. There were lines at the corners of his eyes and mouth that hadn't been there when they had been affianced and the scar was new, but she was sure he could still turn a woman's head. Which was what had happened to her, when she had been young, naïve and vulnerable to the point of stupidity.

'The reason I am here, Lucy, is because I wish

to enlist your aid in a matter that is of extreme importance.'

Containing her surprise, Lucy stared at him, raising an eyebrow, hoping it would convey her scepticism. 'My aid? For what, may I ask? Four years ago you did not need me or my aid. Why now?'

Getting to his feet and clasping his hands behind his back, he turned and looked back at her, watching her with a disconcerting gaze. 'The past is behind us. For the present that is where it must remain. There is the serious business of a war going on and it has demanded my complete attention for the past four years.'

Lucy realised he was serious in his request. He was a tall man, over six feet by several inches, and he seemed at that moment to fill the room. Watching him warily, she didn't understand where this conversation was leading, although she had a strange tingling in the pit of her stomach, a tingling suggesting she would not be pleased with what he had to say.

'Please continue.'

For a moment he seemed to lose himself in contemplation. When he next spoke it was in a musing tone. 'What you don't know is that from the beginning of the war against France I have been working with a branch of the government which operates completely in secret, a branch which reports only to the Prime Minister. I have been given an assignment in Portugal. It concerns the Duke of Londesborough—who happens to be a very close friend of the Prime Minister.'

The tingling had become an aching dread. Wishing her mouth were not so dry, Lucy cleared her throat. 'What are you saying? That you are a spy? What nonsense is this? You'd best explain yourself, and quickly, for I have no time to listen to this.'

Nathan did not smile, nor had Lucy really expected him to. Becoming thoughtful, he turned his back on her. Turning to face her once more, he moved closer, pinning her with his penetrating gaze. 'I spent twelve months in Portugal, where I was wounded and sent back to England to recuperate. When I was restored to health I did not intend going back, but on being given this assignment I am left with no choice but to return. The families concerned mean a great deal to me. I consider it my duty to help them.'

Lucy made an impatient gesture with her hand. 'I see—although I really don't see what all this has to do with me. I know absolutely nothing about politics and spying, nor do I wish to.'

'I can understand that. The majority of women find the subject of no interest and if I remember correctly you were one of them. But I do need your help.'

Lucy had to look away because he was staring at her with such intensity she found it most disturbing. She straightened her skirt as if to straighten her thoughts. The atmosphere in the room was beginning to weigh on her. She was tired and her head was aching.

'My help?' she repeated. 'I really do not see how I can be of any help to you.'

'I want you to come to Portugal with me—to work with me. I have done such tasks before when a certain degree of discretion is required—it would appear I am rather good at subterfuge. But this time it is different.'

'How?' she demanded.

'Because you will be with me.'

She stared at him incredulously. 'You want me to become a spy? That is rather far-fetched, even for you. It's quite ridiculous.' She laughed, although she did not feel amused. 'I am an actress—just that. Nothing more and nothing less.'

He gave a low, sardonic chuckle. 'I'm not asking you to become a spy. It's true, you are an actress, which is one of the reasons why I have chosen you to help me. You also have other qualities that recommend you. Not only are you beautiful, Lucy Lane, but wise, too, and witty and clever. You have too many talents for a mere actress. I would like you to know that what happened between us before has no bearing on my decision to ask you to assist me in this. It was a purely practical decision. It is my opinion that you are ideally suited for the mission I have been set.'

For a span of several heartbeats she said nothing, then, 'I will not agree to do whatever it is you require of me. I refuse to do it. I will not. Let me remind you that I have no talent for the—the profession you propose, that it is altogether strange to me. You are asking me to give up the theatre—for if I agree to this mad scheme that is what it will amount to and I cannot afford to let that happen. I have a safe and comfortable profession, one that I happen to like. I will not give it up for something so uncertain. What is it you would have me do? What is so important about this mission?'

Her angry reaction to his request came as no surprise. 'At present I cannot tell you the whole of it for I have not been fully informed. All I know is that an English woman and her child have been captured by a band of ruthless deserters—soldiers from both sides—and they are being held for ransom in the mountains.'

'I am sorry. Are they terribly important, this woman and her child?' she asked, horrified by the woman's predicament.

'To her family, yes, she is. You will be working with me. I can't pretend that it won't be a great undertaking for you. Where we are going is exceedingly dangerous. Going through the lines is perilous in the extreme. You will be put at risk.'

Lucy's eyes opened wide. 'And you would expose me to such danger?'

'With reluctance, believe me, but it is necessary.'

'But—why me?' she asked, slightly bewildered. 'Surely the risks would be lessened were you to take someone who is accustomed to Portugal—to the mountains—a soldier, perhaps.'

'If I could be certain the captives have come to no harm then, yes, it would. Unfortunately the woman was wounded when she was taken hostage. If she has not died of her wound then she will be considerably weakened by her captivity. The journey out of the mountains will not be easy. I need a woman to take care of her—and her child.'

'But—how can you ask this of me?'

'You are the only one I can ask, the only one I can trust. I ask you to trust me, Lucy.'

'Trust you?' She shook her head in disbelief. 'I think not. Either I am mad, sir, or you are.'

The savagery in her tone startled him. 'We don't have much time. I ask you to think about it.'

'I have. We haven't seen each other for four years. Much has changed. *We* have changed. My answer is no. Now I would like you to go. We have nothing else to say to each other.'

He cocked a brow nonchalantly. 'No? Tell me, what have you been doing for the past four years? When I left for Spain I heard you had left London with a travelling theatre company.'

'I did—not that it is any of your business. For three years I worked in the provinces, gradually building my reputation before returning to London. I was lucky. I got the breaks I needed.'

'I am sure talent had something to do with

it—having observed you on several occasions on stage.'

Taken off her guard by this, she stared at him with surprise. 'You have? I didn't know.'

'How could you? I was careful not to let you see me. However, I would add that many women are beautiful, but very few have that personal magnetism that marks them out. I believe your aunt Dora had it, too. She was the toast of the town in her day.'

He was right. Aunt Dora had been an actress by profession. She had seen Lucy's potential and put her on the stage. It had paid off.

Lucy was too beautiful not to have been the recipient of many admiring looks and advances from men. Usually she brushed them aside with a laugh that conveyed the message but gave no offence. Nathan was not like that. When he had remarked on her beauty he had been stating a fact. He did not flatter. He did not smile invitingly. They knew each other too well for that. There had always been an arrogance about him. Now he seemed harder and self-absorbed. Had the war done that to him? she wondered.

Her expression was one of contempt. 'Why, what's this? Flattery from you? Coming from you it is insincere and I prefer you didn't use it on me.'

'It's not flattery. I am sincere in what I say. You know, you make me almost sorry for the past. You were beautiful then but now, with a maturity about you, you are more so. No man could help but desire you. It suits you to be angry. It makes your eyes sparkle.'

He let his eyes dwell appreciatively on her lovely face and caress the long, graceful throat and the proud curves revealed by the low-cut bodice of satin and lace. 'Don't play the fool with me, Lucy. You are an accomplished actress. Moreover, you speak French like a native. That is a valuable asset for what would be expected of you.'

'I have no mind to get myself killed for a cause that is nothing to do with me.'

'You cannot refuse to at least give me the opportunity to change your mind.'

'It would be a waste of time. My mind is made up.'

'Is there nothing I can say to induce you to agree?'

'No. Nothing. That is my last word. There is no point in our meeting again.'

'Shall I command you, Lucy?'

Her eyes blazed. 'No man commands me.'

She turned her back on him to walk away. Suddenly her arm was grasped in a vice-like grip and she was spun round. So surprised was she that it took a moment before she realised that his arms were encircling her and he was drawing her against his hard frame.

'No! Don't you dare! Leave me alone—you—you brute! Let me go…'

He smothered her objection with a hungry, wildly exciting kiss. Temporarily robbed of her anger that had fortified her resistance, Lucy's traitorous body lost its rigidity and the scream of warning issued by her mind was stifled by her pounding heart and the shocking pleasure of being held in the strong arms of the man she had believed she would never see again.

His mouth opened and twisted across hers, his tongue thrusting through as his arms crushed her in his embrace. Her world careened crazily as his mouth became insistent, demanding, relentless, snatching her breath as well as her poise. The whole of her body seemed to burst into flame. The feel of him, the smell of him, all combined to transfix her. She was caught up in the heat of a battle she could not hope to win. Her weapons had died, her wits fled. The hard, muscular chest, warm through the cloth of his coat, tightened against her meagrely clad chest, and she was aware of the heavy thudding of his heart while her own throbbed a new frantic rhythm.

His warm lips moving on hers, the sensation of his body pressing against hers—it was all so achingly, poignantly, vibrantly familiar to her. Trailing his mouth across her cheek, brushing insistent kisses along the sensitive curve of her neck and ear, Nathan let his hands slide into her hair, tilting her face up to his, and his eyes held hers, teasing, challenging.

'I'm glad to see you haven't forgotten how to kiss, Lucy.'

Before Lucy could utter a reply, his parted lips came down on hers again in another long, searching kiss. Lost in a stormy sea of desire, confusion and yearning, Lucy felt his hand splay across her lower spine, forcing her closer to him, but instead of resisting she slid her hands up over his shoulders, unwittingly moulding her melting body to the hardening contours of his. A shudder racked his muscular body as she fitted herself to him and Nathan's arms tightened, crushing her.

Fighting back the wild urge to lay her down on the carpet and take her then and there, Nathan dragged his lips from hers and drew a long, unsteady breath, slowly expelling it.

Surfacing slowly from the mists of desire, Lucy stared into his hypnotic eyes, dazedly watching their colour and mood change from the smoky darkness of passion to their usual enigmatic pale blue, while she felt reality slowly return. Her hand was still curved around his neck and it finally dawned on her what she had done. Retracting her arm, she stepped back, but his hand shot out and gripped her wrist.

Nathan's eyes narrowed and his jaw tightened. 'My compliments,' he said curtly. 'I see you have not forgotten all that I taught you—and that you have learned a great deal more in the past four years.'

Outrage exploded in Lucy's brain. 'Are you complaining? Four years ago I imagine you found me excruciatingly naïve. Things have changed, Nathan. I have changed. Now, please leave my house. We have nothing further to say to each other.'

'I disagree. We will speak of my reason for

seeking you out in a day or two when you have had time to think it over.'

'I will not do it,' she hissed, pulling her wrist free from his grip.

He looked down at her with disdain. 'No? You will—in the end.'

For a second, Lucy thought she must be going mad. There was a red mist before her eyes and a storm of utter fury in her heart such as she had never felt before. How could she have let him kiss her? How could she have been so weak?

'Just what are you implying?'

'I know that you need the money, Lucy, that things haven't been going well for you of late. If you behave sensibly, as I hope, and do as I ask, then I promise you will be paid handsomely—a princely sum that will enable you and your aunt Dora to live the rest of your lives without having to worry where the next penny is coming from, without having to work yourself into the ground on the stage.'

For the span of several heartbeats she said nothing, then, 'I happen to *like* what I do. Now, get out,' she whispered fiercely. 'Get out and don't come back. I hate you! Oh, how I hate you!'

He gave a twisted smile and his heart flinched

before the cold fury in her glittering green eyes. The pallor of that lovely face, the anguish so clearly written there, touched some forgotten chord and had their effect on his cynical nature. He opened his mouth to say something, then thought better of it, shrugged, like a man seeking to shift a burden from his shoulder, and crossed the room. With his hand on the door handle he paused and looked back at her.

'I forgot to wish you happy birthday, Lucy.' He smiled softly. 'You see, I do remember.'

Chapter Two

When Nathan had left, Lucy stared at the closed door, the energy that had fortified her for the length of his visit deserting her as she walked slowly over to the window and stood staring blindly out into the darkness of the garden. She felt as if she had just done physical battle with an army and lost.

After all this time, his smile and his kisses could still make her burn with longing. A moan escaped her as she leaned her head against the cool glass of the windowpane. Shame and fear surged through her as she covered her face with her hands and bitterly faced the awful truth. She had been so confident that if ever they should meet again he could never make her feel anything for him. And all it had taken to prove her wrong was a smile and a kiss.

Physically, she was no more immune to Nathan Rochefort than she had been four years ago. The very nature of his kiss had wreaked havoc on her body, her soul and her heart. Despite all she had learned, everything she had acquired in sophistication and experience, despite everything she knew of him, he could still twist her insides into tight knots of yearning as he had done when she had been nineteen years old.

Where he was concerned, she was still as susceptible as she had ever been. What kind of sorcery did he employ that he could have this effect on her, when she harboured no illusions about any tender feelings he might have for her?

Striding off into the night, Nathan reflected on his meeting with Lucy. This was not the same woman who had been excited and enthusiastic four years ago. Now she spoke crisply, with a confident authority, all traces of wide-eyed naïvety gone. There was something feline about her. She was quiet in her movements, beautiful, but she had claws, he knew, and he also knew she had the intelligence to use them skilfully if need be.

The flash of anger in her eyes when he had confronted her and kissed her told Nathan that he had gone too far and that if he were to continue in this vein the success of his mission would be seriously imperilled. He remembered how, when she had broken off their engagement without explanation, his anger had been fierce, but at the same time he had been confused.

He had tried numerous times to see her, to demand an explanation, only to be told she didn't want to see him, then that she had joined a troupe of travelling actors and gone to the provinces. Having no time to pursue her since he was to leave for the Continent, he had left London, determined to forget her. Only it had been impossible. She was too deeply embedded in his heart and mind for him to do that.

After that, when anyone asked about her, he would answer dispassionately, his reply devoid of concern—not even his eyes showed interest. Lucy was gone. Since he knew damned well that he had done no wrong, the only remaining conclusion was that she had left him for someone else. Having seen the way other men followed her with their eyes, drooled over her when she appeared on stage, the existence of a lover was the only thing that made any sense.

With this thought in mind, he hadn't considered

trying to contact her again. She became dead to him and he didn't give a damn where she went or whose bed she occupied. She had a highly refined sense of survival and she'd land on her feet wherever she went.

But seeing her tonight he had wanted her all over again. The truth was that he missed her. He missed her far more than he could ever have imagined. Numerous times he had picked up his pen to write to her, but his pride had refused to let him put pen to paper. *She* was the one who had ended it. It was Lucy who must make contact with him.

But then his hand had been forced by duty and now here he was.

His father had been a bishop, his mother first cousin to Lord Wilmslow. Never having married, Lord Wilmslow had died without issue. Nathan was his heir. It was Lord Wilmslow's influence that had taken Nathan from Oxford University to the Foreign Office where his command of languages, his sound mind, reliable judgement and quick intelligence had ensured a swift rise. Introduced to men of note, he had been given responsibilities and entrusted with confidences. His reputation had led to his first major appointment when war had broken out with France.

British spies had proved effective in following Bonaparte's activities, and with the information they gleaned, more than ever the British Government was convinced the French leader was determined to invade England. As an important member of the British intelligence system Nathan had been sent to France and then to Spain to work against Bonaparte, an appointment which was as lonely as it was secret.

But the savage war was done for him when a French sword had pierced his side. When his wound had healed, and at thirty-two years old, he had decided it was time for him to think of marriage and raising a family. When he had been summoned and given this assignment, he knew he had to go back.

It was an assignment that drew his full attention since it affected him personally and would enable him to avenge the death of a young soldier, a brave soldier called Harry Connors, who had been the son of a close friend, a soldier whose death he himself had inadvertently caused. He would never be free of the guilt of what he had done until what he considered to be an act of murder had been avenged.

Another reason why this mission was so important to him was because it involved rescuing the wife and young son of his closest friend, who had been killed in battle. He would not be able to live with himself if he did not try his utmost to rescue them from the murderous rabble holding them captive.

But he could not do it alone. After spending weeks in captivity it was likely the woman and child would be in no fit state for a long trek down from the mountains, so it would be better if his companion was a woman. He knew many women, but not one of them was suitable to carry out such a mission.

From a strictly logical standpoint he had chosen Lucy Lane to help him—the last woman on earth who would want to.

She would be perfect for what he had in mind. Of course he had expected her to react angrily to his appearance and his offer, but how long that anger would last he didn't know. She had already been angry with him for four years. She would fight him, but no matter. Before approaching her he had been quietly watching her for some time.

Making discreet enquiries into her circumstances and discovering she was in financial straits, he realised the money she would be paid for accompanying him on his mission might tempt her.

Also her relationship with Jack Lambert bothered him. Lambert had a manly quality that endeared him to women. He was also a notorious rake with a well-deserved reputation for profligacy. He had heard the rumour that Lambert found the beautiful actress a challenge and that he fully intended luring her into his bed by offering her marriage—not that he had any intention of carrying out his promise. Lambert wasn't the only one to be attracted by her, Nathan reminded himself, for Lucy was a beautiful woman, and there was the allure of her profession, as well. But Lambert was a no-good wastrel who, from sheer perversity and extreme boredom, had unscrupulously flayed the reputations of dozens of pretentiously proud females, but he had never once attempted to rebuild one of those demolished reputations.

Standing in the shadows outside the theatre, Nathan had pressed his lips together at the unexpected stab of jealousy that tore through him as he watched Lambert kiss Lucy's lips. He had told himself it didn't matter if she did return his kiss. He couldn't have cared less. But deep down he would hate to see Lucy become just another of Lambert's victims and become an object of ridicule. But then, Lucy was not without guile. She was no naïve innocent, but desperate to solve her financial issues, the lure of Lambert's wealth might prove too strong a temptation for her to resist and she might admit him to her bed, hoping it would end in marriage.

Whatever the truth of the matter, that had been the moment Nathan had determined to recruit her to serve his purpose.

There was no softness in his gaze as he strode on, only the calculating gleam of a man on a mission. Despite what was between them he knew that he had not been mistaken in choosing Lucy Lane. She would be perfect for what he had in mind.

The next afternoon Lucy received a note from Nathan, asking if she had given the matter he had discussed with her some thought.

She'd already made up her mind that what he asked of her was preposterous. There was a time when she would have gone to the ends of the earth for him, but that was in the past. She had given him her heart, her devotion and her love—in short, she had given him what was the sum and substance of Lucy Lane. She had loved no man before him and no man since and he had betrayed her with her closest friend, Katherine Tindall.

Looking back over the days before she had ended it, she realised it had been in their faces, in their eyes and the way their bodies met, familiar with one another. Katherine, a widow whose military husband had been killed in India, had acted strangely. In her naïvety Lucy had asked her if all was well with her. She recalled Katherine's evasive disinclination to tell her why she was acting secretive, the way she had laughed nervously and accused her of imagining things—and all the while…

And Nathan! He, too, had seemed withdrawn, secretive, his thoughts elsewhere. She had asked him what was wrong—with him, with her, with them. She didn't know. She couldn't tell. He had told her nothing was amiss, that it was in her imagination. His face, though, had belied his words. Normally they had no secrets from one another and she had known he was hiding something from her.

And then there had been Mrs West, an older woman, a widow, an actress herself, who had been among their circle of friends. She had taken Lucy aside and told her in low, conspiratorial tones of the rumour that was being whispered about town of Katherine's closeness to Nathan, that they were often seen together having a tête-à-tête. *You're an intelligent girl,* she had said. *Surely you must have noticed.* Lucy hadn't and she wildly shook her head to deny it, telling Mrs West with bitterness and pain that she didn't believe it and hating her for what she had said, that they were nothing but malicious lies. But could this be what was behind their odd behaviour, the changes she had noted in both Katherine and Nathan?

A shiver passed through Lucy as she remembered the moment she had seen for herself and could no longer ignore the horrible truth. The scene she had witnessed just days before their wedding had become frozen in her memory. Early one morning she had gone to call on Katherine, who was to have been her matron of honour, to discuss some minor details concerning the day itself.

About to get out of her carriage, she had paused

on seeing the door open, shrinking against the squabs when she saw Nathan come out of the house accompanied by Katherine. After embracing her and placing what had looked to her like a lover's kiss on her cheek, he had walked away. That was when something inside her, no more than a tiny crack, began to form at the foundations of her belief that she and Nathan would be together always.

Every nerve in her body had stiffened against the onslaught of her bitter anger and the pain of betrayal. She had wanted to hurt him badly, make them both pay. She wept in the dark of the night with the pain until she thought she would die of it. Her spirit was battered and desolate, but when she rose from her bed and put pen to paper, telling Nathan that she had changed her mind, that it would be folly for them to wed, that she had been mistaken in her feelings for him and that he was not the man she wanted for her husband, she was clear-eyed and icy calm.

When he had called on her she adamantly refused to see him and did not leave the house. Nor did she discuss the matter with anyone, not even her aunt Dora. After two weeks his visits ceased and she later learned that he had been posted to

France. Feeling a desperate need to get out of London and to leave the memories and heartache behind, she had joined a travelling theatre company.

Now, to confuse her totally, he had swept back into her life, just as handsome, just as intriguing, and with him he had brought an offer of money as well as adventure. He knew too well how difficult it would be for her to refuse such an alluring combination, but she must.

Refusing to let him intimidate her, angrily she tore up the note and threw it into the fire.

Another note was delivered the next day, and when she failed to respond he turned up at the house.

'I've given you my decision,' she told him irately when Polly showed him into the parlour, where she was poring over the housekeeping books, wishing there was more money in the pot to pay the outstanding bills and to spend on a few luxuries. 'I want no part of it. Now, please don't pressure me anymore. There have been times in the last four years when I have wondered if I did right in breaking off our engagement. Now I am very glad I did. I was right to do so, for now

I see you for what you are. You are a monster. You keep nibbling away at my reserves like a mouse. You will bide your time until the moment is ripe—until I have nowhere else to turn—and then you will pounce.'

Keeping a firm check on his expression, Nathan stepped closer with a respectful glance. 'I apologise if I expressed myself badly the other day. Do you need more time to think about it?' Her angry reaction to his proposal had come as no surprise. He was aware of her stubborn independence and he would have to soothe her ire as much as possible. It was up to him to convince her to work for him.

'No. I've given you my decision. There's too much at stake. I am happy as I am. I enjoy my work, work that is comfortable and familiar to me, work in which I take great pride. I will not leave all this and enter a very different world. I also have my aunt to take care of. Should anything happen to me, who would look after her? She isn't strong. Who would pay her bills?'

'That would be taken care of.'

She looked at him incredulously. 'By whom? You?'

'Yes.'

With an exasperated sigh she looked at him. 'Are you simply unable to comprehend the word *no*?'

'I do have a difficulty with that particular word,' he conceded, smiling crookedly.

'I'm not surprised,' she answered. 'You probably do not hear it very often.'

'Rarely,' he agreed. 'I am arrogant, I dare say,' he went on, 'and everything else of which you accused me of being. I admit it freely. However, I ask that you overlook my flaws and agree to go with me to Portugal.'

Lucy held her breath. It was a physical effort not to close the gap between them, to reach out for this man whose body had once been as familiar to her as her own. Her hands clenched into fists at her sides, her nails digging into the palms of her hands as she fought against an attraction so strong it almost overwhelmed her.

When she failed to answer he took a step towards her, holding out his hand as if in silent appeal. 'Lucy—'

She stepped back, away from him. 'When it comes to persistence you have it in abundance. But my answer is still no. Now, please go. Nothing can be gained from this.' He flinched. Her lips tightened. She must not show weakness now.

She kept her gaze fixed on something beyond him. Her body was rigid, her control as brittle as glass. If he reached out and touched her now those fragile defences would shatter. She prayed that he did not realise the power he still held over her. The memory of his kiss was enough to shatter her defences into a thousand pieces.

Nathan stared at her, his eyes hard and angry. After what seemed like an age he seemed to come to a decision. He went to the door where he turned and looked back at her. 'I'm not giving up, Lucy. One way or another I will persuade you. Believe me, this is important. You have no idea how important. Think about it.' He left quietly.

A bitter taste of disappointment and anger filled Nathan's mouth as he walked away from Lucy's house. He was a worried man. It would soon be time for him to leave for Portugal.

When Lucy had ended their courtship he had thought never to see her again. She'd finished it and he still didn't know why, but he'd had time to wonder. It wasn't until the eve of his departure for France, when he'd run into Katherine and she told him that Lucy wouldn't see her either, that his mind had begun to backtrack.

He wondered if Lucy had seen something she ought not to see. Might she have stumbled across some stray detail in his closeness at that time to Katherine and formed her own conclusions? But that was impossible. He knew he had grown very comfortable with Katherine, which his friend Lord James Newbold—the second son of the Duke of Londesborough—who was enamoured of the lovely fair-haired young widow, had warned him to be wary of. But he was too experienced to have done something careless.

But he thought it strange that Lucy had ended her friendship with Katherine and for this reason he would have to keep the identity of the woman he had to rescue secret until Lucy had agreed to work with him and they had arrived in Portugal.

His memories of their time together had never left him. A softness warmed his eyes as he remembered the long summer afternoons they had spent together and the nights, long and filled with loving. He remembered the mornings when they had wakened side by side and she had smiled at him, glad to have him with her. She had been soft in his arms, her lips eager for his kisses, her eyes slumberous and warm with her love.

Cursing softly, he quickened his step, unwilling to contemplate the idea of failure. He had to persuade her. Too much hung in the balance. He had a job to do. Lucy's obstinacy could not be allowed to get in the way.

The first of Lucy's creditors to present an unpaid bill arrived at her door two days later. He was soon followed by another.

'I'm sorry, Miss Lane,' the man collecting for the milliner said, his voice neither sympathetic nor accusatory, 'but Mr Matthews insists that the bill has to be paid. He's been lenient, giving you more time, but that time's up. He needs to be paid now.'

Lucy stared at him numbly as an embarrassed redness suffused her face. She managed to scrape up enough money to pay the bill outright, but when the chemist came asking her to settle up for Aunt Dora's medicines, she could only pay half.

And so it went on. The house came under daily siege as angry tradesmen and women clamoured for payment of their accounts. They gathered like noisy vultures, ready to pick what remained of her assets down to the barest bones. Lucy felt herself plummeting to near despair. To make matters worse, rehearsals for *The Merchant of Venice* had begun and her financial worries were getting in the way. She had read and memorised the script and would be word perfect on the opening night. Unfortunately, on several occasions she was late at the theatre, which did not go down at all well with Mr Portas. He commented on her tardiness and told her in no uncertain terms that he would not stand for it.

For want of money to meet her obligations, Lucy had to do something. Her pride forbade her to turn to Jack for help. There was only one thing for it. She would have to ask Mr Portas for an advance. The production was due to open one month hence and, as far as Lucy was concerned, she hoped it would run and run.

If Mr Portas refused to give her an advance on her future earnings, she would have no choice but to move out of her rented house and go and live with Aunt Dora. But even then she would need money to continue living.

The next afternoon she left the house and headed towards Covent Garden. It was a wonderful neighbourhood with a magical, carefree air and on any other day she would breathe deeply the better to absorb the smells, the sights and sounds as she entered the market. It was a noisy, crowded place with an aura of decadence, but Lucy loved it. The market was the very heart of Covent Garden, which, along with its mellow buildings, the piazza and arcades and the theatres, gave it such flavour and vitality.

But today she had too much on her mind to appreciate any of this as she walked quickly through the labyrinth of cobbled streets towards the Portas Theatre. Having grown up surrounded by people who were the theatre's lifeblood, it had always been an enchanted place for Lucy. Whenever she entered the foyer of the Portas Theatre, with its enormous gilt mirrors adorning the walls, along with posters advertising whatever was playing at the time, she always felt as if she had been transported into another world. Golden cherubs were set into the vast ceiling and huge scarlet curtains hid the stage and matched the material on the seats.

But today as she entered by the stage door at the back of the theatre, she saw none of this. The interior was dimly lit with coils of rope on the floor, discarded scenery and props littered about and racks of old costumes dusty with age. Stagehands hurried about their business, preparing for the evening performance. Some greeted her cheerfully and others got on with their work. She stopped a chap rushing past her carrying a Greek urn to ask where she could find Mr Portas.

'On the stage, luv. But be warned—he's in a foul temper today. I'd come back tomorrow if I were you when he's calmed down.'

Lucy watched him hurry away, stepping back to avoid a man carrying a potted palm towards the stage. Mr Portas wasn't on the stage and she eventually tracked him down in the corridor outside one of the dressing rooms. With his hair tumbling over his forehead and wearing black breeches and a white shirt with sleeves rolled up over his elbows, he was giving a man with a late delivery of theatrical merchandise a dressing down. After seeing him on his way, he turned to Lucy, his eyes flashing dangerously.

'Miss Lane! What are you doing here? Still, I'm glad you are. You've saved me the trouble of sending for you. I have something I must tell you.' He glanced at her sharply. 'Is there a problem?' he asked impatiently.

'Yes—I—I find myself in difficult circum-stances.'

'You do?' The eyes he turned on her were pierc-ing. 'How difficult?'

'In the light of my new position I—I wondered if you could see your way to letting me have an advance on my future earnings. I—I wouldn't ask, but—I am quite desperate.'

He stepped back, his expression irate. 'No, Miss Lane, I think not. In fact, the reason I am glad you came is so that I can tell you I have hired someone else to replace you.'

With a sinking heart, Lucy stared at him, un-able to believe he could do this. She could feel two spots of colour burning on her cheeks. 'But—the part was mine. You said I was perfect to play Portia.'

'And so you are—I mean you were. I have al-ways admired your skill in the past, but I'm sorry, Miss Lane, I've changed my mind. You are al-ways late. I cannot spare the time to wait on your convenience. I have a theatre to run, a play to get out and yet you persist on being late, which makes me think the role is too much for you.'

'I am sorry, Mr Portas, truly. I've had other things on my mind of late—'

'Whatever they are they do not concern me,' he retorted, seemingly unmoved by her plight. 'My priority is the production. But don't be too downhearted. You'll have other offers from other managers. You got good reviews from your last performance. You certainly don't need me.'

'No, I'm sure I don't,' she said, aware that others had stopped to listen. 'I got along quite nicely for a number of years without you.'

'There you are then,' he said, wiping his hands on his trousers and looking about him in an agitated way. 'I wish you luck. Now I must get on. Things to do.'

'Yes, of course. I won't keep you.' She halted and half turned. 'Do you mind telling me who is to play Portia?'

'Coral Gibbons. She is ideal for the part. I should have seen it sooner.'

She could only stare at him, all her dreams of the future suddenly dissolving around her. At length, she said, 'Yes, yes, she is. I see. Thank you for your time, Mr Portas. And now if you will excuse me, I am needed elsewhere.'

Lucy had to be alone. She felt suddenly numb with misery, disappointment and a growing anger. She had not realised until then how very much she had depended on playing Portia. If her replacement had been an inconsequential supporting player going on thirty-five and losing her looks, she wouldn't be so angry.

But Coral! Her closest friend! She was lovely, a perfect replacement, and Lucy had no doubt she would be a resounding success.

With the witnesses to her downfall slinking into the shadows, Lucy swept towards the exit with her head high, only to come face to face with Coral as she was about to leave by the stage door.

For one vivid instant the air between them shivered with tense friction.

'Lucy—oh, Lucy…'

'What have you done? Can you not see…?'

Lucy's voice was lifeless. It was as though Coral had taken something precious from her, some secret treasure she had hoarded and which was now revealed, something which had given her life and a recognition of her own value.

But if Coral was disconcerted by Lucy's abrupt manner, she hid it quickly under a mask of sympathy. 'Lucy!' she murmured, taking her friend's hand and drawing her away from the curious gaze of a stagehand. 'You have seen Mr Portas.'

'Yes,' Lucy replied, trying without success to hide her resentment for the full, rounded curves, the lovely blond hair falling about the small, fascinating face. 'Just now. He—he told me that the part of Portia is no longer mine.'

'I'm sorry, love. No one could have been more surprised than me when he offered me the part. I was tempted to tell him where to go—but I couldn't, not really. Please don't be angry with me, Lucy.'

Lucy sighed, shaking her head dejectedly. 'I'm not angry with you, Coral. Getting angry accomplishes nothing. But I can't pretend that I'm not disappointed.'

Coral shook her head as though in dismay at her own gullibility. 'I can't blame you. I would be livid had it happened to me.'

Coral said the words quietly, sincerely, and Lucy felt a tugging inside and knew she mustn't give in to her disappointment and simmering anger against the unfairness of it all. She smiled. There was a new radiance about her friend, a glow to her creamy complexion and a sparkle in her vivid hazel eyes. Her abundant blond hair tumbling about her shoulders and glistening with gold highlights, she looked absolutely stunning

in a gown of pale blue taffeta with narrow silver
stripes. Never had Lucy envied another woman
as much as she did Coral at that moment. But she
was not bitter that her friend was to play Portia.
If the part had to go to someone else, Lucy was
glad it was her.

'I wouldn't have wanted you to turn it down,
Coral. Of course you had to take it and I wish
you every success. You are perfect for the part
and it's about time you had a major role to play.'
What Lucy said was true, for ever since Coral's
appearance in a minor role two years ago, she had
been a favourite with the public, one of the most
popular supporting players in the Portas Theatre.

'Thank you for saying that. It's more than I deserve from you. I would never hurt you deliber-
ately, you know that. I value our friendship too
much. What will you do now?'

Lucy shrugged. 'I'll look around. Trail the theatres. Someone might take me on.'

'I do hope so. What happened, Lucy?' Coral
asked, upset and deeply concerned for her friend.
'I can't for the life of me understand what went
wrong.'

'I don't know, Coral. I've been so busy trying to make ends meet. Aunt Dora hasn't been

well of late—I'm going to have to move out of my home and go to live with her. At least it will lessen the cost.'

'Have you seen Jack?'

Lucy shook her head, suddenly realising she hadn't seen him since the night of the party. Perhaps Nathan's arrival had something to do with it. 'I'm sure he's busy—and he knows I have rehearsals—had rehearsals,' she corrected herself. She smiled bitterly. 'I think he's finally given up on me. Goodbye, Coral. I must go.'

Coral caught her to her. They hugged tightly, emotionally. 'Goodbye, Lucy. Take care,' she whispered. 'I'll come and see you soon.'

'Yes—yes, please do.'

Determined to find work, Lucy had gone from one theatre to another. Unfortunately none of them needed actresses at present, not even with her credentials. Angry and resentful, she had kept on looking, but it was the same at every one. Frustrated and defeated, she had turned for home.

Once inside her room she turned the key in the lock and leaned her head against the hard wood of the door frame. Not even Polly was allowed to witness the collapse of her brave façade as all her courage drained away and she sank to her knees and wept.

When Lucy called on Aunt Dora at her house in Bayswater, a basket of fruit over her arm, she found she wasn't her only visitor that day. Nathan was standing on the doorstep, waiting to be admitted, slapping his leather gloves against his muscular thigh. His broad shoulders were squared, his jaw set in implacable determination, and even in this restrained pose he seemed to emanate the restrained power she had always sensed in him. He was looking every inch the handsome, elegant gentleman today, with his blue superfine coat and darker blue trousers, his striped blue-and-gold waistcoat and his immaculate white linen.

'Well, well!' she exclaimed drily, trying not to show her surprise on seeing him as her heart quickened its beat. 'You are persistent if nothing else.'

Nathan turned his head and looked at her, a look of unconcealed admiration on his handsome face as he surveyed her jaunty yellow dress. Around her neck she had tied a matching yellow scarf, knotting it on the side, with the ends flipped over her shoulder.

'Have you rung the bell?' she asked.

'Two minutes ago.'

'Sarah must be busy. She serves my aunt's every capacity. If you don't wish to loiter in the street, perhaps you should come back later—or not at all,' she said coldly.

'It's no bother. I'll wait.'

'I think you should go. She hasn't been well. I don't want her disturbed.'

No sooner had she spoken than the door was opened by Sarah, a pretty young woman with an open face and friendly brown eyes. 'Good day to you, Miss Lucy. I'm sorry to have kept you waiting, but I was settling Miss Sharp in the drawing room. Please come in.' She smiled at Nathan, flushing prettily and bobbed a curtsy. 'She's expecting you, sir.'

He is no doubt accustomed to this sort of feminine reaction everywhere he goes, Lucy thought irately. She looked sharply at him. 'Do you mean to tell me you have already paid a call on Aunt Dora?'

'I came to pay my respects yesterday. Unlike

her niece she was pleased to see me and was keen for me to call on her again today.'

'I can imagine,' Lucy remarked drily, brushing past him into the house, leaving him to follow her or remain outside. Handing the basket to Sarah, who closed the door after Nathan, she walked towards the drawing room. 'What are you doing here? What do you want?'

'Now, why on earth should you think that? I am paying a social call on your aunt Dora. That is all.'

'Why?'

'Just because my former betrothed cut me out of her life doesn't mean that I should stop seeing Dora. We were friends, good friends, and when I called on her she was happy to see me—unlike her niece.'

Knowing it was some ulterior motive that had brought him here and not to make idle chit-chat, Lucy glowered at him and opened the door.

Dressed in a green-brocade dressing gown over a white-muslin shift, her silver hair loosely dressed beneath a pretty lace bonnet, Aunt Dora reclined like a pale and beautiful spectre on a chaise longue, seemingly unaware of the tense, charged atmosphere that existed between the two people who had just entered the room. She had been unwell for four weeks. A persistent cough had kept her confined to her bed and all the cures and remedies applied since then had done little to remedy it.

'Good afternoon, Aunt Dora,' Lucy said, crossing to her aunt and hugging her warmly. She worried constantly about her aunt's frail health and wished she could do more for her. 'How are you feeling? A little better, I hope. I met this gentleman on the doorstep. I hope you are feeling up to visitors.'

'Most assuredly,' Dora protested, sitting up so that Lucy could place a cushion behind her back, the effort of doing so making her breathless. 'Nathan was kind enough to pay me a visit yesterday. I do so enjoy his company—I always did—and he's in London for such a short time.'

'I think we both know that he always has a reason for what he does,' Lucy retorted, avoiding meeting Nathan's steady gaze.

Though he was arrested by the beauty of the sunlight streaming in through the small bay window behind her, illuminating her hair and shoulders in a subtle halo, the look she gave him made it clear that she was in no mood to be placated.

'You are wrong, Lucy. I would be most offended had he not called on me...' Dora's voice
trailed off as a cough she had tried to restrain got
the better of her.

'Oh, Aunt Dora,' Lucy whispered, hating to
see her weakness. Handing her a glass of water,
she held it while she took a sip. 'Is that better?'
Her aunt nodded, resting back on the cushions
and dabbing her lips with a handkerchief. 'I've
brought you a basket of fresh fruit from the market, along with a book of poetry I thought you
might like to read. I've given them to Sarah.'

'Thank you, dear,' Dora said, casting her niece
a worried look, 'but I wish you would not spend
your hard-earned money on me.'

Lucy gave her a loving smile. Aunt Dora had
no idea of the dire straits she found herself in,
but the time had come when she would have to
be told. 'I like to spoil you. How I would like to
take you to the country where the fresh air will
make your chest better.'

Dora airily waved a slender hand. 'You must
try not to worry so, dear. I do so hate to be a
bother. As you see I am better than I was—and
I do so hate the country, as you well know. I'm
only at my best when I'm in town close to my

friends, and you, Lucy dear—although I was so sorry when Nathan told me you are no longer to play Portia. What is Mr Portas thinking of to give the role to someone else?'

Lucy threw Nathan a reproving look. 'I'm amazed Nathan was able to give you the news when it is yet to be made public. I would have preferred to tell you myself.'

'I called when you were out, looking for work,' Nathan explained, his voice quietly sympathetic. 'Your maid—Polly?—gave me the unfortunate news. I'm sorry, Lucy. I know how much that part meant to you.'

'Don't be too downhearted, Lucy,' Aunt Dora said, giving her a comforting pat on the hand. 'There will be other parts. Although I confess I am extremely disappointed with Mr Portas.'

'I am more than willing to provide a sympathetic ear and a shoulder to cry on, if so desired,' Nathan offered.

Lucy dragged her gaze towards his tall commanding figure. He was gazing at her with an air of surprising openness, as he stood in front of the fire in a casual, manly pose, his arm draped along the mantelpiece. 'I do not desire. At present I am extremely angry and disappointed.' He raised that damnable eyebrow at her, so knowing, so thoroughly in control.

'I can understand that.'

Lucy glared at him, hating that mocking smile that twitched infuriatingly at the corners of his mouth. 'I don't think you understand the enormity of what has happened to me,' she retorted, going to stand in front of him and glaring into his eyes. 'I did wonder if for some malicious reason you might be the perpetrator of my downfall,' she said angrily, for the suspicion had briefly crossed her mind.

'I want you with me, Lucy, but I would not stoop that low.'

She was relieved to hear him say that. Her emotions told her she could not possibly survive the pain of it if he had.

'What nonsense is this, Lucy?' Aunt Dora piped up, her voice reproachful. 'How can you accuse Nathan of such a thing? He does not have a malicious bone in his body. You accuse him most unfairly.'

Nathan's smile was almost sweet. 'Your aunt is right. You are letting your imagination run riot.'

Lucy's temper flared. 'I am not accusing you, but my troubles began the day after you came to see me. It began with the trade's people I owe money to. Have you any idea how humiliating it is to have people coming to your home and demanding money.'

'You could put an end to this situation.'

'How? By agreeing to go with you to Portugal?'

'Portugal?' Aunt Dora cried, the mere idea of her niece disappearing into a war zone bringing her upright. 'Why on earth would you go to Portugal with Napoleon's soldiers running wild all over the place?'

Lucy was quick to reassure her. 'Please don't upset yourself, Aunt Dora. I am going nowhere.'

'Don't be distressed, dear,' Aunt Dora said. 'I have a little money put by. We are not destitute. It's not the end of the world.'

How Lucy wished that were true. 'It certainly feels like it to me. Don't you see? No one is going to employ me now.'

'But you are a talented actress. I'm sure something will turn up.'

'You have more faith than me,' Lucy murmured. 'I've been to every theatre in London looking for work, but no one is taking on new actresses.'

'Lucy...' Nathan wanted to go to her.

She lifted her gaze solemnly to his. 'Yes?'

When he saw the painful sadness dulling her beautiful eyes, remorse dragged his spirit down into the depths of a dark abyss. 'I am sorry things are as bad as that.'

'But—how will you manage?' Aunt Dora wanted to know.

How shall we *manage?* Lucy thought, for Aunt Dora no longer had the money to pay her own bills. She would never know the enormity of them. Not that Lucy minded while ever she was working and could afford it. Lucy's parents had died shortly after her birth and Aunt Dora had raised her as her own. There had never been much money and Lucy had spent most of her childhood hanging about theatres in the company of actors, but they had managed and Aunt Dora had done her best. Lucy would be grateful to her for ever and she loved her dearly.

'I shall have to look for some other kind of work and of course I shall have to give up my house. Things will be difficult for a time. I'm afraid we'll both have to tighten our belts.'

'Then you must move in with me. You can have your old room. It will be like old times having you close by me.'

Lucy smiled at her fondly. 'Thank you, Aunt Dora. I think I shall have to take you up on that.'

'You have work if you want it,' Nathan said quietly.

Her gaze passed over him scornfully. 'With you? I think not.'

'Why are you so angry with Nathan, Lucy? As you will remember, Nathan, my niece can be quite volatile at times. She is a woman of mighty will.'

'So am I,' he replied firmly.

In spite of their broken engagement, Lucy knew that in her heart Aunt Dora had always held an image of Nathan as her betrothed. She had been deeply disappointed when they had parted. 'Nathan is anxious to preserve me to use for his own ends, Aunt Dora, but I'm afraid that will never happen.'

Nathan lifted a brow questioningly as he dared to delve into those shining green orbs. 'And you're certain of that, are you, Lucy? I wonder if you have really considered the full depth of your predicament.'

'I am fully aware how dire my situation is and I know you to be the most persistent. I resent very much your high-handedness in arranging my life. I have done quite well without you in the past four years and will continue to do quite well without you in the future—without further interference from you.'

His voice was calm when he spoke. She could not seem to shake him. 'You seem to forget that it was you, not I, who ended our engagement, Lucy.'

'Out past relationship has no bearing on the future.' Turning her back on him, she went to her aunt. 'I must go now, Aunt Dora. I will come and see you tomorrow with better news, I hope.'

'Must you go so soon?' She sighed and kissed her niece. 'Very well, Lucy. As I said, something will turn up. I am sure of it.'

Purposely not looking in Nathan's direction, Lucy went out.

'Go with her, Nathan,' Dora said. 'Talk to her and come and see me again soon.'

Chapter Three

With long, purposeful strides, Nathan drew level with Lucy as she left the house.

'What do you want?' she asked without looking at him.

'To talk.'

'We have. Now, go away. I have to look for work.'

'Come now. Your earnings as an actress were not great.'

She felt insulted. 'I may not earn as much as the leading actresses at Covent Garden or the Opera House, but I have so far managed to earn my way quite comfortably.'

'So far.'

'So far, and I will continue to do so—when I can find someone who will take me on. If not, I will find other kind of work until they do.'

'You must be concerned about the bills that are accumulating.'

'I'm concerned about everything just now.' She glanced at him. 'You sound as if you care.'

'I do. I'm worried about you and your aunt. That is one of the reasons why I am offering to pay generously for your services. Your aunt is worried about you,' Nathan rushed on to reason with her before she could express further indignation.

'Aunt Dora worries about most things.'

'Mostly about you. Which is why I'm willing to pay you five thousand pounds if you come with me to Portugal.'

Lucy halted and stared at him incredulously. 'Five thousand pounds?' Letting out a small sound of frustration, with a toss of her head, she stalked ahead, her hands clenched by her sides. 'You jest, Nathan Rochefort,' she hissed when he fell in beside her. 'How dare you play with my mind—with my feelings in this way? You really are quite despicable.'

Taking her arm, he brought her to a standstill. 'I'm being serious about this offer,' he stated firmly. 'I want you with me.'

She raised her head with an impassioned air. 'Doesn't it matter what I want?'

'Of course it does.' The intensity receding slightly from his stare, he smiled. 'It matters to me a great deal what you want. Just don't ask me to believe that you are indifferent to the money I am offering to pay you.'

He spoke the truth. Of course she was tempted by the amount. Who in their right mind would not be? Five thousand pounds would mean she never had to work again and enable her to get the best possible care for Aunt Dora. But could she tolerate being with Nathan day in and day out, feeling his presence, his gaze, for ever watchful, commanding her, when she had struggled so hard to put the past and him behind her?

'But why me?' she cried. 'Why pay me all that money?' Her eyes locked on to his face and her gaze did not waver.

Seeing that his offer of five thousand pounds had taken the wind out of her sails and that passers-by were beginning to stop and gape at them, taking her arm, he began to escort her along the street. 'I would prefer to carry on this conversation in private—at your house.'

* * *

Neither of them broke the charged silence on the way home, but no sooner were they over the threshold and the parlour door had closed behind them than Lucy faced him.

'I'm not at all cut out for what you are asking of me. I would probably turn and run at the first sound of gunfire.'

Nathan gentled his gaze when he saw her staring at him with a stricken look. 'Lucy,' he said quietly, 'I will always keep you safe.'

She bristled as though he had given her some great insult. 'No.' She shook her head, glaring at him accusingly. 'No one can promise that.'

'I can be very determined,' he answered, with a half smile, as he saw he should push her. It was obvious he'd already touched a nerve. 'I am not perfect. Far from it, in fact. But if you come with me, I will do all in my power to see that you come to no harm.'

'How?' she demanded, her green eyes glittering with remembered pain. 'How can you claim you will do that? And why is there no one else you can ask?'

'Because I know you. You are exactly the person I am looking for. You speak French for a start. As I recall it is very good.'

'Aunt Dora taught me. She spent many years in France as a child. She considered French an important part of my education. What else?'

'You are an accomplished actress—the only actress I know. Your talents may be required of you to play a part. You are also witty and wise enough to know a fool when you see one.' He moved to stand directly in front of her, encouraged that she did not step away from him. 'You have confidence, too, as well as a sense of humour—although I have seen very little of that of late. And your compassion for others compels my admiration and respect.'

Lucy trembled, staring at him.

'You are also brave,' he continued as she turned away abruptly. 'The fact that you have worked your way through adversity in your profession and the care you take of your aunt is commendable and bespeaks your courage and good sense. It makes me feel that I can trust you, trust in your integrity, which is a rarity for me. It is not often I come across a person I can trust.'

She looked at him, listening like a doe in the woods, but poised to flee from him. She was rendered helpless by his words. It was difficult to argue with a man who praised her not for superficial things, as Jack had done, but for the very qualities that she most valued in herself. It would seem he did understand her a little better than she had given him credit for.

The tantalising channels in his cheeks deepened as he offered her a smile that seemed every bit as persuasive as it once had been. 'Will you not relent, Lucy?'

She hesitated. All things considered, she could do worse. Feeling herself weakening, before she could do so completely, in a moment of desperation, she said, 'I don't know. And now I would like you to leave. I have much to think about.'

Shaking his head slowly, he moved to stand in front of her. Perhaps it was time to try another method of persuasion. 'Not yet.' His eyes delved into hers, seeking he knew not what. 'I'd appreciate a few more moments of your time. We have much to reminisce over.'

His voice was low, incredibly warm, melting her. Lucy feared, from the inside out. She couldn't believe what he was able to do with her emotions and with such little effort.

Sighing softly, he touched her cheek with the

tip of his finger. 'I remember our time together and our conversations and the first time I ever heard you laugh—the first time we kissed and the first time we made love,' he said, his voice low and fierce and wrenching to hear. Suddenly he was catapulted backward through time while the image of the beauty before him abruptly blended into another image—that of an enchanting, curly-haired young girl who had once looked up at him with unconcealed love glowing in her eyes.

He could not prevent his thoughts from returning to what it had been like to be with her. The exquisite tease of her ankle caressing the back of his leg beneath a table, the feel of her arms coming up around his neck in a wave of delicate scent, the heat of her body. Most of all he remembered her face after they had made love, the genuine pleasure of her smile, pleasure that his kiss had given her, pleasure she had not been able to hide from him.

All that passion was within her still. It simmered just under the surface. He had been driven to unleash it and that was coming back to taunt him now, for he wanted to unleash it again. Within him, he felt a pang of nostalgia, mingled with a sharp sense of loss because the girl he had known was gone now.

'I remember how it felt to hold you, how your skin felt to my touch. I remember how you looked in the moonlight with your face upturned to mine, wanting me to kiss you.'

'Stop it.' She felt her face grow hot beneath his eyes and turned from him, trying to still the trembling in her limbs.

Nathan moved to stand close behind her, bending his head so that his lips were close to her ear, his breath warming her neck. 'I remember how you liked me to touch you, how you would say my name over and over again, of how you filled my senses until I could not think.'

Lucy placed the back of her hand over her mouth and caught back a sob of pain and fury. 'You are cruel, so cruel,' she told him in a fierce whisper. 'You should not say these things to me when we both know it is only to get me to do what you want that impels you to say them.'

'*You* accuse *me* of being cruel after what you did to me? You killed what we had without giving me an explanation. It is you who has been cruel, Lucy, to deny me that.'

'Stop it,' she cried, moving away from him. 'I will not listen to this.'

'Close your ears all you like, but I remember everything and I cannot believe you have forgotten. If you have, I will make you remember. I swear on my life I will.'

Turning round and staring into those translucent eyes that ensnared her own, Lucy felt as if she were being swept back in time. Drop by precious drop she felt her confidence along with her resistance draining away. How could she have deluded herself into believing she could sway him from his purpose? Not once since she'd met him had she ever emerged the victor in any conflict with him.

Drawing a ragged breath, she turned from him, passing cool fingertips across her burning eyelids. She was tired, so very tired of trying to find work, tired of being turned away from one theatre after another. She would miss her work and she worried so much about money and how she was going to pay her creditors. She couldn't even pay her immediate bills. And how was she to care for her aunt?

But she could not do as he asked—could she?

Folding her arms across her chest, she turned and looked at Nathan.

Nathan saw her struggling with indecision. 'Do say yes, Lucy,' he said in a quiet voice.

Perhaps it was the use of her name. Perhaps it was the change in his tone. She thought for a moment, then said, 'I can't fight you any longer. You should congratulate yourself, Nathan. You have outmanoeuvred me. You have been very clever. It would seem you have left me with no alternative. Very well. I will work for you.'

He looked at her steadily, knowing just how difficult this was for her. 'I cannot tell you how relieved I am to hear you say that.'

'I am sure you are. However, there are conditions you must adhere to. Ground rules must be established between us.'

'Which are?'

'That whatever there was between us in the past is over and done with. What you have just said will not be repeated. We are two different people. If this new arrangement is to succeed, you will not try to initiate any kind of intimacy. We must be careful to keep the two strands of our lives from becoming tangled. You have to promise me this otherwise I will not go with you. If I do, I will do my best not to let you down. I will be singularly focused and our future relationship must be a working one if I am to succeed in the mission I am to be presented with.'

He looked at her long and hard for a moment, then he said, 'The past is a part of everyone, Lucy, and I know I will never be entirely free of my own. But you have my word. A working relationship it will be.'

'Thank you.'

'Now you have agreed to co-operate we have much to discuss.'

'I expect we have. How long do I have before we go to Portugal?'

'Two weeks at the most.'

Her heart flipped over. She had hoped for more time. 'As little as that?'

'I'm afraid so. You can ride?'

'I can, but I haven't for a while.'

'Have you ever fired a pistol?'

She shook her head. 'Will I have to?'

'Maybe. I will try to teach you the basics before we leave.'

'And Aunt Dora? She will be against my going. Provision must be made in—in case something happens to me.'

'I promise that will all be taken care of before we leave.'

'I would appreciate that. I've already decided to give up this house. Polly can go and live with Aunt Dora. One consolation is that Sarah looks after her as attentively as if she were her own mother. I'm sure she will appreciate another pair of hands to help her care for my aunt.' She looked at Nathan as a more pressing issue occurred to her. 'Another thing I feel I must mention is the outstanding bills. I would appreciate it if, perhaps, you could see your way to settling that particular problem.'

'Leave it with me.' Now he'd accomplished what he'd set out to achieve there was no time to lose. 'I'll leave you now,' he said, striding to the door. 'I'll be back in the morning at eight o'clock. Your training will begin immediately. Get a good night's sleep. You're going to need it.'

As it got closer to the time when Nathan was to arrive, Lucy found she was becoming more and more nervous, which was ridiculous, considering she had been running her own affairs for over four years and making her own decisions. What was happening to her life? It seemed to be spiralling out of control. Everything was happening too fast.

More immediate was the problem of what she was going to wear. She rushed upstairs and surveyed her wardrobe. When she was ready she went down to the parlour and sat at her desk to wait, making a list of all the things she had to take care of before she left for Portugal.

Eventually her mind began to wander and she began thinking about Nathan. She knew he had been in Spain and that he had been wounded. There was so much more she would like to know. Was he married? Had he married Katherine? It seemed likely since she, too, had gone to Spain. But Lucy would not ask. The reason she was doing this was because, for some peculiar reason, only she could help him in his mission to do whatever it was—and because he had left her with no choice. But most of all she was doing it for the money.

But, she asked herself, finding it difficult to be honest with herself, to examine her feelings where Nathan was concerned. Was it solely for the money that she had agreed to go to Portugal with him, or was the temptation to be close to him once more just too hard for her to resist?

For so long she had tried not to think about him, burying her head in the pillows at night to muffle her sobs at the memory of those last loving times she'd had with him before he'd become distant, as if he had other, more important things on his mind. Of late these recollections were so real, so vivid. Like a storm they would not be halted, the crucifying memories crept inexorably back, back to that time when they had first met.

It had been a summer's evening at a party given by a mutual friend. They'd met often after that and courted openly. She remembered the first time they had made love. Having walked into the countryside, they had lingered in a barn full of sweet-smelling hay and it had been so wonderful when he had kissed her, when he had held her in his arms, desiring her as much as she desired him. All their hitherto cautions and restrained behaviour had been swept away in a tide of wanting and she lost her virginity eagerly.

Hearing a knock on the outside door, giving herself a mental shake she set the pen aside and stood up. Adjusting the elbow-length sleeves and smoothing her skirt with the palms of her hands, she smiled. It was a pretty dress, pink and white sprigged with pretty flounces around the hem and with a modestly low bodice. She felt a nervous anticipation as she waited for Polly to show Nathan in.

He strode into the room, carrying a parcel beneath his arm. He was wearing a tan jacket and white-silk neckcloth, buckskin riding breeches and gleaming brown-leather boots. His dark hair was ruffled and fell over the top of the scar that ran beside his left eye to his cheek. It gave him a sardonic, mocking look when his face was in repose. Only laughter or a smile softened the rigour of the scar.

Despite this he was devilishly attractive to look at. Lucy's pulse raced. She was unsure as to the cause—her handsome riding instructor or her fear of what was in store. He stopped a couple of yards in front of her, gazing at her with a half smile curling on his lips.

'Are you ready to begin your training?'

'As ready as I'll ever be.'

His eyes passed over her. He shook his head. 'That won't do. Here,' he said, handing her the parcel.

Lucy took it and set it down on the table in front of the sofa. 'What is it?'

'Open it.'

Totally bewildered, she did as he asked. Dumbfounded, she stared at the contents, holding them up.

'You would deck me out in these? But—I can't possibly. Why, they're indecent and inappropriate.'

He laughed. 'You don't know the difficulty I had getting these made for you. Every tailor thought me mad when I described what I wanted and no one believed that I desired to put them on a woman. I had to pay a goodly sum to have them made.'

Lucy continued to stare at them. 'But—they're *men's* breeches. I am expected to wear these?'

He nodded, amused at her dismay. 'Unless you prefer to be constantly tangled up in skirts. You must have worn breeches in some of your roles on stage.'

'I have—but that was different. I was playing a part.' Frowning, she continued to inspect the breeches. 'I doubt they're my size.'

'I have a good memory, Lucy.'

She flushed, lowering her gaze so she didn't have to see the knowing look in his eyes. 'Four years is a long time. I've put on weight.'

'In all the right places if my eyesight is to be

believed. I assure you I had these made with all good intentions in mind. Do not fear that I'm making sport of you. You will find it easier and more comfortable to ride a horse wearing breeches. It's more practical. As a woman you will attract attention—some of it unwelcome. For your own safety, it will be better if those we meet think you are a male to begin with.'

'You'll be telling me to cut off my hair next.' When he didn't say anything she glanced at him sharply. 'You *want* me to cut my hair?'

He grinned. 'You have beautiful hair, but you will not be as conspicuous with short hair. It's— practical. It will soon grow.'

Lucy didn't relish the idea of cropping her most prized asset, but perhaps he was right. She would attract less attention and it would be less trouble. 'Very well. I'll have Polly cut it before we leave.' Shaking her head, she glanced dubiously at the breeches once more. 'I'm becoming more con- fused by the hour. These breeches look awfully tight. I really don't think they're my size.'

'They'll do for the time being. Go and put them on. We're wasting time. I want to assess your horsemanship and you cannot sit astride a horse in that dress—pretty though it is.'

Without further argument, Lucy left with the offending garments.

Feeling terribly self-conscious, she reappeared ten minutes later. The breeches, which disappeared into riding boots, were skin tight, showing off her long and perfectly shaped legs, the short jacket cut so high to reveal her attractive round derrière. Nathan admired the sight with glowing eyes, before cocking an eyebrow and ushering her outside.

The coach carried them north out of town and approached a pair of tall iron gates. A gatekeeper stepped out of the keeper's cottage and after Nathan had spoken to the man they were permitted to pass. They swept along a curving drive with extensive lawns to the right and left of them. Lucy's eyes became fixed on a large imposing house that appeared against a backdrop of sweeping parkland, rising to a height of three storeys. Evidently it was the property of a man of some consequence.

'What a beautiful house,' she murmured, unable to tear her eyes away from the twinkling expanse of mullioned windows. 'Who does it belong to?'

'A relative of mine. My uncle. He's away in foreign parts at present.'

'Is he a spy, as well?'

'No,' Nathan replied, helping her out of the coach. 'He's a gentleman. Come along. I'll introduce you to your mount. We'll ride out so you can get used to being back in the saddle. Tomorrow you will receive instruction on how to use a firearm—something small that is adaptable to a woman's hand. You will have to learn how to use a dagger. I pray you never have to use either weapon, but it's as well to be prepared for every eventuality.'

The stables were at the back of the house, a dozen stalls set around the stable yard. Most of them were occupied. Grooms and stable boys were going about their daily chores. Nathan was familiar to them and they greeted him in a friendly enough fashion. One of the grooms approached them, leading a chestnut mare.

'Come and make friends. Her name is Jess and she's as docile as the proverbial lamb.'

Lucy loved her. It was good to be back on a horse, to ride across the vast green acres of parkland. However, not having had the opportunity to ride for a long time, she was soon stiff. Nathan informed her she sat like a sack of potatoes and held the reins all wrong. She told him to take a flying leap and said she was going home. He told her she'd leave over his dead body. She said it was not a bad idea.

A look of sorely strained patience crossed his face as he caught her by the waist and lifted her down from the saddle after one particularly gruelling session. 'God help me if I ever injure my back,' he quipped.

'God help you if you ever turn it,' she snapped, her body sore, aching and exhausted, but she was beginning to enjoy herself.

The following day she had instruction on how to use a dagger, lunging and sidestepping and often being thrown to the floor and dancing out of her instructor's way. Nathan was filled with admiration, telling her she fought well, that he had no idea a woman could be so ruthless.

'There's Lady Macbeth,' Lucy pointed out with a wicked twinkle in her eye.

He laughed. 'There is that. Most women of my acquaintance are not trained in such matters. You may not even need these skills. However, it is always best to be prepared for the worst.'

Learning how to use a firearm was not as difficult as she had imagined. She surprised both herself and Nathan. He presented her with a pocket flintlock pistol, its small size making it more adaptable to a woman's hand. After showing her how to load it, he handed it to her, watching as her graceful fingers trained for etiquette now gripped the firearm.

Her instruction was given in an outbuilding adjoining the stables. She proved to be an exceptional shot. Her aim was true and she was an apt pupil. However, it was one thing to try to aim at a makeshift target, but she wondered if she would ever have the courage to actually pull the trigger if the situation arose.

Try as she might to keep herself aloof, her entire being was attuned to her instructor's presence. It was necessary for him to come close, to stand behind her and guide her arm. Her composure was sorely strained. He was so close she could feel his warm breath on her neck. It was familiar. At those times everything else ceased to exist for her except for the man in such close proximity to her.

It was disturbing. Did he feel the same? Did he feel anything for her at all? She held her breath, hoping his arm might snake around her waist and draw her to him, that he would say he was sorry for hurting her, that there would be forgiveness and things could go back to the way they were before.

But he made no move to touch her in any intimate way. And why should he? she asked herself reproachfully. She had, after all, laid down ground rules. And after sending him away without a by your leave four years ago, the thought must be anathema to him.

And then the lessons were over and it was almost time for them to leave for Portugal.

'When do we leave?' she asked.

'I'll let you know.'

'I'll be ready.'

From her bed where Sarah had tucked her in, reclining on a mountain of pillows, Dora glanced up from her book as her niece, still dressed in her breeches, came in and padded in her stocking feet to the fire. Dora watched anxiously as she collapsed into a chair and rested her feet on the fender. There was a troubled, faraway look in Lucy's eyes. It had been there for days now.

'Are you all right, Lucy dear?'

Lucy was staring into the depths of the fire as though her very life depended upon it. She was caught up in her meditation and Aunt Dora's voice brought her back to the present with a start. 'I'm sorry. I'm just tired, that's all.' She sighed, settling herself against the cushions and suppressing a yawn with the back of her hand. 'It's been a long day.'

'You look thoughtful.'

'I was thinking of Portugal. I feel a great deal of uncertainty, I must confess.'

'Ah, yes, but you may find it interesting.'

'I believe I will.'

'Does it worry you—going to a foreign country?'

'Yes, it does—with the war and everything. I suppose it will be strange at first. I shall have to have my wits about me at all times.'

'At least if you encounter any French soldiers you will have no difficulty with the language. You'll be glad I taught you. You're very brave to be doing this.'

'Brave? Me? It's a nice thought, but I haven't seen it like that. I'm simply doing what Nathan has asked me to do—whatever that may be. I'll soon be back in England and safe—and richer by five thousand pounds.'

'It's a great deal of money.'

'Yes. I think we might buy a bigger house.'

Dora laughed. 'I am perfectly happy here.' Her expression became serious. 'Just come home safe, Lucy. I couldn't bear it if anything happened to you. What is Nathan doing out there? Has he told you?'

'He's involved in matters of a sensitive nature. He hasn't told me much, only that we're to rescue a woman and her child who are being held captive in the mountains. He has told me there will be dangers. I'm sure he knows what he's doing.'

Dora gave her a thoughtful look. 'I really do hope so. Is everything all right between you and Nathan, Lucy?'

Lucy was about to answer in the affirmative, but the words would not come. In any case she never could hide her feelings from her aunt. 'Not really.'

'Do you want to tell me?'

'I'm not sure I can. I'm not sure I even know myself.'

'Oh dear. That bad?'

'Yes. It feels so strange being with him again with all that is between us.'

'Is it possible that you were mistaken in him—and Katherine?' Dora asked tentatively.

Lucy shook her head. 'The evidence at the time was quite damning.'

'Which I thought very strange. Katherine was always so charming, so friendly with us all.'

'Precisely,' Lucy agreed. 'I felt so lost and bewildered at the time, but I know what I saw—heard the rumours—and for a while, before we parted, there was a coldness about him when we were together. There was no mistake.'

Resting her head on the back of the chair, she closed her eyes. There had always been an element of doubt in Aunt Dora's mind. She never believed that Katherine could be so calculating, that Nathan, in whom she could see no wrong, would do anything to hurt her.

'I never imagined that I could feel so much for one man,' Lucy went on quietly, 'but Nathan had become indispensable to the point where it was impossible to visualise life without him. Which was why the blow when it came gave me twice the heartache. He threw away any happiness we might have had. Now I prefer to leave the past where it is.'

'You poor dear. Katherine went to Spain, I believe. Have you heard what became of her?'

'I assume she and Nathan went together—that she became one of the many women who follow their men into battle. It is common practice for wives to accompany their husbands on missions abroad, apparently. I heard she married. Perhaps she married Nathan. I don't know.' The thought struck her that if Nathan had married Katherine, why had he kissed her so passionately when he had arrived at her house on the night of the party? She sighed, too tired to think about that just now.

'Nathan has never mentioned having a wife. I'm sure he would have. You must speak to him.'

'I'd rather not and I would appreciate it if you didn't mention it, either. I cannot forget how humiliated I felt—how angry I was with him at the time.'

'That's hardly surprising, but you'll never know what really happened unless you ask.'

Lucy pondered the matter. 'It isn't as straightforward as that. The emotions are too painful. I don't want to resurrect the past.'

'For heaven's sake, Lucy, you are going to be

alone with him for weeks—perhaps months, in a foreign country. He will be your only friend— if you can still call him that. I think you should have a frank discussion about what went wrong. You may find the truth unpalatable, but it needs to come out. Until the whole truth is out in the open, you cannot address it. The past cannot be ignored when it impinges on the present and threatens to blight the future.'

Lucy looked away. Was Aunt Dora right? Had she handled things badly? If she had, she had no idea how to put it right. It crossed her mind that Nathan might not want her to, that he didn't want to go back to how things had been and his mind was set on his mission. If he were to reject her, she didn't think she could bear it. The thought of further humiliation made her cringe inside.

Nathan found Lucy in the small, cosy sitting room at the back of the house in Bayswater. It was an intimate room, snug and informal, books and papers scattered about, a fire burning in the fireplace, a large window looking out over the small and flower-filled back garden.

Lucy had ensconced herself in the window seat, her delicate feet not quite touching the floor. She held a book and was lost in reading when he approached.

The first thing that struck him was her newly cropped mop of chestnut hair. The light lent gold highlights to it, which sat like a cap of curls about her head, stray wisps caressing her forehead and cheeks. Her profile was towards him and he admired her high cheekbones. Her long neck was as graceful as a swan's. Her violet-coloured gown opened in front to display her white petticoats. The bodice, lined with white lace, plunged downwards, and he watched her breasts rise with each breath. Her hands were tiny, the fingers slender and graceful.

She was as lovely and desirable as he remembered and he felt the heat rise in his loins.

After a moment he walked farther into the room, suddenly filled with regret at what he was expecting of her. He had sent many men into battle and he had been sorry to see them go, but always he had known that it had to be done. But he'd never had to place someone he knew well, a woman, a woman whom he had loved—might still love—in such danger.

'Lucy,' he said at last. He watched with amusement as she started, nearly dropping the book.

She glanced up and he smiled at her. She did not
return the greeting. Instead she put the book face
down on her lap and ran her fingers through her
hair.

'Well? What do you think? I had Polly cut it
earlier. Does it suit me?'

He laughed softly. 'Polly could have shaved
your head and you would still be beautiful.
Where we are going you will find it less trouble.'

Her face became apprehensive. 'Is it time to
leave?'

He nodded. 'Tomorrow. First thing.'

'The sooner we leave, the sooner the mission
will be over.'

'The idea of being on the road with me, alone
and far from the places that you know, doesn't
daunt you, then?'

'Not unduly,' she lied, dropping her gaze, feeling the old familiar ache of desire wrenching at
her insides. She should not have agreed to this.
It was wrong—madness. If she did not know
how it felt to be in his arms, to be loved by this
man, then she would not be suffering this terrible longing now.

'You are forbearing, Lucy,' Nathan murmured,
having no idea of her thoughts. 'After a gruelling

two weeks of intensive training, most women would have objected most strenuously.' He smiled faintly and his next words were softly spoken. 'But then you are not most women, are you?' He saw she was unsure how to respond to that. 'I meant that as a compliment. Very much so.'

Lucy's heart beat a little faster. 'I'm flattered.'

'I meant it.'

'I have tried very hard to learn. I am determined to help you succeed. I hope we can rescue the woman and her child. I also hope I don't let you down.'

'You won't do that. Are you nervous about travelling so far from home?'

'I would be lying if I said I wasn't apprehensive about what will happen when we reach Portugal,' she answered truthfully. There were times when she thought about it that the very idea of going all that way filled her with terror. That was when she would remind herself of the money. It was a fortune for her and her aunt. But even the thought of such an enormous sum was not enough to calm her. 'It's the first time in my life that I've ever travelled—abroad, that is. I'm apprehensive yet excited by the prospect of gratifying my curiosity in seeing foreign parts. Is there anything else I have to know before we leave?'

'I think I've brought you pretty much up to scratch. Make sure you wear a hat at all times to conceal your hair. It's best if people think you are a youth at first glance. We don't want to attract attention to ourselves.'

He looked at her gravely. Knowing full well that he was taking her into a situation from which she might not escape was torturing him. But he had no choice. He did so because he had to. But he would do all in his power to keep her from harm. That, he was sure of. And if anyone should hurt her, or kill her, then that person would cease to live.

'It won't be easy, Lucy, I want you to understand that.'

'I know. You have already told me.'

'You must see Lucy comes to no harm,' Dora said, entering the room with the aid of a walking cane at that moment. 'I want her back safe and sound, otherwise your life won't be worth tuppence, young man.'

'I give you my word, Dora. I've an investment in her. I've achieved something remarkable getting her to join me. There will be no bullying, no browbeating, I promise.'

Lucy scowled at him, but a teasing light in her eyes lessened its severity. 'Don't believe a word he says, Aunt Dora. He's done nothing but browbeat and bully me ever since he arrived. I have the bruises to prove it.'

'Well, I think you're very brave,' Dora said, settling herself into a chair.

'Me? What nonsense you talk, Aunt. I'm only doing what any woman would do when she can see nothing but penury ahead of her and is suddenly offered a substantial amount of money.'

'I don't think every woman would. I think there are special women and you are one of them. What say you, Nathan? Do you agree?'

'Absolutely. I would not have asked her to assist me in my mission, had I not thought so.'

'How long do you expect to be gone?' Dora asked quietly.

'It's hard to say. If all goes to plan, we should be home within three months.'

'You will not be home for Christmas?' Dora sincerely hoped they would be, but nothing mattered as long as her precious niece came home safe and sound.

'I doubt it, but we shall see.' Nathan went to the door where he paused and looked back at Lucy. 'Get some rest. We have a long couple of days' hard riding ahead of us to reach Portsmouth.'

'What will happen to the horses? Will we leave them there—in Portsmouth?' Lucy hoped not. She had become extremely fond of Jess.

'They are going with us. It will save us the trouble of having to purchase mounts in Lisbon.' He smiled, his eyes caressing her face. He wanted to say something to reassure her, to ease her fear, but he could not. 'Go to bed. We'll be leaving at dawn.'

The sky was beginning to lighten. Soon it would be dawn and the city would start to stir. Kitted out in the clothes supplied by Nathan and a variety of clothes and other things she would require for the journey, Lucy gave a slight pressure with her heels and Jess fell into step beside Nathan's horse. She was confident that Aunt Dora would be well cared for, although Lucy had almost been moved to tears when she had bid farewell to the woman who had taken care of her all her life.

They were on their way to Portsmouth, where

they would take ship for Lisbon. Nathan, focused and marginally optimistic, turned his mind to their forthcoming journey. Barring setbacks, they would be in Portugal in two weeks.

The day was fine and it felt good to be setting off at last. Lucy could not regret leaving London behind in spite of the comfort it offered. She had always been happy to be on the road when she had played the provinces. But this was different, she reminded herself. This time it would be dangerous.

Now they were focused on their original purpose it gave them something else to think about other than what had happened between them in the past. Lucy wasn't sorry for that. The thought of being alone with Nathan for long periods of time was a lowering one. They rode in an easy silence, but there was still a vague sense of constraint between them. They had agreed to concentrate on the present and leave the past as just that, but their affair and what they had been to each other still hung in memory, not to be forgotten. They had rested the night at a country inn. Unused to riding such long distances, sore and quite worn out, Lucy had sought her bed after a hasty meal. Next morning, roused at daylight by the twittering of birds and people moving about inside, she had dressed and found her way down the stairs to find Nathan waiting for her. After breakfast, they had resumed their journey.

After two days of hard riding, with just the occasional break to rest the horses and get something to eat, it was dusk when they finally reached Portsmouth. It was the most fortified town in Europe, with a network of forts circling the city. With a large, industrial complex of arsenals, storehouses and army and navy barracks, it was dominated by the dockyard.

Lucy's gaze was drawn to a line of decrepit-looking ships in a line out in the harbour. She drew her horse to a halt.

'What are they?'

'Prison hulks. They're ships that are no longer seaworthy, introduced about forty years ago to alleviate the pressure in prisons—although I have to say that the hulks are worse than the prisons.'

'Do you mean they're full of convicts?'

Nathan nodded. 'They're also used for prisoners of war from the Peninsular Campaign.'

Lucy shuddered. 'I can't believe anyone could exist on them. They look grim.'

'They are, believe me. But come,' he said, urging her on. 'We'll find somewhere to stay for the night. We'll make an early start in the morning. The horses will have to be put on board ship and I must submit to the money changers before we board ship.'

'Why? What do you mean?'

'You cannot spend the English shilling where we are going. Our money will have to be changed into Spanish escudos. Unfortunately we'll lose out, but there's nothing to be done about that. It's a particular hardship on the soldiers, who must take money with them wherever they are going, where another man can take goods. To a mercantile man it will often be a gain, instead of a loss.'

As they rode through the cobbled alleys, Lucy was not enamoured of Portsmouth. It was dirty, smelly and crowded, and the oil lamps gave out small light. Nathan chose a popular inn close to the docks. They entered to the strains of a melancholy tune a sailor was singing. The man was tall and gaunt, but his voice was baritone. Some men around him sat quaffing ale and listening. The inn was devoid of women, except for a couple of serving girls carrying jugs of ale to the tables. A fire crackled in the hearth and an aroma of roast meat rose into the air, making Lucy's mouth water. Nathan went to talk with the innkeeper as she went to sit at a table in the corner, sliding into the chair.

Lucy looked around her. The inn had dark oak panelling on the walls with heavy beams running across the ceiling. A layer of sawdust had been strewn across the flagstone floor for warmth and to collect the mud and wet from people's boots.

Nathan came and sat across from her. They were served food and drink, which Lucy accepted gratefully as her stomach growled for nourishment. Despite her male attire and her wide-brimmed hat covering her hair, her flushed cheeks, soft lips and glowing eyes were impossible to conceal and were as tempting as any man could want. There was no disguising the fact that she was a woman.

Lucy failed to notice the stares she drew from the men, nor the seedy-looking man who sat across the room from them, already well into his cups. Her attention was divided between her food and listening to the song of the sailor.

Chapter Four

After they had eaten, they followed the landlady to their rooms for which Nathan had made arrangements. The landlady made herself scarce, leaving them to settle down for the night. For a few moments Lucy waited for Nathan to leave also, but he lounged in a chair and seemed in no hurry to go. On a sigh she pulled off her hat and ran her fingers through her hair to smooth the curls. Aware of Nathan's eyes on her, she turned and looked at him.

'Nathan, it has been a long day and I am very tired. If you don't mind I would like to go to bed.'

Without a word he shoved himself up out of the chair. He touched one of her glossy curls before he strode to the door. 'I'll be just next door.'

Then he was gone and Lucy sank on to the bed. Pulling off her boots and removing her breeches and jacket, she blew out the candle and climbed under the bedding. A dingy light from a lantern in the courtyard below, caught in a strong wind, cast its moving shadows in the room. Closing her eyes, she settled herself, secure in the knowledge that Nathan was next door. Sleep came quickly.

It seemed an eternity had passed when she was drawn from the depths of slumber. Terror goaded her to full awareness. A hand pressed tightly over her mouth, smothering the scream that rose to her lips. Her eyes flew open and in a frenzy she clawed at it. Then a face loomed up close above hers in the darkness and her fear increased. It was the drunken roué she had seen below.

The air in the room turned cold somehow, lapping against Lucy like winter waves on a river. For a moment it held her in a circle of deathly chill and she could feel the blood in her veins freeze.

'Don't make a sound, lady, if you know what's good for you,' the intruder hissed, his liquor-soaked breath fanning Lucy's cheek and almost making her retch. 'Tease, that's what you are, tryin' to pass yerself off as a lad—though a mighty fetchin' lad you make, deary.' Removing his hand from her mouth, he waved a bottle in front of her. 'I've brought somethin' ter enjoy—afore we get down to business.'

Lucy made a move to the other side of the bed, but his hand shot out and grasped her wrist, pulling her to him with a strength that almost snapped her bone.

'Not so fast,' he said, relaxing his hold to remove the cork from the bottle with his teeth.

Lucy regained her courage and snatched her wrist away, dragging herself across the bed. Standing up, she gave the man a crisp warning. 'Get out. My friend is next door.'

'Aye, I saw him. I figured ye'd be needin' some company.'

'I told you to get out,' she retorted. 'I will most certainly scream if you don't.'

'I'll be well gone before he drags himself from his bed.' The drunk set the bottle aside and his eyes fastened on her in burning lust. 'If yer friend were any kind of man at all, he'd be 'ere with yer now. I wouldn't leave a pretty little thing like you alone.'

He lunged at her, but Lucy had avoided many a grasping plunge in the theatre from overzealous devotees and, scrambling across the room, she snatched her pistol from her bag and held it with both hands in front of her, pointing it at her assailant's head. She had felt very safe and secure in the knowledge that Nathan was close by, but suddenly she felt very vulnerable.

'I told you to get out. I assure you that blowing a hole in your head would give me the greatest pleasure.'

The drunk froze, his eyes on the pistol. 'Now listen 'ere—'

'I said get out.'

'You heard the lady,' Nathan said from the doorway, his sword gripped in his hand. His sudden appearance and his towering, threatening presence in the small room had the drunk scrambling back in terror.

'I meant no 'arm,' he mumbled.

At the same instant Nathan's long sword went to his throat. The intruder saw the lethal power of the plain and shining steel in the light of the road lamps. The blade was held at Nathan's full arm's length, its tip barely quivering at the drunk's Adam's apple.

There was silence in the room.

Lucy sensed Nathan's anger. Her own had not diminished. 'What are you doing?'

Nathan spoke softly, each word clear and slow. 'I was thinking of running my blade through his neck or skinning him alive. However, it is with regret that I shall have to let him go.'

Lucy looked at Nathan and the light from the street lamps lit the left side of his scarred face, a face implacable and frightening, and she felt the fear. She recognised his competence and hardness. She recognised, too, the temptation that Nathan had to kill the man at this moment and might have done exactly that had he met with a similar situation on campaign. The man must have seen it, too, for he trembled violently, his eyes darting around the room, as if searching for a hole in which to disappear. The sword arm moved at last.

'Get out,' Nathan said, his voice as cold as the steel blade of his sword, 'before I change my mind.'

The man didn't need telling twice. In a trice he was across the room and through the door as if he had the devil himself on his tail.

Nathan watched him go. He looked at Lucy, unable to tear his eyes off her. Her shirt barely reached the thighs of her long shapely legs, which he remembered had once been wrapped around his own. Her eyes glowed feverishly in the dim light. She had never looked more glorious and yet the glory as she watched the man stumble out of the room was cruel, as cruel as he could be when faced with the enemy. He stiffened uneasily, strangely disturbed by it.

Her head was flung back, her lovely hair wild about her head, and her mouth, which every man, just a short time before, would have given a year of his life to kiss, curled in a snarl of something they would not care for.

'He's gone now, Lucy. You can put the gun down.'

Nathan's voice was slow but steady now. Placing his sword on the bed, he stood before her, holding out his hand for the pistol. His face was dark and inscrutable. His mouth was firm, his lips clamped tightly together. His eyes looked dark in the reflection of the candlelight, dark and as sombre as the deep swell of the Atlantic Ocean they were soon to sail into. His eyebrows were drawn down above them and in the curve of his jaw a muscle jumped.

'He should be punished, Nathan. He cannot go around trying to attack women in their beds.'

Her voice was quiet, steady now, with none of the impassioned wildness of the past few minutes.

'Are you saying I should have run him through?' She shook her head. He sighed. 'Leave it, Lucy. The man was drunk and will no doubt sleep it off in some gutter.'

She stared at him. 'But—don't you care what he—he—nearly…?'

'What?' Nathan's eyes bored into hers. 'Thank God I'm a light sleeper and I arrived before any real harm was done.'

'Why—you conceited ass. By the time you came I had the situation under control. You could see that. You taught me how to defend myself. Don't think you have to wet-nurse me.'

'I don't and I don't intend to, but don't go around thinking that because you know how to fire a gun you can shoot people willy-nilly.'

'I wouldn't do that. I know this is what you warned me against. You taught me well.'

Nathan looked at her hard before taking the pistol from her. Placing it on the bedside table, he lit the candle, more concerned by what had happened than he revealed. When he'd heard the man stumble up the stairs and heard a door open and close, he'd known instinctively what was afoot.

Panic had beset him. Lucy was in danger, immediate and terrible, and with every instinct in him, he had leapt from his bed. He'd been ready to hold her close, to comfort her, for he had been profoundly moved to think he might not have been in time to stop the swine raping her.

'I was furious when I realised that drunk had come into your room and what he might have done to you, but you also have my admiration for quickly overcoming your initial fear. I am proud of you, proud of the way you reacted.'

Lucy's look was wary. 'But?'

'The man was drunk. Did you intend to shoot him?'

'No—of course not.'

'I'm glad to hear it. Save it for Portugal.'

Irate because he didn't seem concerned, plunking her fists in the small of her waist, she glared at him. 'So is it your opinion that I should have done nothing, that I should have let that filthy drunk have his way with me?'

Nathan shook his head. 'Lucy, where did you get that notion? And don't look like that. You're like a disgruntled hedgehog and just as prickly. Of course I'm glad you put up a fight.'

Lucy continued to glower at him, her fingers

drumming upon her hips. Nathan's face was taut, emphasising the scar on his cheek. The candle behind him made an aureole of light around his dark head. He regarded her in silence. Despite what had just happened she was profoundly aware of him and the state of her undress. He was an extremely handsome man and, no matter how she tried to fight it, she was not immune to him. There were too many memories, too many struggling to come to the fore to resurrect feelings and emotions, which was disconcerting.

Too accomplished an actress to allow any of these emotions to show on her face, she folded her arms. 'Just what does a disgruntled hedgehog look like? I really have no idea. I see there's no danger of my head swelling from any compliments from you.'

'Please forgive me,' he said simply.

She nodded. 'There is nothing to forgive,' she answered quietly.

For a long moment Nathan's gaze held hers with penetrating intensity. It was as enigmatic as it was challenging and unexpectedly Lucy felt an answering frisson of excitement. The darkening in his eyes warned her that he was aware of that brief response. Something in his expression made the breath catch in her throat and the warmly intimate look in his eyes was vibrantly, alarmingly alive. Not for the first time since he had come back into her life she found herself at a loss to understand him. Suddenly his presence was vaguely threatening. As they continued to face one another, she naked except for the flimsy shirt that hung down to her thighs, she craved his lips against hers, her body within his arms.

'I—I think you should leave, Nathan. I'll be all right now.'

As if he had read her thoughts, bending his head, without thought to the consequences, he pressed his lips to hers. His arms slipped with infinite care about her. His embrace enfolded her, bringing her in close contact with his lean frame. Lucy felt the hard, manly boldness of him and she closed her eyes as his searing lips slowly traced along her throat and shoulder. His hands caressed her, leisurely arousing her, stroking her breasts and moving downward over her belly.

Lucy's whole body began to tremble as his lips descended to hers and she sought to forestall what her heart knew was inevitable by reasoning with him.

'This isn't what we planned,' she whispered,

shuddering as his lips trailed a hot path across her cheek to seek the inner crevice of her ear. 'You promised...'

He smothered what she had been about to say with his mouth, kissing her long and deep until Lucy shivered with the waves of tension shooting through her. The instant he felt her trembling response, his arm tightened, supporting her.

'Don't worry, Lucy,' he murmured huskily. 'I'll stop whenever you tell me to.'

Imprisoned by his protective embrace, reassured by his promise and seduced by his mouth and caressing hands, which had found their way under her shirt to bare flesh, Lucy clung to him, sliding slowly into a dark abyss of desire. Heedless of what he was doing, Nathan forced her to give him back the sensual urgency he was offering her, driving his tongue into her mouth until Lucy began to match the pagan kiss. Lost in the heated magic, she touched her tongue to his lips and felt the gasp of his breath against her mouth.

Nathan kissed her again and again until her nails were digging into his back and she was gasping for breath. Lost in the exciting beauty of her, the same uncontrollable compulsion to have her that had seized him four years ago had overtaken him again and he kissed her until she was moaning and writhing in his arms and desire was pouring through him in hot tidal waves. Out of sheer preservation he forced his hands to stop the pleasurable torture of caressing her breasts, but his mouth still sought hers, sliding back and forth against her parted lips, but softer now.

An eternity later he raised his head, the blood pounding in his ears. Lucy stayed in his arms, her cheek against his chest, her body pressed to his, trembling in the aftermath of the most explosive, inexplicable passion Nathan had felt in a long time.

Gradually Lucy's breathing became even and the sounds from the inn below began penetrating her drugged senses. Drawing a shattered breath, she gently disengaged herself from his arms, struggling valiantly to make the transition from heated passion to some semblance of normality.

'That should not have happened,' she whispered, combing her trembling fingers through her tousled hair. 'You agreed we would not do this— *we* agreed. We are just two days into our journey and already you go back on your word.' She spoke steadily, without reproach, for she could not deny that half the blame was attached to her.

Nathan shook his head and his face became gentle. His eyes were steady and honest, and he did not avoid her gaze as he spoke. 'Lucy, I will not lie to you and deny that I do not want you. There is something special, something fine about you, an indescribable magnetism which draws me to you. It always did, so nothing is changed. I saw the challenge in your eyes, though I am sure you were unaware of it.'

'Yes—yes, I was. But I did want you to kiss me, to hold me. That I cannot deny.'

'This was not premeditated. Men are weak creatures when their manhood is involved,' he murmured with some bitterness, 'and cannot resist it. But you are right. It should not have happened. If we are to fall into one another's arms every time we are alone, then we are in danger of failing in our mission.' Distracted by raucous voices raised in song from down below, he turned away and retrieved his sword from the bed. 'I think we should try and get some sleep. I doubt you'll have any further trouble. The door has a bolt on it. Slide it when I've gone.'

Returning to his room, Nathan knew he would get no sleep that night. He thought long and hard about what had just occurred, on the way Lucy had looked at him when he'd entered her room, her head thrown back in triumph, her eyes filled with some gladness—satisfaction—as though a promise had been fulfilled. It made him wonder why it was that her actions and her words, which should have pleased him, satisfied him, left him with a deep unease, which, though he would see no difference in her over the following days, he would carry with him in the coming days and weeks.

He could not bring himself to believe she would have killed the man. To reach for a weapon was the kind of reaction everyone—men and women—would have in the heat of the moment and she'd had reason enough. Yes, he had taught her how to shoot, taught her well, yet she was so fine, bright and brave and true. He could not make her as he was, to see her tarnished by war and the corruption that war brings to a soldier— the death and the killing—and to feel the terrible guilt he would carry with him to his grave over the needless death of young Harry Connors.

He would do his utmost in the coming weeks to guard Lucy from the hazards which would be strewn across her path. But he must stand back.

He would not coddle her, spoil her as before. There must be no repetition of what had just occurred between them, which would only serve to weaken their resolve to see this mission through to the end.

Lucy awoke to find it was not yet fully light. She had slept heavily, and now she got out of bed and padded across the floor. Pouring water from the ewer into the basin, she splashed it on to her face. Shivering from the cold, she glanced at her male clothes draped across the back of a chair. Already longing for the day when she would be able to don her gowns, she quickly dressed, arriving downstairs as Nathan came in from the street.

'You must have been up early. Where have you been?'

'I've arranged for the horses to be taken on board the *Harris*—that's the vessel we will sail on. I've managed to acquire a couple of berths. I've also taken care of the money.'

'My, you have been busy. You should have given me a knock—although I'm glad you didn't. I was quite worn out when I went to bed.'

'I'm hardly surprised—considering what happened.' He raised a questioning brow. 'No after-effects?'

For what, she wondered, the drunk's intrusion or their shared intimacy? She shook her head. 'No. I slept well.'

'When we've had breakfast we'll go on board. Hopefully the ship will be under way by early afternoon.'

It was a grey day, the sky the colour of old pewter with a hint of rain in the cool air. The noise and the sheer energy and vitality of Portsmouth's docks Lucy could not have imagined. Men hammered and sawed, and carried huge things on their shoulders. Casks, ropes and chains were everywhere. A jumble of ship's spars and masts towered above her head until she could barely see the sky. Tidily stacked piles of wood were lying about—stout oak for hulls, pine for masts. Figureheads at the prow of each ship reared at regular intervals. The redolent aroma of timber mixed with salt and tar, with every smell of a great seaport, filled her nostrils.

Which vessel were they to board? Lucy wondered as she tried to keep up with Nathan's long strides. She could not believe that she would be standing on the deck of one of these great ships, to command a view of the swaying sail and lines, to stand at the prow and feel the wind and spray on her face. To know the rise and fall of the vessel as it leaned into the jaws of a squall. To feel the warmth of the sun brush her cheeks as they sailed close to Portugal.

There were several ships in the fleet. They boarded a sixty-four-gun ship with its large guns run out at the porthole. Depending on the weather, it expected to make the run to Lisbon in under two weeks. It was carrying soldiers. Some of them who had been wounded and sent home to recuperate were returning to their regiments. There were several women aboard, some with children, taking the voyage to join their husbands, willing to run the dangers of war to be close to their loved ones.

Nathan took in provisions for themselves of biscuits, coffee, sugar, butter and other edibles that could be purchased. He managed to secure Lucy a small cabin—not much bigger than a cupboard, but she was glad of it. She would appreciate the privacy.

* * *

It was dusk when she went to the quarterdeck to look around. Now they were underway she experienced a strange sensation in which anticipation mingled with excitement. The chill wind that was driving tattered regiments of cloud across a watery sky brought with it a sudden and vicious spatter of raindrops. As the ship sailed down the Channel, she watched the coast recede.

There was no way of knowing what she might find when they reached Portugal, but she was relatively confident that she would be up to it. Nathan obviously thought so, otherwise he would not have sought her out to make her part of his assignment.

Nathan came towards Lucy from the shadows and stood beside her. The deck was almost deserted. He was conscious of her closeness. She lifted her head and looked into his relaxed, unguarded face in the pale light of the newly risen moon.

Standing close to her, Nathan took in the vague and subtle perfume of her skin. She had a smudge on her cheek, which he found endearing. Since

Lucy had broken off their engagement, all his contacts with women had been restricted to polite intercourse and nothing else. With her presence, it was inevitable that she would evoke thoughts and memories he had tried to bury. War made life uncertain, but he hoped at the end of it there would be a future—a home and a family and a woman's love.

'Are you all right—not too cold?' he asked as a brisk breeze played among the rigging, billowing and snapping at the sails.

Lucy shook her head. 'I've never been on board a ship before. It's a new experience for me.'

'We'll soon be leaving the Channel and sailing through the Bay of Biscay. It can be rough so prepare yourself. Even the strongest stomach can be affected by seasickness.' Turning sideways, he looked down at her. His gaze went deep into her eyes. 'I'm sorry about what happened to you in London. I know how much the role of Portia meant to you. You are a good actress, Lucy. Portia was a role worthy of your talents. I've rarely read such plaudits. Your anger and disappointment must have been overwhelming. I imagine you will by pleased if the performance fails.'

'On the contrary. I sincerely hope it will be a great success.'

'And it will not sour your friendship with Coral?'

'No, of course it won't. Initially I was angry and resentful, but we have been friends for too long to let something like this come between us. I am happy for her. Coral has proved herself a consummate actress. She will be pure perfection as Portia. She radiates vitality, wry good humour and overwhelming charm in a performance that is sheer enchantment.'

'You're a good friend. You are indeed generous.'

'Not generous. I'm simply being honest.'

His eyes fell to her face and his voice was hoarse when he spoke. 'Somehow I can't imagine you being anything else.' Her beauty still stunned him and her sparkle, gentle humour and indomitable caring for others had held him in a thrall of admiration. Four years ago she had become part of him, a part of his flesh and his spirit. His lover of the night had been an added bonus.

There was still a sweetness about her, a candour so disarmingly endearing. Her consideration and concern for Coral despite her playing the role she herself had coveted was real, admirable and instant.

Uneasy beneath his watchful gaze, Lucy looked towards the darkening sky with the silver moon riding low. 'You've travelled to Lisbon before, Nathan?'

He nodded. 'In my line of work. Portugal was in a state of collapse—it still is.'

'What was it like? What did you do there?' she asked, curious that he never spoke of his life in the Peninsula.

His stare did not waver from the sea and he did not immediately answer. When he spoke his voice was distant, as though all emotion had been carefully erased from it.

'One of my assignments was to discover if it was worth defending and whether it was prudent to keep British troops there. That was the task I was given to carry out.'

'And when you made your assessment? Was it on your advice whether the troops remained in Portugal or withdrew?'

He shook his head. 'The decision did not rest with me. It was up to me to supply the facts to the Foreign Office, but of course I was not working alone. I had contacts over there and the use of the army's couriers to send military dispatches to the British Embassy in Lisbon. From there the Ambassador sent them unopened to London.'

'It all sounds very complicated—and dangerous.'

'It was. When I was wounded and returned to England, I told myself I wouldn't go back.'

'What happened?'

'Another assignment. This one to be precise.'

'Where we are going, will there be conflict?'

'I sincerely hope not. We will be going into territory that is unimportant to the English and the French. Events are moving in Wellington's favour. Bonaparte's invasion of Russia in June has ended in disaster. As a result Bonaparte is unable to spare fresh troops for the Peninsular Campaign. At the same time, reinforcements continue to be fed into Wellington's army.' A sudden gust of wind blew cold off the sea. 'Come, enough talk of the war. We'll be in Lisbon soon enough.' He escorted her to her cabin—such as it was. 'If you should need me, I'm bunking down next door with the midshipman. To avoid a repetition of what happened to you last night—not that I think you will be disturbed—make sure your door is fastened.'

'I intend to. Thank you for telling me about your time in Portugal.'

They looked at each other. He fingered a short tendril of her hair that had escaped her hat. She reached up and caught his fingers and squeezed them lightly.

'You're a lovely woman, Lucy. I would be every way a fool if I didn't see that.'

He moved his hand to her cheek. He felt her blush, although in the dim light he couldn't see it.

'Goodnight, Nathan,' she said a little breathlessly, and before he could reply she had slipped inside her cabin and closed the door.

Lucy had slept little the first night, not being accustomed to the rolling of the ship. The following morning she returned to the deck. Seagulls screamed and wheeled above the churning wake and the acres of straining canvas overhead sang to the rush of the wind, while spray drove over the bows in a fine, stinging veil of mist. Passengers and crew went about their business. When she was alone she kept to herself. Eyes were drawn to her at one time or another, but never was anything said or done to suggest they thought of her as anything but the young man she appeared to be.

It was common practice for naval officers to tyrannise over their men so that they trembled at an order. Thankfully the captain of the *Harris* was an amiable sort. It was evident that his men were fond of him. One of the sailors told Lucy that he had sailed fifteen years under him and never knew him to punish a man without the crew being convinced of the justice of it, nor did he punish cruelly. He was, however, when necessity compelled, very strict and then he punished with severity. This kind of management made him respected, both by those who were under his command and those who were merely onlookers. As a result of this the ship moved forwards without noise or confusion just as if no order had been given.

On the second day they lost sight of land. Lucy had viewed the receding shore with a degree of regret. A melancholy gloom spread over the soldiers, except those who had been abroad before. As night fell, spirits gradually lowered, and all was silence, except for the whistling of the wind in the shrouds. Several of the passengers were laid low with seasickness. Lucy couldn't believe her luck that she had escaped—so far.

Their principal amusement on board was playing draughts and Lucy and Nathan would sit at the game for hours, the board balanced on a barrel. Lucy was fascinated at seeing porpoises tumbling and rolling about in the sea. They appeared in small groups, their small heads and triangular fins frequently seen popping up in the sea.

After three days, the wind changed and now their real troubles began as the crew was roused and sent up to take in sail, lashing them tightly in place, with ropes strung across the decks to provide hand holds for those who must venture on them. The ship ran gallantly before the ever-stronger gusts, clawing through the crest of each wave, then sliding down into the troughs.

Most of the passengers were struck down with sickness and kept below decks. Lucy had not succumbed and could only look on in sympathy. She rarely saw Nathan, who spent most of his time calming the horses and doing what he could to help out on deck. When he did stumble into her cabin to check on her, he was usually shivering and chilled to the marrow of his bones. After eating some buttered biscuits and drinking the coffee Lucy managed to procure from the galley, he would leave her.

During the night the wind rose to a perfect hurricane, drowning out the noise of the cursing captain, who, however, gave the men two or three drams a piece. The dismal noise in the rigging reverberated as if against a forest, in one continued roar. The waves came rolling towards them, like mountains piled on each other—the sea appeared white as snow.

When the lightning ceased, the tremendous thunder which accompanied it stunned their ears. There was no comfort to be had. The ship's timbers strained and creaked as she rolled from side to side. The rain came down in torrents and the lightning set the whole atmosphere ablaze, so that they could distinctly see as well as in daytime.

Lucy found what an excellent seaman their captain was. He certainly kept the ship steady when he directed the helm. At such a time, the wrong direction of the helm would have sunk the vessel.

On the fifth day, the captain told them they were in the Atlantic, approaching the Bay of Biscay. Nathan ordered Lucy below. She went, reluctant to leave the deck. It was cold and dark down there. Below deck, no braziers could be lighted during the storm, or even lanterns—Nathan had explained to her that these precautions were taken in case of fire.

As the storm raged, unable to bear the confinement below deck, Lucy ventured from her cabin. Bright veins of lightning briefly illuminated the ship, making the intervals of darkness seem even blacker. Her stomach knotted with fear as she staggered and groped her way along the companionway and up the stairs, gasping as she emerged on deck. The rain was cold and slashing, and she was soon drenched. Yet she breathed easier in the open. Everything that wasn't fastened down rolled about the deck. The captain and the helmsman stood beneath the lantern by the wheel and, as the *Harris* tossed, they seemed to float about against the darkness as if detached from the ship.

Swallowing convulsively, she looked for Nathan. He was looking out at the hostile sea when he saw her. Concern for her safety made him angry.

'Lucy! What are you doing! Don't you know you could be washed overboard?'

She could scarcely hear him for the howling

wind. As he was speaking, the ship heeled to one side. She lost her hold and was driven with amazing force against the capstan, and from there to the other side of the ship against one of the main beams. It proved her protection from the sea, for it saved her from being plunged into the abyss, without the faintest probability of rescue, but her head made contact with something hard.

She levered herself upward, but her legs remained twisted beneath her. The deck seemed to reel about her and she saw it as through a long, dark tunnel. It was Nathan who moved first to assist her. All his anger had drained away when he saw her predicament.

'Lucy! Dear God, Lucy.'

Before she could accept or reject his assistance, placing a strong arm beneath her back and sliding another underneath her knees, he lifted her from the deck and stood her gently on her feet. She teetered unsteadily, unable to stand alone.

'Lucy, are you hurt? Damn it, look at me!'

She opened her eyes to find him looking down at her, his large body shielding her from the worst of the blinding rain, his fingers cupping her face.

'Are you in pain?'

'Not much,' she mumbled, taking stock, 'except for the ache in my head.'

'My God, you gave me a fright.' His breath was warm against her cheek. 'Here, let me help you.'

Quickly he slipped an arm about her shoulders and half supported her against his broad chest. She was glad of his support when she had to negotiate the wildly rolling deck again. Carefully he helped her below to her small, low-raftered cabin, where he made her sit on the bed. He risked lighting a lantern, securing it to keep it from falling and setting the ship on fire.

Nathan drew in a breath. Her hat had been whipped from her head by the wind. She looked pale and bedraggled, even pitiful, as she huddled there, shivering. Something in his chest tightened. In the glowing light, he could see at once that her wound wasn't fatal. There was a small amount of blood caused by a superficial laceration on her brow.

'Lucy,' he murmured, sinking down before her, 'are you all right?' Placing a gentle finger under her chin, he compelled her to meet his gaze. 'What is it?'

'Would you…' Lucy whispered, her teeth chattering, 'do you suppose…you could hold me?'

Wordlessly he opened his arms, and when she came into them, he could feel her body trembling. 'There's nothing to fear now,' he said gently, stroking her sodden hair. 'You've suffered nothing more serious than a cut to your head. Already it has stopped bleeding. I dare say you'll have a headache, but it will pass—as will the storm.'

'It wasn't the storm. I thought…I was afraid I might be washed into the sea—that I would drown.'

Nathan pressed his cheek against her hair. He had been afraid, too. Afraid that he had lost her to the sea. 'Don't ever,' he breathed, remembering that devastating moment when he had looked down to see that mountainous sea sweep over the deck, remembering the helplessness he had felt, 'disobey me again.'

'I won't. I'll not venture out again until the storm has passed.'

Nathan repressed a smile, suspecting her docility was a measure of her fatigue.

'Come now,' he urged, 'if you will allow me I will help you out of those wet clothes. You'll be warmer without them, then you must get into bed.'

He knelt before her and began chafing her cold hands. He saw she was watching him quietly with wide, expressive eyes that looked trusting and vulnerable. She sat unresisting as he pulled off her boots. He hesitantly unfastened her breeches and peeled them off, stripping off her stockings in the process and rubbing her shapely calves to bring the blood back. Fortunately the rain hadn't penetrated to her undergarments so he left them alone. He then removed her jacket and unfastened her shirt, pushing it off her shoulders. He stood up, bringing Lucy with him, his head brushing the rafters.

His gaze was drawn to her face, to her cold, trembling lips. Slowly he bent his head, covering her mouth with his, warming her. When he heard her sigh, he deepened his kiss, thrusting gently into her mouth, warming her tongue with his. When she shivered, he didn't think it was from the cold, but he left off kissing her to finish peeling the wet shirt from her shoulders. Leaving the chemise she wore next to her skin, she stood before him, pale and cold, and he could see that gooseflesh covered her bare shoulders and that the nipples of her high, firm breasts were chilled and rigid beneath the fabric that covered them.

His blue eyes darkened at the sight. Lucy tried to cover herself with her arms, but Nathan caught her hands and pulled them away, scrutinising her carefully for further injury. In the lantern light he could see a reddening on her shoulder and his mouth hardened. Gently, he reached out to touch the faint discoloration. She raised an eyebrow as if in question. He hardly dared speak, he hardly dared breathe. He moved his hand, sliding it gently on to her back so that his fingertips touched the skin of her spine. She closed her eyes, seemed to sigh, and he pulled with his hand and she came, so easily, into his chest.

The restraint they had both forced on their nature since leaving Portsmouth broke, as they again felt the fierce thrill of being in each other's arms. Lucy was overcome by her ardent desire to surrender herself to him once more. As his lips touched hers, she gasped, the sound betraying her longing for him. The force between them had grown powerful and impatient in its long captivity and the longing could not be denied. His kiss was long and deep, with all the ardour and passion of his being.

Lucy could think of nothing but the urgency of his mouth and the warmth of his breath, the feel of his arms about her and his strong, muscled legs pressed against her own. Her body quickened with the sweetness of overpowering surrender— that incredible remembered joy. The blood pulsating round her body obliterated all reason and will as her whole being burst with heat threatening to overwhelm her. Lost in that wild and beautiful madness, Lucy ran her hands up over his chest, her fingers brushing his neck.

With iron control, Nathan straightened his body, and through the haze of heated passion she was aware of his strong and surprisingly gentle hands taking hers and drawing them away. That one kiss had been too much and too little, leaving both of them hungering and aching. Then, without conscious intention, his hand moved up to the curving swell of her breast to brush a hard nipple with one finger.

Lucy's reaction was immediate—she pushed his hand away and stepped back. 'Please, Nathan, don't do this. We can't go back. We said we wouldn't.'

Nathan stared at her, remembering with a surge of desire that her reserve hid a woman of passion and he wanted her. Wanted to draw her back into his arms and fill himself with the feel and taste of her, to span that impossibly narrow waist with his hands and draw those inviting hips beneath him, to have those long, lithe legs wrapped around him.

The fierceness of his wanting startled him. It was with a tremendous effort of will that he stepped away from her. 'I apologise, Lucy, and you are right to remind me. Any minute now I am likely to forget I shouldn't be here, alone with you…like this. I think you'd better get into bed,' he forced himself to say in a voice that was deep and husky.

Unable to look into her wide green eyes a moment longer without dragging her down on to the bed and making love to her, he opened the door and went out. He should not have kissed her, should not have resurrected those feelings and emotions so long repressed.

In the past Lucy had loved him with a pure and simple love that forgave, that understood. She had loved him, laughed with him, teased him. When he had gone to war he had taken with him a picture of her in his mind. She had been a memory that had not faded, a passion he could not forget.

She had seethed with life and possessed a child-like faith in love. She had given herself to him and never doubted the wisdom of the gift as he had sometimes doubted it.

He was aware that the days of being around her, of wanting her, of self-denial and frustration had finally driven him beyond restraint. She had torn the heart out of him when she'd left him, so that she became a painful, humiliating memory, and he'd sworn that he'd never get close enough to anyone to let them do that to him again. On reaching Spain his restless spirit had driven him from one achievement to the next, but the achievement never seemed to satisfy.

Staring at the closed door through which Nathan had disappeared, Lucy wanted to call him back. He represented safety, warmth and security, and she did not want him to leave her alone. But they had put down ground rules, rules that must be kept if they were to see this assignment through to the end. Extinguishing the light, turning back the covers on her narrow bed, she crept beneath them, pulling the blanket over her head, seeking the haven of darkness and solace from the turmoil of her emotions.

* * *

The next day the weather cleared a little. The *Harris* continued on course, the sun appearing at intervals. After making sure that the horses had suffered no ill effects from the storm, Nathan went in search of Lucy. She wasn't in her cabin so he concluded she had gone up on deck. He found her at the stern. Having retrieved her hat, it was pulled well down on her brow.

Lucy was watching the work of the crew. Some of the masts had been damaged during the storm and she watched, fascinated, as the seamen clambered up and down them, as sure-footed as monkeys as they tried to repair them. She gave a start when Nathan came up behind her and whirled to face him.

'So this is where you've been hiding yourself. I didn't expect you to be up so early. How are you feeling?'

He thought she had simply been startled by his taking her unawares, but she visibly stiffened at his words. She didn't look all that pleased to see him.

'I was not hiding,' she said stiffly, forcing the words past the tightness in her throat. Her mind burned with the memory of what had occurred between them the previous night. She wouldn't humiliate herself further by letting him know how much she craved his kisses, his touch. 'I believe I mentioned that I prefer being on deck than being confined down below. I am feeling better. I have a bump on my head, but otherwise I am unhurt.'

Her tone, her very posture, was cool and aloof. She knew he was watching her, trying to read her expression. No doubt he hadn't been sure what to expect. An acknowledgement of what had passed between them, she supposed. She decided not to reopen the subject and she was relieved that he felt the same, for he made no reference to it.

'I'm glad to hear it,' he said quietly. 'As you said, you could have been washed overboard.'

'But I wasn't, so we can get back on course and do what we set out to do. At least the storm seems to be behind us. In fact, I'm sure I saw land in the distance when I came on deck.'

She was right. They had their first glimpse of the coast of Spain, and later they could see the entrance to Corunna. At first the coast appeared as a mist on the edge of the horizon. They could distinguish the broken mountains and then the trees and houses. Then the wind shifted in their favour and they ran before it.

Two days later, they came within view of the Rock of Lisbon, which at first seemed to be only a blue speck.

They had lost sight of the fleet some days before, but now fell in with numbers of shipping crowding in and out of the Tagus. Here the river was about a mile wide, but after it passed the city it widened to four or five miles, where it separated into many small divisions, one of which ran as far as Madrid, the capital of Spain.

As they approached the shore, they found it dotted with pretty villages and they could distinctly make out the oranges on the trees. To add to all this, the day was fine and the weather inviting.

A large pilot boat shaped like a canoe and painted in gay colours with about thirty men at the oars guided them in. Nathan told Lucy that the city of Lisbon was about eight miles up the river, with Belem Castle projecting into the river. The landscape was enchanting and Lucy was surprised to see a large number of windmills, which were a feature of the country. They eventually dropped anchor midafternoon.

Having collected their baggage, Nathan and Lucy left the ship and climbed into one of the boats that came alongside to carry the passengers ashore. When Lucy asked about the horses, Nathan told her they were to be taken off the ship later.

The weather was pleasant, the sun shining and the temperature as warm as it was in England in August. When at last they arrived in Lisbon to a cacophony of church bells—Nathan informed her how the Portuguese were very fond of the bells—they were relieved to put their feet on dry land once more.

Chapter Five

Nathan hired a carriage to take them to their destination, Lucy looked about her with great interest. In this part, close to the port and the river, the streets were narrow and crooked and on the whole unclean. The city was built on a hill, many of the streets steep, some of the houses seven- or eight-storeys high. The journey became more pleasant as they left the port behind. Lisbon was surrounded with a number of fine gardens, well stocked with orange, lemon, lime and fig trees. The carriage climbed several hundred feet above the river to an area which commanded stunning views. Nathan informed her that it was a place where all persons of note resided.

Eventually they arrived at the home of Lieutenant Colonel Sir Robert Connors in his Britannic Majesty's army. It was a large square house standing high above the Tagus. With white-washed walls, the shutters painted blue, it was bathed in sunlight reflected from the river and framed by orange trees.

'We are expected,' Nathan told Lucy when they got out of the carriage and he paid off the driver.

Sir Robert Connors, a man of medium height and in middle age, appeared on the front porch. He looked with some fondness at the tall nephew of his good friend Lord Wilmslow, who did not enjoy the best of health. 'Nathan, good to see you. I thought you might be on the *Harris*. How's the wound?'

'Totally mended, Robert. As you see I'm as good as new, which is why they've sent me back to work.'

'I'm glad to hear it. Come inside. Maria will be glad to see you.'

'I trust you are both well, Robert?'

'In excellent health, dear boy. I only hope those two sons of ours are safe. At present they are with Wellington in the south. Cadiz, I think, but one can never be sure.'

'They will be,' Nathan replied with a confident air. 'They take after their father.' His expression became sombre, his voice quiet. 'I've already expressed my regrets about young Harry's death. If I could have done things differently I would have. You know that, Robert.'

Sir Robert nodded. 'I know that,' he said, his voice rough with emotion. 'It's war, Nathan. These things happen. We miss him, but for the short time he was in the army he did us proud.'

Lucy had been silent throughout this exchange. She assumed they were speaking of one of Sir Robert's sons who had perhaps been killed in battle and her heart went out to him. She would have expressed her sympathy, but she didn't want to intrude. Nathan turned towards her. 'Robert, this is Miss Lucy Lane, and this is my old friend, Lieutenant Colonel Sir Robert Connors semi-retired—who in my opinion is still fit enough to lead the troops on a winter campaign.'

Sir Robert laughed heartily and clapped Nathan on the shoulder. 'I could inscribe my name in glory, if I felt so inclined, or consign myself to the eternal torments of warfare, but I've become rather partial to idling my time away in semi-retirement with my dear wife.' He smiled at Lucy, his eyes twinkling as he took her hand and raised it to his lips in an old-fashioned manner. 'I'm happy to meet you, my dear. I suppose

Nathan has been completely neglectful of telling you anything about us.'

Lucy glanced at Nathan with wide uncertainty. 'I'm afraid he has.'

'You must forgive him, my dear. As ever he will have much on his mind. I trust the voyage wasn't too rough?'

Lucy returned his smile. Sir Robert had a strong face, deeply lined, dominated by brown eyes topped with busy grey eyebrows. He might give the impression of age, yet his twinkling eyes and ever-willing smile were the epitome of eternal youth. 'For a while—in the Bay of Biscay.'

'It invariably is, I'm afraid. I'm sure it must have crossed your mind that this is a strange time to be travelling abroad—during a war.'

'What is life without a little danger?' Nathan remarked, flashing a very dangerous smile indeed at Lucy.

She dropped her eyes, severely reproaching herself for the pink flush she could feel stealing into her cheeks. 'I have travelled extensively in England, but I have never been out of the country before.'

'Then I hope you won't be disappointed in Portugal and that your mission will bring you safely back to Lisbon. Come inside and meet Maria. She is Portuguese, but speaks English like a native. She's been looking forward to meeting you.'

Robert ushered them inside the house. It was simple, white and spacious, and, as Lucy was to discover, the surrounding garden was an earthly paradise in miniature—a paradise in which nature, almost unaided, had played the role of gardener. Maria hurried to join them, a broad smile on her face.

'Maria!' Nathan hurried forwards to hug the woman and they spoke in Portuguese, a language that Lucy did not understand.

Lucy thought Maria to be in her fifties. She was still very beautiful. Her skin was olive-coloured and flawless, and her hair, which cascaded down her back, was coal black and wavy. Her light, filmy clothes, in spite of an abundance of delicately coloured ribbons, did little to conceal her perfect figure and served, in fact, to bring out something of the Portuguese quality of her dark beauty. Her eyes were dark, too, and as Lucy watched her, Maria suddenly turned her attention to Nathan's companion and smiled a radiant smile that revealed small white teeth.

'Welcome to Lisbon,' Maria greeted her warmly

in perfect English. There was an air of kindliness and generosity about her and Lucy liked her immediately. 'It's lovely to meet you, Lucy. I have a room prepared for you—and a gown,' she said, her eyes passing over Lucy's apparel with disapproval. 'For one night at least you can drop these gipsy ways Nathan has imposed on you and become a lady.'

Lucy laughed. 'That I will never be. I am an actress and have been for many years.'

'And a good one, I'll warrant, otherwise Nathan wouldn't have recruited you to assist him in this venture.' Maria put a gentle arm around the younger woman. 'My dear, you must be simply famished after that long voyage, with nothing but ship's biscuits and dried meat to eat. Come, I will show you to your room. Hot water will be brought so you can bathe.'

Left alone, the two men went out on to the jasmine-covered terrace where they sat to discuss Nathan's assignment over a brandy. Sir Robert had been one of Nathan's contacts for secret work in Portugal before he had been wounded and sent back to England.

Crossing his legs in front of him, Sir Robert

looked at Nathan, at the fine lines around his mouth and at the corners of his eyes that had been absent before. He was as cool and aloof as if he were a nomadic king holding himself back from a distasteful event.

'When you went back to England to recuperate, I feared you were too ill to return to Portugal.'

'And therefore you would get no more work out of me?'

'That is what we thought. But it is agreed that you were one of our best operatives. When Lady Newbold and her son were taken hostage by the rebels, it was partly down to your close friendship with her husband and also because you have first-hand knowledge of the mountainous terrain in the north that you were chosen for the assignment. I am glad you are recovered sufficiently to take it on. There will be no bugles, battles or bags of glory this time, Nathan. You will be working alone.'

'How many hostages are being held?'

'That we don't know and it is for you to find out. It is true that Lady Newbold and her child are not the rebels' only hostages, but they are the ones you must concentrate on. The Duke of Londesborough is to pay the ransom. I must also inform you that the partisans and the British army are to launch an attack on the rebels' stronghold after you have secured the release of Lady Newbold. If all goes to plan, the remaining hostages will be freed and the gold will be reclaimed and returned to the Duke of Londesborough.'

'And the partisans?'

'You will make contact with their leader—a man by the name of Arturo Garcia, at the convent north of Santarem. You know the place?' Nathan nodded. 'It is known the rebels are holed up in some ancient fortress in the Sierras, but little else. Once you have secured Lady Newbold's release, you will meet with Garcia again and give him information of the rebels' hideout: the number of men, their arms and where the hostages are being held and their condition—in short, anything you can glean that will be useful. You understand they want to minimise the risk of injury to the hostages.'

'If they let us go and don't kill us once they have the ransom money. They may be deserters, but they are not fools. They are trained soldiers. They know how to fight.'

Sir Robert fixed his gaze steadily on the

younger man. 'That is right. Deserters are dangerous. They know their lives are forfeit if they are captured, so they will not flinch from any crime, no matter how cruel or vile. There is another reason why you were our first choice for such a vital and delicate operation.'

'Oh?'

'Because you are familiar with the leader of the deserters.'

'Who is?'

'A Frenchman. Claude Gameau—also known as Le Chien Noir—the Black Dog.'

Nathan went cold, his expression grim. 'So, Gameau has deserted.' He shrugged. 'I'm not surprised. He's a man violently inspired who didn't think much of soldiering.'

'You saved his life.'

Pain filled Nathan's eyes. 'For him to go on and kill Harry—reason enough for me to regret ever letting him live and granting him parole to be exchanged.'

'I'm sure you do—and I do know how deeply Harry's death affected you. But you must stop torturing yourself, Nathan. It wasn't your fault. You allowed Gameau to live. It must count for something. He owes you. For that reason alone we believe he will allow you to leave unharmed.'

Nathan's lips twisted with irony. 'I fear Gameau is off the map of chivalry, Robert.'

'He may not mind his manners, but you must mind yours if you are to carry it off.'

'Is he aware I have been given the assignment?'

'No. I have to ask you about Miss Lane. Is she up to the task, do you think?'

'I hope so. Lady Newbold and Lucy are...old friends.'

'And you think that is enough?'

'Miss Lane has courage and good sense. I can trust her, trust in her integrity. She is also reliable and will stay the course, I am sure.'

'And she cares enough about Lady Newbold to help rescue her.'

'I have yet to tell her it is Lady Newbold we are going to rescue.'

Robert gave him a quizzical look. 'And—is that likely to be a problem?'

Nathan shook his head, swirling his brandy round his glass. 'I don't think so—not when I explain everything.'

'That is something. I told you Lady Newbold was wounded when she was taken. Unfortunately we don't know how badly. She may not make it to Lisbon unaided. We felt we had to suggest that you found a woman who is trustworthy, someone who would be up to the task. You cannot care single-handedly for an injured woman and an infant.'

Maria showed Lucy into a room that was low-ceilinged with pale blue curtains and bedspread. It was a charming, restful room and what delighted Lucy was the balcony overlooking terracotta roofs and the River Tagus.

Hot water was brought and she bathed and changed into a lovely pale blue dress laid out for her by Maria. Lucy could not help giving a shiver of pleasure as she touched the soft material. Maria, quite rightly, thought she would appreciate disposing of her breeches, if just for one night.

For what was left of the day, they were entertained in a manner Lucy had not thought possible by strangers. Maria had met Sir Robert when her parents had taken her to London when she was a young woman. When Sir Robert had retired from the army after serving in India and later in Spain, and having become used to warmer climes, he and his wife and their three sons, all military men and serving with Wellington, had decided to settle in Lisbon. They still grieved for the loss of Harry, their youngest son, but they put on a brave face for their guests.

Maria was as gracious and kind as she was witty and warm. Her light-hearted charm was infectious and Lucy felt the tension melt away with the laughter. The evening swept past in a relaxed and congenial atmosphere. In the presence of the older couple, whom he had known for many years, Nathan seemed at ease. While dining, Lucy even managed to remain calm beneath his unwavering stare.

Nathan was the one who felt the bite of discomfort as he admired Lucy in the pale blue satin gown, the gentle sway of her hips as she walked ahead of him to the flower-decked terrace and the incredibly narrow curve of her waist.

Sitting on the terrace with the cicadas chattering, breaking the stillness of the evening, Lucy felt she was in heaven as she sipped chilled wine and nibbled on olives and cheese.

* * *

Later, when Sir Robert and his wife rose to seek their bed, Nathan held back.

'We have to talk.' She met his gaze and nodded. Picking up a cashmere shawl Maria had left, Nathan went to where Lucy stood and draped it gently about her shoulders. 'You're shivering.'

'Thank you,' she said, drawing the shawl around her gratefully. 'It has turned cold. I always imagined Portugal to be a hot country.'

'And so it is in summer, when the sun bakes the plains into dust, but in winter it can be freezing.'

It was a beautiful starlit night, and as Lucy strolled to the edge of the terrace her mood lightened. The moon was a great golden orb in the sky and the sounds of the town below hung on the air.

'It's a beautiful night,' she commented.

'So it is,' Nathan agreed, watching her. 'Would you like more wine?'

'No, thank you. I drank enough over dinner. The food was delicious and your friends have made me feel very welcome. So,' she said, turning to face him, 'now we are in Portugal, perhaps you would like to tell me more about this assignment you have been given? I would like to know what is facing us. I have to know if all this is worth it—I sincerely hope it is because when I return to England nothing will be the same for me.'

A tiny smile twisted one corner of his mouth although his eyes remained without warmth. 'In what way?'

She gave a brittle laugh. 'My life, my career, everything I have worked for.'

'You don't have to work any more, Lucy.' Nathan spoke quietly, watching her, making no attempt to move closer to her.

'No, I suppose not. I'm glad you guaranteed payment before we left London. For my own peace of mind I feel better knowing Aunt Dora will be taken care of should anything happen to me.'

'It has been taken care of. As you have seen for yourself a bank account has been opened in your aunt's name and the amount I promised you has been deposited.'

'Yes, I know. Thank you for that. So, tell me about this assignment and what it is that you expect of me. You have already told me we won't be going into a war zone.'

Without preamble, he said, 'No. As you know

a lady is missing. I have been ordered to find her and return her to her family.'

She smiled. 'You're a soldier, Nathan, and a lady needs rescuing. Is that not what soldiers throughout history have done?' Relieved that she wouldn't have to face a regiment of French soldiers, her smile widened. 'I hope it won't be too difficult and I understand why you need a woman's help. Do you know where to look for her?'

He nodded. 'Yes. That is not the problem.'

'Then—what is it?' She had a sudden feeling that she wouldn't like what he was going to tell her. 'Who is it you want me to help you to save? What is the lady's name?'

'It is Katherine, Lucy. It is Katherine who is missing.'

The name fell between them like a cannonball. Lucy's smiling face closed instantly. She gave the impression of not understanding what he was saying. Her feverishly glittering eyes were riveted on Nathan's face, searching it desperately for some sign that she had not heard him correctly. But, no. She swallowed. 'I see.' Crushed by a deep hurt and disappointment, she turned her burning face away from him. 'Nathan,' she beseeched, 'don't ask that of me...not you!'

Moving close to her and placing his finger gently on her cheek, he turned her face to his. His blue eyes slid towards her and trapped her in their burning gaze. 'I do ask it of you because you are the one person who can help me.'

A sudden revulsion seized her, making her oblivious to everything—where she was. 'How can you of all people ask this of me?'

'At this time nothing matters but rescuing Katherine. It is important that I find her, and if that meant recruiting you to help me, then so be it.'

A sudden spasm of pain tore through Lucy. 'You knew this all along. Little wonder you wouldn't tell me. Had you done so you know I would *never* have agreed to it. You deceived me cruelly. I will never forgive you for this, Nathan,' she said, her voice shaking. 'Never.'

'I regret that the deception was necessary.'

'I realise now why you would not tell me of the woman's identity in London.'

He lifted his brows, as if silently asking her what she expected him to say.

'I have no wish to revisit the past. Such things are best left.'

'Not always. If they remain hidden, they can fester and become harmful. It's easier to hide behind it than speak of what is painful. Whatever went wrong between you and Katherine is your affair. Although—I don't think it is mere coincidence that she received the same cold treatment from you as I did.'

Lucy listened with incredulity to his flow of calculated insult, delivered in a cordial, conversational tone. Was he mocking her, or was he trying to show her that the warmth of their relationship which had developed in the past had changed into a quiet, amiable contempt. If that was it, she thought, she could not bear it.

She returned a non-committal look and lapsed into silence. Nathan was reluctant to press her on the past any further, for fear of alienating her altogether. But when he thought of the passion they had shared, the enjoyment they had found in each other, how could she suddenly have turned so cold on him four years ago?

Lucy turned from him. 'I—I heard Katherine had gone to Spain—about the same time as you did. Later I heard that she had married. Did—did you make her your wife?' The question almost choked her to get it out, but she had to know. She dreaded what he would tell her.

Nathan frowned. 'What are you talking about?'

'Did you marry her, Nathan?'

'No, I did not. Did you have reason to believe I would?'

His answer brought Lucy immense relief, but she did not show it. 'I could see she meant something to you.'

'We were friends, Lucy, good friends, nothing more than that. It is becoming clear that you read more into that friendship than there was.'

Lucy turned to face him, her expression stiff and angry with memory. 'You say that now. My eyes did not deceive me, Nathan.'

'What are you saying?'

'When we were together I never imagined you would look at another woman and in my wildest dreams I did not imagine that you would be blackguard enough to associate with a woman who was my closest friend, a woman of whom I was extremely fond. There was deep affection between Katherine and me. We shared the same ideals, hopes—and the same man, it seems,' she said, unable to hide the bitterness she still felt. 'I always thought she was honest, that her friendship was genuine. But I was wrong about her—about you.'

'And you are sure of that are you, Lucy?'

'Katherine was a beautiful woman—I am sure she still is, but how would I know, not having seen her since the morning I saw you leave her house—embracing her and bestowing a lover's kiss on her cheek. I thought she had no man in her life, but of course she did. My betrothed. How you must have laughed as you played your little games behind my back.'

'I never realised you had so little faith—or trust—in me.'

His mind reeling, the magnitude of his error in not taking Lucy into his confidence that it was Katherine they were coming to Portugal to rescue was enormous, but even worse was the knowledge of what she must have suffered four years ago. Her pain and her vulnerability touched him more deeply than anything else could. But he remembered how she had turned her back on him and how he had left for the war an angry young man full of rage and hurt pride, and how she had almost destroyed his faith in women.

Would either of them ever again experience that grand passion they had known together? *There will never be anyone else for me.* Those words she had once spoken were in his head. They tormented him, echoing through his brain as he tried to get on with his life.

'You fool, Lucy. I went to see Katherine for the very best of reasons. What you saw was quite innocent.'

'It was?' She stared at him silently for a moment. 'Are you telling me there was nothing between you?'

'That is exactly what I am saying,' he said firmly.

'But there were rumours—cruel rumours that hurt me terribly. Mrs West—you will remember Mrs West—she told me the two of you had been meeting in secret—that you were often seen alone together on several occasions.'

His expression hardened. 'And on this you condemned me—and Katherine. Lucy, could you not see that Mrs West, the biggest vindictive busybody in London, bore a grudge against you— and Katherine.'

Lucy stared at him in amazement. 'Did she? I had no idea. But—why would she?'

'You are attractive. Beautiful, talented—and worst of all, young. Mrs West didn't find it difficult to dislike either of you.'

Looking back, Lucy remembered how she had

felt sorry for Mrs West, who had been an actress herself. She knew how much she had loved the theatre and had been loath to give it up when the parts dried up. Lucy realised Nathan was probably right and that Mrs West's bitter jealousy had turned to deadly treachery.

'But what about you, Nathan? Your behaviour towards me became different. You were distant, preoccupied. I knew you had something on your mind. We were to be married and yet the times we were together became less. I thought—I believed, all things considered, that it was all connected and that Mrs West was right. I thought you didn't love me any more. I couldn't bear it. I—I thought you would leave me. I couldn't face it. And then when I actually saw you with Katherine, it was evident to me that Mrs West had been right all along and that you had both played me for a fool. What else was I to think?'

'So you walked away.' Nathan sighed, shaking his head. 'It would seem you had forgotten that I was a military man about to go to war.'

'Then why didn't you talk to me about it?' she cried. 'I began to think I didn't know you any more.'

'And I thought you trusted me.'

'How could I trust you when you were up to your eyes in deception? How were we supposed to have any kind of life together if you didn't tell me what was going on?' she demanded indignantly.

'It was—difficult—I had a duty!'

'One that apparently mattered to you more than I did.'

'No. That is not true. You were the most important thing to me in the world. I had to protect you by keeping you out of what I was about to do. The two disparate halves of my life had begun to collide and at the time I had no idea what to do. There was evidence that Bonaparte presented a very real threat, that he was implementing plans to invade England. I had been recruited by English intelligence and I was being sent to France to spy against him. Telling you I was to leave you immediately after the wedding would change the whole picture for you and I did not assume you would be pleased to be left stranded in London.'

'Had you so little faith in me that you thought I would not understand? You should have told me.'

'I couldn't. I was forbidden to tell anyone. Telling you about my assignment also meant placing the security of the whole secret web in your hands. It would have become another risk to all the other agents in the field. How was I to know you were convinced I was having an affair with Katherine? If you thought that then you should have confronted me with it, not run away.'

'I had to. I was angry, humiliated and deeply hurt. I didn't want to see either of you. I had to get away. Why didn't you try to find me?'

'Why?' he said, arching a brow, his voice hardening. 'May I remind you that I tried—as well you know—day after day. I wrote to you—sent you flowers, begged you to see me. You never did reply.'

'You should have tried harder,' she told him, feeling utterly wretched.

'You went away and I had to go to France. I did not betray our love, Lucy. You did. If I'd known all this from the start and thought you would misconstrue the situation, I'd have set the matter straight. You did not give me the chance.'

'No,' she conceded. 'I accept that.'

Her voice was quiet with regret. This latest revelation turned everything on its head. At the time she had told herself that the bitterness that consumed her helped no one, least of all herself, but had tossed the thought aside, not wanting to think about it. Instead she had wrapped the pain, the grief of her loss and her anger about her like a blanket and found a strange comfort in it. Until now.

Tears burned the backs of her eyes, and she said brokenly, 'I was a fool, an angry misguided fool. Aunt Dora was right when she said I hide my feelings. It has become a habit with me and perhaps a defence, too.'

'A defence against what?'

'Becoming hurt again. I realise now that I made a mistake about you and Katherine, but it wasn't an unreasonable conclusion to jump to.'

'Perhaps not. But there is no turning back the clock, no going back.'

His words were meaningful, firmly, quietly spoken. In that moment Lucy knew Nathan had moved on with his life. The passionate lover had been absorbed into the rigidly autocratic figure of his rank. He was a man of strength and small pity. His face was proud, the face of a man hardened by military experience, mellowed only by the beautiful blue of his eyes.

'No. Neither of us can do that.'

'There's been enough misunderstanding between us. I wouldn't like you to think I misled you by anything I have done or said since our meeting in London.'

He was referring to the intimate moments they had shared, Lucy was sure of that. But she wouldn't allow him to see how deeply being in his arms once more, to feel his lips on hers, had affected her.

'Why did Katherine go to Spain?'

'To be with her husband—James Newbold— who you must know is the Duke of Londesborough's son. You must have seen how it was between the two of them. He danced attendance on her at every event we attended.'

'Yes—I do remember,' she murmured lamely.

'He was killed in action.'

Lucy stared at him in horror and disbelief, seeing Nathan's pain and how deeply the death of his friend had affected him in his eyes. 'Oh—I didn't know,' she said, her heart heavy with his loss. 'Katherine's first husband was killed in action. That marriage had been of short duration, too. Poor Katherine—to lose two husbands in similar circumstances. I liked James. Who could not? He was very handsome. He—he did have an eye for Katherine.'

'He loved her, Lucy.' Turning from her, with his

hands clasped behind his back, Nathan walked to the edge of the terrace, looking down past the twinkling lights of Lisbon to the Tagus, its waters shining silver in the moonlight. 'I do understand what a sacrifice I am asking of you, I really do, but you and Katherine were friends once, good friends. If you value the friendship you once shared, then you must try to help me set her free—her and her son.'

'Yes, of course. Tell me more about where she is being held.'

'The organised band of deserters holding her are hiding out in the mountains to the north, which, with winter approaching, is a haven for deserting soldiers from all sides, soldiers who defy both the French and the English. They subsist by terrorising the countryside, taking what they want and murdering those who dare to oppose them. They take hostages—ladies of good families being a speciality—and hold them for ransom. Their leader is a Frenchman, Claude Gameau—also known as Le Chien Noir, the Black Dog. He's ruthless, a man to be reckoned with.'

'How large is the ransom he is demanding?'

'One thousand guineas—in gold. Gold is a useful commodity.'

Lucy stared at him in amazement. 'How on earth will we transport such a large amount of money across Portugal? Why—we could be set upon by bandits and robbed.'

'It is a chance we will have to take.'

'Did you bring the money with you from England?'

He shook his head. 'It is here. The duke has been in contact with Sir Robert. He has the matter in hand.'

Lucy frowned, suddenly thoughtful. 'Perhaps they won't let us go. After all, we will have seen their faces and be able to identify them. As deserters, if captured, the penalty is death. How do you know they won't take the ransom money and kill us both?'

'Gameau owes me. I am relying on that. These men are cutthroats, rapists and murderers—a gang of scum. Because Katherine was wounded when she was captured, caught in an ambush when she was in a convoy returning to England, it will make our task more difficult. Since the Duke of Londesborough lost his eldest son in Spain, followed closely by James, the child is his heir. Gameau is unaware of this, otherwise he would have demanded a king's ransom. The child is no more than a baby. I have no idea of Katherine's condition—she might not even be alive still.'

He sighed heavily, brushing back a lock of hair from his brow with his fingers. 'To be perfectly frank, Lucy, when I learned she had been taken, I would have returned to Portugal anyway to try to rescue her, without being ordered to do so. James was my closest friend. It is the very least I can do to try to find his wife and son. I knew from the beginning that I was going to need help to get them both out of the mountains. That was when I thought of you. I suggested this to James's father and he agreed that under the circumstances it would be a sensible move—if you were willing. It is the Duke of Londesborough who is paying you the money for the assignment.' He was studying her closely. 'How do you feel about being dragged from hearth and home and forced to endure the hardships that will test your courage to the point of madness?'

'I was not dragged. I came of my own accord—although not without some coercion from you.

The loss of my job and mounting debts had much to do with it.'

'Not to mention the five thousand pounds,' he reminded her lightly.

She smiled. 'That was the decider, I admit.' Turning from him, she walked slowly across the terrace deep in thought. Suddenly, when she thought about Katherine and how she and her young son must be suffering at the hands of her captors, the money didn't seem important any more. But where did she go from here and how could she turn her back on Katherine now? She could see what she had to do, knew what she must do. She bowed her head.

'How far away is she?'

'Several days' hard ride. The terrain will be difficult.' Nathan looked at her, steadily assessing her. 'I understand if you are afraid.'

'Of course I'm afraid,' she said, turning to face him. 'I would be lying if I said otherwise—and you would know.'

'But?'

'I am deeply sorry for what happened four years ago, but you must understand why I behaved as I did. Despite all that I want to help you secure Katherine's release.'

'So, you are willing to sacrifice yourself for a cause which is not even yours?'

'You have just made it my cause. I am a professional in all that I choose to do. I have a job to do now and I will see it through to the end. What do I have to do?'

He looked at her for a long moment. 'We have to stick together. You have to stay alert and aware, but I will tell you if there comes a point where you should be afraid.' He shook his head, staring wistfully into her eyes. 'Initially I had no intention of involving you or any other woman in this. Believe me, Lucy, when I tell you that I did not want you to have to live in fear.'

Lucy was deeply affected and touched to hear this. 'No—well—if things go to plan I may not have to. When do we leave?'

'In the morning.'

'But what about the horses? They are still on board the *Harris*.'

'They will be well tended. I've arranged for them to be brought to the house tonight.'

'But the poor things have spent the journey in the hold. Don't they need time to recuperate?'

'They're tough. They'll soon pick up again,' Nathan assured her. 'We'll make an early start.'

'I'll be ready.' Clutching the shawl about her, she turned to go. About to enter the house, she turned and looked back. 'I can only say that I am sorry, Nathan—for what happened.'

'So am I.'

His eyes lingered on her for a moment, but the look in them was inscrutable. She turned from him. 'I'll go to bed now. Goodnight, Nathan.'

'Lucy?'

'Yes.' She paused and looked back at him.

He smiled at her. 'I'm an ungrateful wretch and I don't think it even occurred to me to thank you.'

She smiled back at him, happy to see a softening and friendliness in the blue eyes. 'I'll see you in the morning.'

Grim-faced, Nathan watched her go. Then he cursed under his breath. He shouldn't have let her go like that. She'd tried to make a conciliatory gesture which, after all that had passed between them, must have taken a good deal of courage and he'd behaved churlishly.

Lucy went to her room with mixed emotions. An uneasy feeling of doubt about what Nathan had told her about his relationship with Katherine was nibbling away at her. In the past, before they had become lovers, Nathan, a red-blooded male, had been unable to resist a pretty face. That thought made her yearn to be in his arms again, but she could not relent completely, not until she knew the whole truth. She wanted to believe him, to trust him, but what he'd been doing that morning when she had seen him leaving Katherine's house still remained a mystery.

She stood at the window and looked out at the night. But neither the cool breeze that lifted her hair away from her flushed face, nor the moon shining silver on the Tagus or the sighing trees that fringed the house, could act as an unguent to her aching spirit.

The following morning she rose before dawn. Slipping into her masculine attire, she was surprised how good it felt to be without the restrictions of female clothing. Before leaving her room, as Nathan had taught her to do, she checked the priming of her pistol and thrust the weapon into her belt, sliding the knife she carried into her boot.

Please, God. She prayed she would never have occasion to use either.

After eating a hasty breakfast with a quietly

focused Nathan, he carried the saddlebags outside, securing the one containing the gold to the spare horse. The other bags were packed with food rations, blankets and a change of clothes, and a few necessities they would need for the journey. There was also a soldier's greatcoat for Lucy, which would provide added warmth when they reached the hills.

Lucy stood back, watching Nathan. Maria came up quietly behind her.

'You had a good evening, yes? You found your room comfortable?'

'Yes, thank you, Maria. I left the dress on the bed. I doubt I shall get the chance to wear dresses again until this is over.'

'A woman should not need an excuse to wear beautiful things. I look forward to seeing you on your return, with Katherine and her child.' She studied her closely. 'You and Nathan talked last night—about his assignment?'

'Yes. He left me in no doubt of the dangers that may beset us on the journey.'

'You are apprehensive, yes, about what is ahead of you?'

'I would be lying if I said no,' Lucy confessed quietly.

'Nathan will keep you safe, you must know that.'

When Lucy flushed, Maria knew she had been right in her assumption that these two had feelings for each other. Perhaps they would do something about it since they were to be alone together for some time.

'Would I be right in thinking that you still have feelings for Nathan, Lucy?' When Lucy cast her a sharp look, she smiled. 'I know the two of you were close before he went to Spain—that you were to be married.'

The truth showed on Lucy's face. 'Yes, we were, but I ended it. I do still care for him, deeply, but so much has changed.'

'But you are still the same two people who fell in love!' Maria waved her hand in the air. 'When two people love each other, they should be together.'

'As much as I ache to bridge those lost years, to reach out to him, to hold him close, to somehow make it right again, too much has happened, Maria. I hurt him very badly—he hurt me. I'm not sure how he thinks, how he feels any more.'

Maria raised a finely plucked eyebrow. 'Then it is up to you to put things right. Nathan can be as obstinate as all the mules in Portugal, but he has a soft heart beneath that fearsome manner of his. Perhaps if you love him enough to accept everything and live only for the moment that will bring him back to you, you might have a chance. However obstinate he may be, the day will come when he can no longer struggle against himself and you. Some things are meant to be, Lucy, and life is too short for regrets.'

Lucy agreed with Maria, and the compulsion to learn more about the enigmatic man who had turned her life upside down from the moment she'd set eyes on him long ago was so strong it couldn't be denied. 'Four years is a long time. I know nothing about his life after we parted.'

'I only know what Robert has told me and that Nathan was the one of the best of the British intelligence officers who rode far behind enemy lines, riding brazenly on the flanks of the French forces. He sent back a stream of information about enemy movements, entrusting his messages and maps to Spanish messengers. It was a lonely, brave life he led, until he was wounded in October last year at the Battle of Arroyo dos Molinos in Spain.'

'Yes, he told me. Was he very badly hurt?'

Maria nodded. 'A French sword in his side. He

was brought to Lisbon, to this house, afterwards. He was very ill. For a time we thought he would not make it. But he is strong and he recovered.'

Lucy turned her face away, feeling a lump of constricting sadness in her chest.

'It happened months ago, Lucy. He seems to be over it now. I hope your journey into the mountains is successful and you bring Katherine and her child back home. My prayers go with you.'

Her emotions under control again, Lucy nodded thoughtfully as she watched Nathan walk towards them. An image of him lying wounded dug viciously into her battered senses and she knew that if she dwelt on the image and the pain he must have suffered, she would be lost.

Recollecting herself, she thought of what was ahead of them. Her heart began to hammer with a mixture of hope and dread, for although she had grown used to the idea of the journey they were about to embark upon, she still dreaded the thought that it could all go wrong.

Chapter Six

They spoke little as they left Lisbon behind. The horses were frisky and eager to exercise their legs in a gallop after their confinement on board ship. The third horse carrying the gold, it was hoped, would provide a mount for Katherine and her son, if the Frenchman, Claude Gameau, kept his word and released her on payment of the ransom.

The scenery was a glorious feast for their eyes. They passed the end of the lines made by Lord Wellington—fieldworks stretching along the top of a range of hills, which, Nathan told Lucy, extended many miles, as far as the seashore, so as to completely shut off Lisbon from the French.

Nathan had carefully planned the route they would take to the Sierras. Heading north-west, at mid-morning they had stopped to take refreshment and to rest the horses. Dusk found them camping in a clearing of tall trees close to a stream, water being an essential consideration for both horses and humans. Nathan tethered the horses to a misshapen, stunted tree. They bent their heads, cropping at the grass. Stars were set against the velvet sky, the air clear. The stream bubbled along the shallow valley floor and beyond the camp to the lonely hills to the north which rolled far away into the distance.

With her arms wrapped around her drawn-up knees, in silent fascination Lucy watched Nathan, glowing with strength, energy and vigour, go down to the stream for water. Her eyes took in the flexing of the iron-hard muscles of his wide shoulders and the length of his sturdy, powerful legs. She remembered how it had felt to feel the warmth of his body close to hers, how his lips had felt on hers, his hands sliding down her eager body, and her whole being reached out to him, yearning for him to hold her and possess her as he had done so long ago.

When he walked back to where she sat, she took a deep draught of fresh, night air in an attempt to dispel her wanton thoughts.

'I'm sorry I can only offer you water to drink,' he said, handing her the water flask.

Hearing the howl of an animal in the distance, Lucy shuddered. 'Are we going to light a fire?'

'No. If there are enemies around, a fire is the last thing we want.'

Lucy stared into the darkness. 'There are some enemies a fire will keep away,' she said, wolves and other things filling her mind.

Nathan's mouth became a hard line. 'No fire, Lucy. We'll manage without.'

'Will we be safe here, do you think?' she asked, looking about her into the gathering shadows.

'Safe enough,' he replied, his gaze doing a quick sweep of their surroundings. She looked at him. 'What is it?'

'I thought you would wear a uniform.'

'No. This is a private assignment. A red military coat would attract unnecessary attention to us. Common travellers attract less notice.'

'Of course. I should have known better than to ask. As I recall you were never one to seek to draw attention to yourself.' As soon as she had said the words she wished she hadn't. Nathan had always been a quiet observer of life and the world in which he lived. Attention always came to him, as if the very light from the sun and every candle fell only on him. It had nothing to do with his looks or his rank, but from his own demeanour and the quiet strength within.

'That is true and it's a fact that the countryside is full of marauders—men dispossessed by war, desperate men, who will go to any lengths to survive,' Nathan said by way of an explanation. 'I'll take first watch while you get some sleep. You can relieve me for a couple of hours later. I'll wake you. Tomorrow we should reach Villa Franca.'

'How far is it?'

'About fifteen miles. We should do it before nightfall. The accommodation should be an improvement. At least you won't have to sleep under the stars.'

'I don't mind,' she murmured, touched by his concern for her comfort. But despite this he was tense, watchful, his eyes constantly on the surroundings. 'We have blankets and at least we are warm so we will be moderately comfortable. I'm so tired I could sleep anywhere.'

All around them the undergrowth was alive with the sounds of nocturnal creatures. Lucy got to her feet to unroll her blanket. Despite what she had said, she was wondering how she was ever going to get comfortable enough to sleep.

Nathan propped his shoulder against a tree, folding his arms across his chest. He looked at his companion. Her eyes were large in the dimness. He watched her, entranced by the line of her throat, the wide mouth, the shadows on her skin above the collar of her jacket.

Sensing his eyes on her, Lucy straightened and turned her face to his. Her eyes were dark in the moonlight that threw shadows beneath her high cheekbones.

'How long has Katherine been a captive of Claude Gameau?'

Nathan's gaze was unwavering. He was aware of her body beneath the male attire, of dark shadows that promised softness. 'She was captured in late July.'

'Why—that's three months ago.'

'Yes.'

'And the child? How old is he?'

'I believe he was six months old when they were taken.'

'That will make him nine months. It must be horrendous for her. What is he like, this Chien Noir?'

'He is clever. He speaks English like a native.'

'How will we know where to find him?'

'We don't. When we get into the mountains, he'll find us. He knows we're coming and will have lookouts posted.'

Reaching up to remove her hat, Lucy stopped what she was doing and looked at him, realising how little she knew about this man. 'What is it like, being a spy? Were there many of you?'

He nodded, shrugging himself away from the tree. 'There's a network of intelligence agents— in Spain, Portugal and France. It all goes on behind the scenes. In a way it's a bit like the theatre. What the audience see on stage is nothing to what is going on backstage, the people, silent and invisible, who work to put on the show.'

Lucy thought it strange, on this perfect evening, the light fading into translucent grey and the screech of an owl sounding somewhere in the trees across the stream, to think of the vast, secret war that shadowed the war of guns and swords.

'How many men have you killed?'

'I don't know.'

'Truly?'

'Truly. I was in Spain a long time.'

'But you're not a humble soldier. You're a spy, a man of intelligence, paid by Britain for information. Are you ever afraid?'

He smiled. 'All the time. I am, after all, only human.'

They were just feet apart and Nathan knew that either could have moved away. Yet they stayed still, challenging each other, and Nathan knew she was challenging him to touch her and he was tempted suddenly to break the rules he had laid down for himself. The full mouth, the cheek-bones, the curve of her cheek, the shadows about her throat were tempting.

'What does it feel like to kill someone?' she asked.

'It depends. Sometimes good, sometimes nothing at all. Sometimes bad.'

'When is it bad?' She turned her head away.

'When it's unnecessary.'

He looked at her face, profiled against the broken moonlight, her beauty overpowering. His hand came up almost of its own volition, slowly, until his finger was under her chin and he turned her face towards him. She gave him a calm, wide-eyed expression, then stepped away from him so his arm was left in mid-air.

'Do you enjoy killing?'

'No. Some men's deaths you can enjoy—the death of an enemy. Yet I do not wish the death of the French—even though we are at war. There's more satisfaction in seeing a surrendered enemy than in seeing a slaughtered enemy. Death stops war from being a game. It gives glory and horror, and soldiers cannot be squeamish about death. There is a moment when rage conquers fear, when humanity disappears and makes a man into a killer. But that rage can keep a man alive.'

'I suppose Claude Gameau enjoys killing. Will you kill him?'

Lucy looked at his face. She could see a pulse throbbing in his cheek beside the scar. His eyes were dark. She raised an eyebrow as if in question.

'I can't answer that. Although I think I would do the British and the French a great service by killing him.'

'Does no one attempt to catch the deserters?'

Nathan shrugged. 'The places where they hide in the mountains are far from both the lines of the French and the English. Besides, they would see a regiment of cavalry coming two miles away, which would give them time to move on. The partisans, who harry the French constantly, move through the hills a good deal easier and will do the job for the army.'

'I expect the soldiers who abide by the rules must conceive a bitter hatred for the deserters.'

'That's true, but I think that hatred is caused partly by envy.'

'What do you mean?'

'Most soldiers, French and English, think at one time or another of desertion, but few do it. All soldiers dream of a perfect paradise where there is no discipline, a glut of wine and women. Gameau's men have come close to realising that dream and the soldiers who go after them will punish them for daring to do what they can only dream of doing.'

'And yet the deserters were like them once.'

'And now they would murder for a few pence. They're scoundrels, drunkards. They would steal off their own mothers for a pint of rum.'

'Do you expect Claude Gameau to keep his word and let Katherine go in exchange for the gold?'

'I've told you. The man is untrustworthy, but it has to be worth the risk.' She closed her eyes and seemed to sigh. 'Tired?' he asked. She nodded. 'Then try to get some sleep.'

'You will wake me later? We should start as we mean to go on.'

He nodded. 'Very well. We have a long day ahead of us tomorrow.'

Lucy sank down on to her blanket, wrapping it around her and using her saddlebag for a pillow. Her bones and muscles were weary from the long day and jolting ride. She couldn't remember being this tired. Everything was so strange, so new. Closing her eyes, she fell into a deep sleep.

Checking that Lucy was sleeping soundly, Nathan flipped open his blanket and, wrapping it around his shoulders, he leaned against a tree, listening to the night sounds and questioning the wisdom of bringing her to Portugal with him. While he was proud of her courage and resilience, he was very much aware of her vulnerability.

Right or wrong he knew only one thing for certain—his assignment would be more difficult without her. The fact that she was going to have to live under a totally different set of conditions bothered him, but he would be understanding and patient. Deep down he felt sure that she was a woman fit for what lay ahead of them.

* * *

He didn't have to wake her for her watch. She knew what she had to do and that he needed rest.

'I've come to relieve you. You must be tired. Get some sleep.'

Reluctantly he nodded. 'Very well. Wake me if you hear anything.'

He didn't like having Lucy look out for them, but it was important that he rested. Rolling himself in his blanket, he dozed fitfully, his senses alert to the nuances of the night. Finally he slept, but restlessly, his dreams marred by premonitions, of what, he did not know.

Seated on the ground with her back propped against a tree, where she had fallen into a light doze when the first signs of dawn streaked the sky, Lucy listened to the strange sounds, only dimly aware of where she was. The snort of a horse brought her to her senses. The sun had risen just far enough to dapple the tops of the trees. She stretched herself, opening her eyes and looking across to where Nathan had slept. His blanket was rolled up on the ground, but there was no sign of him. Looking down the hill, she saw him leading the horses back from the stream where he had taken them to drink.

She shuddered a little in the raw air. The morning was pale and cool, the sun visible but still remote. She inhaled deeply, savouring the freshness of the air carrying the scent of shrub. Overhead, birds wheeled, their wings catching the sporadic golden flash of the sun before they dipped and vanished beyond the treetops.

'Some use I've been,' she said, reproaching herself for having fallen asleep, unaware how soft and vulnerable she looked, her face flushed from her doze. 'I must have drifted off.'

'I noticed,' Nathan murmured without reproach. 'Don't worry. No one bothered us.'

'I'll do better, I promise. I won't fall asleep again.'

After a short trip to the stream to wash her face, Lucy saddled her horse, making sure the saddlebags were well strapped before securing the stiff leather girth. Nathan moved to assist her. Aware of his nearness, Lucy turned her head, her breath soft and fragrant as she looked into his eyes. Her hands grew cold with sweat and her legs began to tremble.

'Dear Lord, Lucy…' Nathan whispered. 'Dear Lord…this is going to be harder than I realised…' His mind reeled and he pulled her slowly towards him. She came easily, each step unimpeded, until she leaned against him and yielded him her mouth with a long sobbing moan.

Their bodies strained together hungrily in a mindless rapture while the horse shifted restlessly. Lucy melted under his fierce, fevered kiss and she clung to him as she gave herself wholly to his passion, becoming so enmeshed in its intensity that she found herself returning it with a wild and free abandon that amazed her as well as him. She felt him lift her in his arms and her heart streamed into his. She had no strength to pit against his will and her own need, yet as he laid her on the soft grass her hand turned against his chest and she twisted from him wildly and flung herself to her feet.

'I cannot do this. I cannot.' She sank to her knees beside him and covered her face with her hands.

Nathan lay quiet as she had left him and watched her, while his breathing slowed in time, and he said very low, 'I want you, Lucy. I have tried to fight it, but I cannot pretend otherwise.

You loved me once. I think you still feel something for me.'

He spoke her name so softly, as she had not heard it since she had left him all those years ago, and so piercingly sweet it sounded to her that the meaning of his other words came slowly. She could hardly think what to do, with her head spinning after that thrilling brush with passion. Events seemed to be whirling beyond her control, but at the same time she must remember that he had moved on with his life—and he had told her on the terrace at the house in Lisbon that there was no going back.

If she could not have the Nathan back that she had known, and his love had been a large part of that, she would settle for nothing less. She wondered how long it was going to take to break through his mistrust of her. If it took for ever—and after spending days dampening her body's eager response to his, she prayed to God it did not—she would make him see he had nothing to fear, that she would rip off her own arms before she would do him harm in any way.

Raising her head, she cried with bitterness, 'Yes, Nathan, I do still have feelings for you. I admit it and I, too, have fought it and will continue to do so until all this is over. Until then we must conquer our feelings.'

One of the horses whickered softly and the stream gurgled on its way. Nathan stirred and put his hand on her arm. 'I agree. I did not mean this to happen, but it has. There will be no repeat of this—unless you wish it.'

'I cannot,' she whispered, though she dared not look at him. 'I cannot,' she repeated. 'At this time, I would hate myself.'

'And hate me?' He spoke low and gentle.

She looked at him with pain-filled eyes. 'Dear God, I could never hate you. Don't torture me with these questions, and let me go', for his hand had tightened on her arm and he put his face close to hers. She gathered all her strength and cried, 'Have you forgotten why we are both here?'

Lucy's words were like a douche of cold water. They brought him to his senses and he stared at her anew. She was right. Each day her hold upon his very thoughts had grown stronger, and he had been hard pressed to withhold his more amorous attentions. He wanted her, but he was too afraid to trust that she would stay with him. And where that mistrust had once led him only to anger and resentment, it now made his heart ache in a way he had not known possible.

My God, could he be falling in love with her all over again? he wondered, then firmly told himself, no, and after that repeated it to himself for good measure. He was not falling in love with her and firmly refused to do so. Her beauty and her closeness might be able to woo his body, but he would never willingly give her his heart again. He would not allow himself to set aside his worldly ways and self-esteem, not at this time when it was imperative that he kept tight hold on his self-control. He had suffered a moment of weakness and he must not allow it to happen again.

Damn it, he could not afford this distraction right now. Lucy's very presence preoccupied his thoughts when he most needed to focus. He drew back sharply and got to his feet.

'You are right, Lucy, and I apologise for allowing my ardour to get the better of me. We need to be focused. Katherine and her child are our main priority.'

All the time Lucy rode beside Nathan or followed him along narrow, winding paths, she was aware of him. All about them was the sweep of the landscape and a sky full of birds rising and wheeling in glittering formations against the puffs of cloud. The kiss had disturbed her greatly. She realised what had nearly happened between them. How simple it would be, she thought, to slip back into their old ways.

But things were different between them now. Nathan had, after all, made no pledge for the future. Although they knew each other as intimately as was possible between a man and a woman, when they had been young, confident, resilient and the future had held no fear for them, things were no longer the same. *They* were no longer the same. Better to keep him at arm's length, prudence whispered. Then the heartache wouldn't hurt quite so much when they parted.

Besides, if she allowed him to have his way with her and as a result got with child—which was something neither of them had given much thought to in the past—his freedom would be jeopardised. She didn't ever want him to feel as if he was tied to her simply because he might be pressed to do the right thing by his offspring.

Deep down, she was beginning to learn that there was a part of Nathan that had escaped her, a part she could not reach no matter how hard she tried. And always, a small fear lurked in the back of her mind that this time that they were together, a time she would cherish, was too good to be true.

As they progressed with their journey, the Tagus never far from their sights, evidence of the conflict that had ravaged Portugal was everywhere. Villages were in ruins with few houses left standing. Lucy was glad Nathan didn't linger in these places.

Portugal was a land of contrasts and after four years of war it was a land soaked with the blood of men, men who had battled for supremacy, for and against Napoleon.

As Lucy rode beside Nathan her admiration for him grew. He seemed to be made of solid steel. Apparently nothing affected this incredibly brave man. Having spent many hours in the saddle, she was tormented by weariness and cramps, but nothing in the world would have made her admit it. She gritted her teeth to stop herself crying out as the saddle chafed her sore legs and jarred her aching back. She said nothing as she struggled on, knowing full well that the success of their mission was more important than her discomfort. As she listened to the birds' carefree singing, she eased her body into a new position with a tough strength, thinking that no matter how arduous the journey, she would bear it, for Katherine's sake.

The sun was setting when they reached Villa Franca—yet another wretched place. Here there was an inn for the accommodation of travellers and also a rendezvous for all manner of miscreants. The landlord asked no questions, responded with a shrug to Nathan's Portuguese, pocketed the generous coin he gave him for a bed and someone to take care of the horses and make sure they weren't stolen, and after feeding them on sorry beefsteaks, bad bread and sour wine, allotted them a small chamber above. Lucy would have preferred a chamber to herself, but she was so tired she made no complaint.

Nathan indicated the bed. 'Get in and go to sleep. You look done in.'

Unable to stifle a yawn, Lucy took off her hat before removing her boots and jacket. Aware that Nathan was watching her closely, she considered it best to keep her breeches on. Turning back the covers, she crawled into bed as he began to undress.

'It's best I sleep nearest the door,' he said, 'in case we have visitors.'

Lucy quickly moved to the other side of the bed. She was reminded of all the times they had occupied the same bed in the past, when sleep had been the last thing on their minds. Now, she was too saddle-sore and exhausted to be distracted by anything other than sleep.

Having placed the saddlebag with its precious gold on the opposite side of the room to the door, seeing there was no lock Nathan wedged the only chair firmly against it. With his pistol and sword close at hand, he blew out the candle and lay down beside her. A lantern outside swinging in the breeze cast its bouncing shadows dimly into the room. To her dismay, Lucy found her shirt was caught beneath him. She waited for him to move, but minutes passed and he did not and then she knew he had fallen asleep with his cheek against her soft curls.

With a sigh of resignation, she settled herself as best she could to pass the night in bondage, but with his presence close beside her, she found security and she sank into the realms of slumber.

* * *

Nathan came awake slowly, as if swimming upwards from the bottom of a deep pool. His mind was filled with the feel of Lucy warm and soft against him. Those tender breasts beneath her shirt were pressed against his back and her thighs were snuggled under his buttocks. His manhood rose as he thought of taking her, not by force, but with gentle persuasion.

Her lovely face swam in a vision, sultry and soft, her lips parted and moist through which her breath came. In his vision her hair seemed to beckon him forwards, caress him as he kissed her. Her arms were welcoming, encircling him, taking him into her as he pressed his manhood home.

His manhood and his mind united to betray him. Honour, self-esteem and self-control became lost in a puff of smoke before the onslaught of his passions. He was about to turn over, to relieve his masculine persuasion, but on opening his eyes, in the cold light of dawn, his hot blood waned and a cold consciousness replaced it. He recoiled with some distaste at having nearly lost himself and, throwing back the covers, rose from the bed.

Hastily shrugging himself into his clothes, he gazed down at Lucy's sleeping form, innocent and tender, still deep in slumber. He was reluctant to wake her, but he knew he must if they were to make an early start. Now wide awake, he was greatly disturbed. His body commanded him where his mind did not, and of late these visions were recurring with more and more frequency. If he wasn't careful they would get the better of him and weaken him, and then where would he be?

Resuming their journey, they arrived at the small village of Cartaxo on the Tagus, which, Nathan told Lucy, had been Lord Wellington's headquarters twice. The church was in ruins, as indeed were almost all the villages they passed through. They reached Santarem late in the afternoon. It was a fine, large town, surrounded with orange groves, but the streets were very dirty.

Nathan didn't intend staying the night in Santarem. He had another destination in mind to the north of the town. Wanting to stretch their legs, they led their horses through the busy streets, strolling along in companionable silence. The saddlebags containing the precious gold were al-

most hidden beneath rolled blankets. Although
Lucy looked about her with interest, she was
alive to the man beside her. It occurred to her
that this was the first time they had done this
and she found it a pleasurable change from being
bounced up and down on her horse.

'Have you been here before?' she enquired ca-
sually, stepping out of the way of a one-armed
man wearing the red jacket of an English soldier,
the empty sleeve pinned to his tunic.

'Once,' Nathan replied. 'The town is divided
into upper and lower and is full of convents.
Many of them have been converted into hospi-
tals for our sick and wounded. Do you see that
building up there?' He pointed out a building of
immense size and height on the skyline.

'Yes. Is it a convent?'

He nodded and when he answered he had to
raise his voice to make himself heard above the
cacophony of bells. 'As you can hear Santarem
is as bad as Lisbon for bells.'

Lucy laughed. 'I've noticed. The noise will
hardly be a blessed retirement and solace for
the sick and wounded when they are all going at
once,' she remarked, already tired of the constant

ringing. 'You were telling me about the convent up there.'

'It's of particular interest. On the top is a telegraph to communicate with Villa Franca and Abrantes.'

'Telegraph? What is that?'

'It's the medium whereby Lisbon knows every transaction relating to the army, before any dispatches can arrive. Outside the town are the remains of some Roman walls, of particular interest to the historian. If we had the time to linger, I would enjoy showing them to you.'

'I would like to see them.' She smiled. 'You will have to tell me about them instead.'

'That's not the same as seeing for oneself.'

'Indeed not, but this is no holiday, Nathan, and we cannot allow ourselves to become sidetracked with other matters. We have to get on. The sooner we make contact with Gameau and find Katherine, the sooner we will get back to Lisbon.'

They stepped aside as two children bolted from an alley, a boy and girl, laughing and shouting their enthusiasm, a barrel hoop ahead of them. Each time the hoop wandered off course, one of the children struck it with a stick and sent the makeshift toy careering ahead. Lucy stopped as the children ran past them. Their faces begrimed with the dirt of the street, they stared with bright innocent eyes at Lucy, for her disguise did not fool them.

'*Olá*, pretty lady,' the boy said in broken English.

The hoop, with no one to guide it, rattled off to the side and interrupted a flock of feeding hens that squawked their dismay and scattered in all directions. The commotion broke the spell Lucy's presence had woven around the children and they scampered back from them towards the safety of a nearby house.

Watching them go, Lucy laughed. 'So much for my disguise. Those children weren't deceived.'

They walked on in silence, emerging into a large plaza, humming with strident voices as people tried to make themselves heard over the noise of the bells. Displaced and wounded soldiers milling with the crowd all around them were a reminder of the war still going on, a war that was all about power and control, of winning and losing, of living and dying.

Lucy glanced at the man beside her. He wore his power lightly, but until this was over she would be subject to his will.

Sensing her preoccupation, Nathan regarded her, wondering not for the first time if he had been wise to bring her here. But she had shown such courage and presence of mind, and never at any time had she treated him to a fit of feminine hysterics. In fact, he thought that she had more spirit and more nerve than many men he'd met. She was remarkable in so many ways.

'Are you all right, Lucy?'

She nodded, keeping her gaze fixed ahead of her. 'Yes, perfectly.'

'You seem uneasy.'

'Of course I'm uneasy. I would be lying if I said I wasn't. I want this to be over. Soon.'

'It will be. I promise.' His gaze settled warmly on her face. 'I thought the journey might tax your strength. You are doing well.'

Lucy wanted so much to believe him, but she was dreading meeting Claude Gameau and his band of outlaws.

They shared little conversation as they rode away from Santarem and headed towards wooded hills to the north. After an hour's ride they reached a narrow track. They nearly missed it altogether, so sheltered was it by looming oaks

and pines and so untravelled it appeared. They
rode on until they came to some tall, rusty iron
gates that stood open. They followed a driveway
lined with tall hedges, past a few decrepit out-
buildings and a huge woodpile. The silence was
complete. As the drive climbed upwards, nothing broke the stillness. So it was with some surprise that Nathan turned into a narrow opening
and Lucy saw beyond a hedge overgrown gardens and a large ancient building standing four-
square, its windows small, deep set and shuttered
and barred in the evidently thick walls.

'What is this place?' she asked. It looked completely abandoned in appearance.

'A convent—a dwelling for cloistered nuns. Because of its secluded situation, it's escaped the
fate of other convents that have been ransacked
by the French. Many a pious soul in spiritual
need have found their way to this place.'

He rode towards a stout wooden door and dismounted. Knocking a few times, he waited. The
sound echoed behind it. At length a grille on the
door slid open. Nathan exchanged a few words
with someone behind it and then stood back as
the door was opened. A nun peered out, dressed
in black, her sombre costume relieved by a white

wimple. Her holy attire had seen better days, but she contrived to look neat. She also reminded Lucy of one of those sturdy country women who fear neither man nor beast.

Nathan spoke quietly to her and only then did she deign to look at Lucy.

'You can dismount, Lucy,' Nathan said. 'We will spend the night here.'

Lucy did as he asked. She had an odd suspicion that they were expected. A man suddenly appeared to take the horses. After helping Nathan to remove the saddlebags he led them away. Lucy followed Nathan inside with a vague uneasiness. She could not quite put her finger on it, but she detected a subtle change in him. Doing her best to shrug off her inexplicable misgivings, she looked around.

The room into which she stepped was dark with no light coming from the windows. Candles flickered in wall sconces, casting weird shapes around the white walls. She was aware of dark beams above her and a black floor beneath. And it was cold.

Nathan spoke to the nun in quiet tones. She said something in reply and looked at Lucy.

'You are to go with her, Lucy,' Nathan said quietly. 'She will show you where you are to sleep and some food will be sent up to you.'

Lucy stared at him in panic. 'Where will you sleep?'

'There is a room above the stable. I will be comfortable there. Besides, do not forget that this is a convent. It is not accepted practice for a man to dwell within.'

'But—are you saying I won't see you until morning?' Lucy asked, unable to hide the panic she felt at being left alone in this strange place.

'That's right.' He grinned in an attempt to dispel her anxiety. 'Don't worry, you'll survive. Take advantage of this time to get some sleep.'

Lucy was bewildered. Much as she wanted to know what they were doing at the convent, she did not ask. She felt detached and a strange passivity, as if everything was beyond her control.

Showing her impatience, the nun held up her arm, indicating Lucy should follow her in the direction she pointed. She followed her along several passageways and passed through several rooms, all small and dark and heavily beamed and with tiny windows. The atmosphere was sombre, the air rank and full of the pungent smell of cooked vegetables. Every now and then Lucy heard whispered sounds of feet treading lightly and fleetingly through rooms, and voices lowered as if in prayer, but she saw no other person. There was nothing welcoming about this place of darkness and shadows, and she was unable to understand why a woman would willingly shut herself away and devote her entire life to serving God in such a place as this.

Eventually they came to a narrow flight of stone steps rising to the upper floor. The room she was allocated was small and square, with just one window overlooking the track that had brought them to the convent. There was a narrow pallet to sleep on and a sturdy chest, with a jug of water and a bowl, a candle and a small crucifix on its rough surface. As she was left alone, that strange feeling of detachment deserted her. Now, as her mind ticked off the minutes, her fear returned and mounted until every muscle and nerve in her was filled with dread. A nun brought her some food. It was basic, a bowl of stew and bread, which she ate slowly, watching the sun go down over the trees from her window, having opened the shutters.

Putting down the bowl, she looked out, hoping to see Nathan. She hated being parted from him, even though the distance was slight. Her gaze wandered to a copse where a flock of birds had risen and took flight. Wondering what had disturbed them, she fastened her eyes on the dark shadows between the trees. One of the shadows moved and she was sure she heard the soft whicker of a horse.

Sure enough, a moment later two men strolled at a leisurely pace into the open—one of them, muffled in a black coat, was leading a horse. His companion who was the taller of the two was Nathan. They talked for several minutes before the man mounted his horse. Lucy watched them carefully as they continued to converse, then the man began to ride away.

A tremor of fear rippled through her. What sort of dark business was Nathan up to that he had to be so secretive? He'd said nothing about arranging to meet someone. Panic threatened to rise with her sudden sense of having no control over anything, of being entirely under his control, but she quelled those feelings, determined to ask him what it was all about.

Without further thought she left the room and made her way down to the door through which she had been admitted. Letting herself out, she ran as fast as her legs could carry her to where she had seen Nathan speaking to the stranger, her heart beating wildly in her breast.

Nathan turned at the sound of her footsteps, his gaze immediately falling on her flushed cheeks and dishevelled appearance. He thought she looked beautiful—she was clearly so angry about something that her eyes glittered, and he wanted nothing more than to crush her into his arms. Something he knew he must not do. He watched her in silence until she reached him. As the breeze brushed her face and caught her hair, she could hear the high-pitched screech of an owl reverberating across the thicket. The man she had seen Nathan speaking to was disappearing down the lane.

Chapter Seven

'Who was that man?' Lucy burst out breathlessly, halting beside Nathan.

He arched a dark brow. 'You don't need to know that.' Nathan saw her eyes narrow.

'There *is* something, then, something I haven't been told.'

She tossed her head. Nathan loved it when she did that. He found it endearing and spirited. 'I didn't tell you because I wanted to protect you.'

'Protect me? But I don't need protecting.'

'Very well. I had no wish to worry you.'

Her lips tightened to a pale line and he saw her hands clench. He had seen her angry in the past, and a veritable hellcat she could be, but never had her anger been so controlled as now. Controlled, he thought ruefully. She was—they both were—older now.

'I need to know everything, Nathan, if I am to help you and Katherine. Do you understand? I cannot be caught asleep if there are plans afoot of which I know absolutely nothing. What have I not been told? Was that man a contact? You arranged to meet him here, didn't you? Tell me. I've come too far with you to have the door slammed in my face.'

Nathan stared at her for a long moment. It was plain to see that she was not going to back down. At last, he gave her a grim and barely perceptible nod. 'Very well. I will tell you. The man you saw is one of the partisans.'

'He had a fierce look about him.'

'With good reason. He hates the French with all the passion of his soul. They killed his entire family and he repays them by killing as many as he can find.'

'You arranged to meet him here, didn't you, Nathan?'

He nodded, folding his arms across his broad chest. 'The convent, as you will have observed, is well hidden. Unless you know of its existence it's an ideal rendezvous—a perfect retreat. The sisters are brave.'

'I thought nuns were supposed to be impartial.'

'They are. Like everyone else they want the French out of Portugal.'

'Why has no one attacked Gameau's hideout before?'

'Because the place where they hide is too far from military lines. The partisans move through the mountains a good deal easier than the army. The difficulties would be too great. The partisans and a troop of British soldiers are planning to attack Gameau's hideout. I want Katherine out of there before it all falls apart. If the deserters get wind of an attack, in all likelihood they'll kill the hostages and escape into the hills. Wellington is not going to ignore the taking of captives by deserters, in particular women and children. An example has to be set. The partisans know the mountains. If they work together, they can take them.'

'So we have to get there before they do.'

'In exchange for information I'll pass on, they've agreed to wait, but not indefinitely. Winter is almost here. It will be more difficult to launch an attack in the snow. What I tell them—such as where the hostages are kept, an approximate number of the deserters and anything I can glean about their weaponry—will be important to them. No one's ever been inside the rebels' hideout and come out alive.'

'And you are certain that we will?'

'I told you, Claude Gameau owes me.'

'It's a dangerous game you play, Nathan.'

'I'm confident.' His expressions softened. 'I would not have made you a part of it had I thought otherwise.'

Looking up at him, Lucy met his look with a little frown, her body taut, every muscle stretched against the invisible pull between them. 'I'm glad you did. It doesn't matter, but I just wish you'd told me about your assignation with that man. I do understand that you need information. Just don't keep me in the dark, Nathan.'

He uncrossed his arms and stared down at her. 'I will tell you, the next time,' he said, his husky voice soft. 'It is not my intention to deceive you, only to keep you safe.'

'I want nothing from you, Nathan—I only want to thank you for making me a part of this. It goes a little way to righting the wrongs of the past.' She pushed a strand of her hair as she watched the throbbing of his tanned throat, trying to hide the pain in her heart, to forget what lay between them.

He glanced at her, his broad hands placed on his hips, a glint of approval kindling in his eyes. 'That applies to both of us.' He turned his head and looked along the path back to the convent. 'We should go back. We must make an early start in the morning.'

She stood there, lost. Alarm rose within her, as if something infinitely special, something elusive, was escaping her. She felt the scalding tears spring under her eyelids so that he and everything around him grew indistinct. Resolutely she fought them back. In a terrible sharp moment of perception, she knew a sense of loss so strong it seemed to squeeze the breath from her body. Whether it was because she was at a low point in the journey, Nathan's tendency to keep things from her, or the dark, sombre atmosphere of the convent, never had she needed him so much. It was a feeling almost too full, too powerful to bear, as passion and a deeper longing stabbed through her like a piercing pain. Why had she misread him all those years ago? She had missed so much not being with him then, so much of his life.

Nathan had taken a few steps away from her when he turned and eyed her closely, his brow slightly puckered. He walked back to her. 'Is something wrong, Lucy?'

Some of the colour had faded from her face. She saw his eyes brighten as if his thoughts were lifted in some eager anticipation. The steady eyes, the resolute, beautiful mouth had not for a long time been so close. She remained still, drawn into his eyes. Wanting him so very badly, she took a step closer, across the chasm of the years they had been apart. 'Help me,' she whispered fiercely. She laid a hand on his arm, the thick skin fabric of his jacket sleeve rough under her fingers.

His wariness, his distant, cool manner were now torn away. His eyes held hers in one long, compelling look, holding all her frustrated longings, her unfulfilled desires, everything that was between them. 'I will always help you!' he murmured, suddenly closing his arms about her.

Then his firm lips were on hers. He was wide and solid, with a strength that wrapped her with a satisfying reassurance. All she was aware of was heat, a blaze of power, the pressure of hard muscles in a strong body, a complete blending of passion and tenderness. There was a curious low roaring in her ears and through the sound she dimly heard the swift thudding of her heart.

Nathan deepened the kiss, feeling her change within his arms and there was madness and magic in the slender body he held and a hot glow in the eyes that looked up at him. For a timeless moment, they stood fused together as his lips took hers as if he could never have enough. Suddenly he was back in London. It was four years ago and the ease and indolence of summer, the careless desires of a young man were present. The long and bitter years since then fell away and the woman in his arms, her body melting into his, with her lips returning his kiss, was the only woman he had ever loved.

And then it was over. Nathan smiled crookedly, and tipped her face. He drew his fingers over the curve of her cheek and said, 'You really are the most unprincipled young woman, Lucy Lane.'

'I suppose I am, as far as you are concerned. You made me like that—years ago.'

He was watching her intently. Then he released her and took hold of her hand. 'Come, I'll walk back with you.'

'Do I have to go back? I rather like it when we spend the night under the stars.'

He laughed softy. 'This is a convent, Lucy, run by chaste nuns. We must do nothing to abuse their hospitality.'

'If you say so,' she replied, smiling up at him, happy to have him holding her hand. 'But I can't help the way I feel.'

Nathan was silent, a deep crease between his brows as he considered her words. 'Now is not the time to think of that, Lucy. Listen to me. Believe me when I say that if I thought we had a chance of happiness together, I'd take it. I've lived all my life taking chances, but not this one. Not now.'

She was stricken. 'You really are saying that I mean absolutely nothing to you?'

He stiffened, then relaxed. 'There you are wrong. You do mean something to me—and have done for a very long time. That is my misfortune. I have had to live with that knowledge—to think of you as unattainable. I don't want to hurt you.'

She was about to flare up in a temper of despair when she saw the expression on his face was unusually compassionate.

Without relinquishing his hold of her hand, he stopped and looked down into her shining eyes. 'Of all the women I have known, Lucy, none has possessed the fire of heart and mind of you. You are beautiful. A temptress. You could kill the man who loves you—drive a knife right through his heart and never know it.'

The sound of a single bell from the direction of the convent resounded in the air. They both looked towards the sound.

'The sounding of the bell calls the nuns to prayers—vespers or compline,' Nathan said absently. 'I don't know the order of their daily devotions, but we should go back.'

Lucy looked at him and wondered where the hot flood of feeling had gone. Suddenly she was aware of everything around her and she shivered, as if coming back from a long journey.

'Yes, you're right. We should go back.'

Nathan walked with her to the door, and only then did he let go of her hand, but not before he had raised it to his lips and placed a tender kiss on her fingers.

At first light, after eating a hasty breakfast and thanking the nuns for their hospitality, they left the convent and continued with their journey. Lucy watched the muted hues of the scenery blur together in a peaceful collage. Orange and purple streaked the sky and she looked over to the east where the sun was rising behind the high Sierras, their jagged outlines silhouetted sharply against the sky. The villages were becoming scarcer now. Soon they would navigate the sinuous mountain passes.

The strange, past days had left Lucy feeling as if she were moving through a landscape composed of nothing but vague shapes with no particular details—like a dream.

'What are you thinking?' Nathan asked beside her.

She glanced at him, smiling wearily, having put what had happened between them the night before behind her. 'I was thinking how unreal all this seems. I keep imagining that I'll wake up at home and discover this was all a dream.'

Nathan cocked her a devilish smile. 'You wouldn't miss me if you woke up and found I wasn't real?'

Lucy had to smile. 'Yes, actually, I would miss you—just a little.'

He laughed. 'Stop daydreaming, Lucy. We have work to do.'

'And hills to climb, if those mountains are an indication of what to expect. I imagine them to be full of bandits and wild animals, all waiting to vent their savagery on two unsuspecting travellers.'

'Not unsuspecting. I am fully aware of the dangers those hills pose. It is fortunate that the British and French never needed them. The savagery of the terrain made them impassable to the artillery and the infantry would struggle, which made them of no value, but to the bands of deserters they are the perfect refuge.'

They spent three more days and nights on the road before reaching the Sierras, which were reported to stretch as far as the Pyrenees Mountains. The hills were wooded with fir and impressed a picture on Lucy's mind which would not easily be erased.

The mountain paths were often perilous. Wolves prowled and rock slides were not uncommon, and the brigands were lawless, descending from the heights to rob villages before melting away like snow. The weather turned colder, and one day and night they had to endure a troublesome drizzling rain, more penetrating than a heavy shower. Lucy was glad of the thick greatcoat Nathan had provided, which protected her from the cold.

He appeared to know the way through the mountains, for despite the absence of paths and the fact that one mountain looked exactly like the next to Lucy, he rode ahead of her unhesitatingly, although he glanced about often to assure himself of both her safety and comfort. At one point they climbed so high that a tremendous precipice was frightful even to look down. Vertigo washed over Lucy as she peered over the edge. Here they appeared to be so elevated above the world below that they were, in a manner, lost to it. Here and there some bold mountains would penetrate the mass of clouds at their feet and raise their aspiring heads above them. At night even the stars and the moon seemed brighter in the mountains. The morning dew and mists of the valleys took a long time to disperse, rolling in volumes, like the sea, below them.

The journey was becoming taxing for Lucy. Not only was her dejection physical in origin, every day she began to feel more discouraged. Nathan was not openly disagreeable towards her, but he kept within the limits of punctilious courtesy which dismayed her far more than any show of temper would have done. There were times when she would have liked to talk of something else beside their assignment and Katherine's captivity. But she was beginning to realise that his thoughts roamed past her and focused on his mission, on Katherine, almost to the utter exclusion of the unhappy woman beside him.

The silence which surrounded them was ominous. His senses having been trained to high alert, Nathan became tense, watchful, his eyes constantly searching the surrounding hills for menace, pausing now and then to listen for suspicious sounds.

With eight days of continuous riding behind them, with not a town or a village in sight, they camped in a low valley close to a small lake. Well sheltered by a thick stand of trees, they were partially hidden by a shallow overhang jutting from a bluff. The journey had held no terrors for Lucy. Until now. Something was different today. There was an edge to the darkness that made her uneasy. She had the feeling something or someone was watching them. Something cold and implacable that was no friend to either of them. She sensed Nathan felt it, too.

She tried to shake off the feeling, for she was so tired when she slipped off her horse that she could barely put one foot in front of the other. She glanced at Nathan, wishing she had half his stamina. Nothing seemed to affect this incredibly strong man. Tormented as she was by weariness and cramps, nothing in the world would have made her admit it.

Lucy had taken the late watch. When the sun began to rise and everything was still and quiet, the gently misted lake looking as polished as steel, and not relishing the thought of another long day of riding ahead of her, Lucy looked with longing at the water. Nathan had told her the night before to remain near him, but, not having bathed since she had left Lisbon, the temptation was too great for her to resist.

Taking a bar of soap from the saddlebags, she slipped away, past a screen of low bushes, and down a short bank. Removing her boots and stockings and rolling up her breeches as high as they would go, she paddled into the water, gasping as the icy water lapped at her ankles. Removing her jacket, she unfastened the top buttons of her shirt. Dipping a handkerchief into the water, she bathed her neck and face. The water felt luxuriously cool and refreshing and she would have loved to remove all her clothes and immerse herself completely but dared not. However, she did take the opportunity to wash her hair. Her ablutions had taken no more than five minutes, but, much as she would have liked to sit on a rock a while, she must not remain out in the open any longer.

A horse whinnied somewhere in the distance. She glanced to the sound and froze. A man sat astride a horse, looking with icy focus in her direction, his coarse manly features impassive. Immediately she grabbed her discarded clothes and scrambled back up the bank and hurried to where Nathan stood with his hands on his hips, obviously concerned with her disappearance.

'Where were you?' he demanded, rolling his blanket. 'I thought you understood the dangers.'

'Down by the lake,' she answered shortly.

'What is it?' he demanded, seeing the fear in her eyes.'

'I saw a man on a horse farther along the bank. He was watching me.'

All of a sudden, Nathan stopped what he was doing and stared into the distance, as still as a wolf in a forest hearing some distant sound.

Suddenly Lucy was frightened. 'Nathan,

what—what is it?' Her voice, thick with worry, faltered as she spoke.

He didn't reply immediately. He peered into the distance, his keen ears searching for sounds. He sniffed the air, but the breeze was giving nothing away. Still, the alertness of a man well trained in trailing a foe entailed more than just the rudimentary senses. An instinctive warning told him that something was wrong there.

'I heard something,' he breathed.

'So did I. Maybe someone's hunting,' Lucy whispered optimistically. Feeling the hairs stir on the back of her neck, she glanced nervously about her, her eyes wide with apprehension. 'Although I don't think so.'

Nathan drew her to him protectively, placing her behind him. He stood erect, listening intently, his rifle drawn and ready for action. Everything was still and what had been peaceful now became pregnant with menace, the very silence an enemy. The horses moved uneasily as Lucy's eyes searched their surroundings.

Suddenly a horse and rider materialised from the trees. Lucy blinked her eyes and tried to focus on the shadowed figure blocking out the morning sun.

The man looked surly and dangerous. His face, his very appearance, was unsettling. Nathan watched him approach. Lucy observed the contemptuous look on Nathan's face and sensed the alertness in his body. The man halted his horse a few feet away from them—the tension between the two men was almost palpable, even to Lucy's eyes. The man's eyes moved to Lucy and lingered with an unblinking gaze. She shuddered beneath his stare and unconsciously moved closer to Nathan.

'Lieutenant Colonel Nathan Rochefort,' the man said. His English was excellent, though his accent was thick enough to carve. 'I have been expecting someone—so they sent you.'

Cocking an eyebrow in haughty question as the offensive bulk of humanity known as Le Chien Noir, the Black Dog, stared back at him, Nathan said coldly, 'Claude Gameau. It's been a long time.'

'I was wondering if you would remember me.'

'How could I not? I saved your life—an act which I have since had cause to regret.'

'I expect you do. For myself I was happy that you did. I remember saying to you that if it was ever in my power I would repay that debt.'

'And I remember telling you that I hoped it would never be in your power.'

Nathan knew without a doubt that had anyone else delivered the gold, they would not have been left alive. Gameau owed him, and despite Gameau's ruthless determination to survive against the odds, that corrupt deserter still retained some semblance of honour somewhere in him, which was why Nathan had been chosen.

'Then you must be disappointed in the way it has turned out.'

'It is one thing for a man to spout such promises, Gameau. It is quite another to consider how he might act when put to the test.'

Gameau's face flushed with indignation at what he considered to be an insult. 'I gave you my word. But be under no illusion. I am tempted to ignore what I said just to see you brought to your knees. I would enjoy breaking that proud neck of yours, Rochefort.'

'I do not doubt that, but you owe me your life, Gameau. Think back to that day. You'd been shot in the leg and you couldn't run. I could have finished you off—and that Portuguese soldier saw you hiding in the long grass and turned back, do you remember? I stopped him before he could cut off your head with his sword. There'd been enough blood and pain and killing that day. Now that same man whose life I saved is holding the wife and child of a friend of mine and you talk of killing me. To hell with you, Gameau! When I saved your life I thought it meant something.'

Shame filled Gameau's eyes. It was fleeting, but Nathan had seen it and knew he was right. Gameau had either contemplated or intended killing him once he had the gold.

'You are safe. I will not kill you this time. But if we meet again I will.'

Nathan eyed him coldly, his expression giving nothing away. 'Don't be too sure of that, Gameau.' As it happened, the partisans and a troop of redcoats were gathering, but Gameau didn't have that vital piece of information. 'And now you are a deserter. So, you no longer owe any allegiance to Bonaparte?'

A sneer distorted Claude's lips. 'When I escaped the British and made it back to my regiment, I was stripped of my rank and tried for the murder of one of my fellow soldiers who tried to double-cross me over a woman. Had I not escaped I would have been shot. By your gauge of judgement, what loyalty should I give Bonaparte?'

'That is for you and your conscience to wrestle with, Gameau. I am not here to judge you. But be assured that eventually you and your band of outlaws will be caught and your long-delayed execution will happen.'

Claude shrugged. 'Perhaps it will, perhaps I'll be lucky, but now I am a man seeking to make a profit where I can.'

'By abducting and imprisoning women and children?'

Again he shrugged. 'It happens. It is necessary for me and my men to survive.'

'How did you know where to find me?'

'I've been watching you for some time.'

Nathan said nothing for a moment. He moved a step closer and when he spoke he did so slowly and clearly. 'I know.'

Lucy stared at him in amazement. Why had he not told her?

'So what's Claude Gameau doing travelling alone? French soldiers, be they deserters or otherwise, don't travel alone. They're too frightened of the partisans. The brutal treatment they mete out to the French, be they soldiers or deserters, is well known.' He had come to stand in front of the ex-captain, now self-proclaimed general, and the Frenchman's dark eyes watched him closely.

'I did not come alone, but I'm afraid of no one, Rochefort. You, of all people, should know that. You have changed little since last we met— though the scar is new and not as disfiguring as my own.' His gaze shifted to Lucy and he laughed, the sound an unnerving rumble deep in his chest. 'Your lady is not happy to see me. Perhaps she fears I might hurt her. You are indeed beautiful, as hungry men will have told you.' His face formed a cruel semblance of a smile.

Lucy looked defiantly at him and did not move, did not speak lest her loathing and fear show. He was a lean hard wolf of a man, a cruelly featured stranger with an ugly scar, a vivid trail against sunburned skin, marring his high cheekbone. He was not as old as she'd imagined him to be, but all the marks of precocious vice were already written there on his face.

Lucy was unable to take her eyes off him. She felt her heart quicken with heavy pulsing beats. He had the look of one who was a predator amongst men and there was an aura of power, of danger, about him, a look she had seen in only

one other man—Nathan Rochefort. This man
was dressed in French blue. His face remained
singularly calm when he looked back at her. His
eyes lowered and Lucy blushed, knowing that he
was staring at her legs in their tight breeches. His
laughter was brutally mocking when he lifted his
eyes to her face, her beauty apparent even with
her damp hair curling about her head.

'You tremble, *mademoiselle*. I think, perhaps,
you are a little bit afraid of me.'

Nathan's features were non-committal as he
looked at Claude Gameau, but he was register-
ing all the subtle indications that an unpleasant
confrontation could occur if he let what he was
feeling get the better of him. For one thing, there
was a smirk of satisfaction on the Frenchman's
face. For another, positioned some yards behind
Gameau were four of his desperados dressed in a
variety of stained and threadbare uniforms from
different regiments of different countries, put together at random. They were bristling with arms,
their body language confident, their faces mocking. Nathan was under no illusion. He had met
men of their kind before. They would kill them
without a second thought and rob their corpses
afterwards if Gameau ordered them to.

'Now that we have exchanged civilities, Rochefort, let us get down to business.'

'The hostages—assuming you haven't already butchered your prisoners in your usual barbarous fashion.'

'You have come for the woman.'

'And the child. That was the agreement. Are they alive?'

The dark eyes opened wide, feigning innocence. 'Alive? Of course they are alive. You give me the gold and they will stay alive.'

Lucy did not know whether to rejoice or despair. Gameau's behaviour ran to such extremes, Katherine might have been better off had she met a quick, merciful death rather than endure whatever diabolical scheme her captor might concoct. Yet amidst her sinking spirits there was a secret joy that her old friend and her child were alive and hopefully unharmed.

'I intend to deal honestly with you,' Nathan said. 'I hope you don't repay me with treachery. How do I know you will release them on payment of the ransom?'

Gameau studied him through narrowed eyes. This was Nathan Rochefort, who had shot three men at Talavera before they'd had time to draw their swords. It was a brave man who challenged Rochefort. He shrugged. 'You don't. You will have to trust me.'

'Trust? That is a fine word coming from you, Gameau. Do you remember Harry? Harry Connors? I have not forgotten.'

'You should. He's dead.'

'You callous bastard. By your hand.'

'The lad got in my way. It was war.'

'It was murder. When I let you live you were taken prisoner by English forces and granted parole. On your honour you undertook not to escape from captivity without permission. Negotiations were underway for an exchange, but you ran. Honour was trampled when you broke your parole and murdered Harry Connors who was guarding you.' Nathan thought of the pleasure it would give him to kill this man. The rage he felt at this moment was impotent. Ever since Harry's death his head had been busy with the need to avenge his death, but now was not the time. 'I asked you a question, Gameau.'

Claude Gameau thought for a moment then he scowled. 'The woman is not well—she is sickly. She is worth nothing to me if she's dead.'

Nathan looked at him, but his face was a mask

showing no reaction to the distress he knew Katherine would be suffering. 'And the child?'

'He is taken care of. You have the money?'

Nathan nodded. 'Where are they?'

'In the mountains. Follow me.'

When they were mounted Nathan looked at Lucy. 'Follow me close. Ride steady. Watch your footing and for God's sake don't slip.'

She was pale as a sheet, but she nodded and didn't ask questions.

The mountains were ragged crests of moving shadows, sharp edged against the northern sky. They climbed ever upwards, amongst rushing streams and rock cliffs. Then the forest with the thick foliage of the trees almost shut out the day. They continued to ascend and after some difficulty scaled the top, which was very rugged. Here the air was sharp and the wind blew colder. Gameau showed no sign of halting and pressed on swiftly, leading them forwards and upwards and across long slopes of scree where they had to dismount and lead the horses, whose hooves slipped and slithered among the loose stone.

After what seemed to be an eternity, they came to a turning in the rocks where a view opened, transcendently beautiful. A large promontory was strewn with what had once been a large castle, built on and into the sheer side of the mountain. It was crumbling and dilapidated, but still formidable, with rusty chains hanging from the walls which had once housed the portcullis. It extended over a large space and some of the walls were still standing. Several towers remained, offering some defence. As far as Claude Gameau was concerned, that was the essential thing.

Riding into a rubble-strewn courtyard, Nathan halted and looked about him, careful to keep Lucy close by him while he took in the layout, memorising what he saw and storing it in his mind for further use. Men loitered about, their expressions insolent and mocking, their eyes suspicious as they watched the newcomers intently. Like their escorts, they wore uniforms mainly of France, but there were a few Portuguese, Spanish and British, their muskets tipped with bayonets.

There were about a hundred all told, but Nathan had the sense of having eyes on him he could not see. Armed, lounging sentinels stood high amongst the ruins. He kept his expression neutral, for he was very aware of the attention focused on them. He knew all the weeks of planning would come to nothing if he gave any hint of what was afoot.

The rebels watched the man and woman follow Gameau into the centre of the courtyard, beginning to close in on them with wild excitement, which was suddenly snuffed out when Gameau barked an order for them to stand back. They stared at him like dogs in the presence of the pack leader.

'Welcome to my hideout,' Gameau said to Nathan. 'The castle is centuries old. It stood against the Moors from Africa and legend says many of them died in the dungeons beneath for refusing to profess Christianity. As you see, my men are waiting to greet you. They are a disorderly lot. They like to live rough. We are a mixed bunch. There is a man from every regiment fighting in the war, from men of rank to the common soldier. But here there is no rank—no airs and graces. We are all as one.'

'Enough,' Nathan uttered sharply, dismounting. 'Where is she, Gameau? Where is Lady Newbold? I insist on seeing her at once.'

'Of course you do,' Gameau said, heaving himself from the saddle. Sauntering over to Nathan's horses, he pointed at the saddlebags. 'First you will give me the gold, Rochefort. Show me.'

'No, Gameau. First you will show me the lady. Where is she?'

Lucy shuddered, watching as Gameau's eyes narrowed on Nathan. This place struck terror into her heart. Her hands gripped the reins as she tried not to show her fear. She knew she was in the presence of traitors and scoundrels, who preferred a life of thieving and murder to more honest work. Where was Katherine? What had they done with her and the child? Her heart wrung with pity. She scrambled off her horse and waited beside him, waited for Gameau to speak.

Without taking his eyes off Nathan, he beckoned to one of his men. 'Take them to the woman.'

Leading their horses, Nathan and Lucy followed the man across the courtyard. Undeceived by Lucy's male garb, a group of men in the red coats of English soldiers leered and let forth a string of crude remarks, their manner becoming predatory. She could feel their eyes wandering over her like spiders on her skin and she shuddered. When one of them, stepping in front of her, made an obscene gesture with his finger, the sword came from Nathan's scabbard so fast that even Gameau, standing close, could not have stopped the movement.

It had been a long time since Nathan had last killed in anger, but the burn was still there to be called upon. He drew his sword in a heart-beat, implacable and without mercy. The steel glittered in the sunlight, swooped forwards, and the tip stopped an inch from the bridge of the man's nose.

'Would you care to repeat that?'

The courtyard was utterly still. The man did not move. A pulse throbbed beneath his cheek.

'I asked you a question. Would you care to re-peat that?'

The man swallowed nervously, his eyes never leaving those ice-cold orbs fixed on his. 'I will not fight you.'

'Then do not provoke one. Apologise to my companion for the insult.'

The man gaped and looked defenceless without a weapon. 'I—I do,' the man hissed.

'You do what?' Nathan persisted, his voice sounding as lethal as his sword looked.

The man kept his eyes fixed on him. 'Apolo-gise.'

The apology had been graceless and Nathan

moved the heavy blade closer to the man's nose. 'You offended the lady. Make the apology to her.' His countenance darkened with an unspoken threat all too clearly read.

Licking his lips nervously, the man shifted his gaze to Lucy. 'I apologise.'

Nathan kept the sword pressed against the man's nose a few seconds longer before leaning back, reversing the sword and thrusting it home. There was a shuffling of feet as the men drew back, muttering curses. Nathan looked at the man waiting to take them to Katherine. 'Lead on.'

Nathan and Lucy followed him towards a heavy door, ornate with decoration. Securing the horses to a post, he turned and gave Gameau a pointed warning before turning to the door. It creaked open and they went inside. They could see little at first, and as their eyes became accustomed to the gloom, on seeing a stoup that had once held holy water and tiles on the floor, they realised they were in what had once been a chapel. The room was empty. Crossing the room, they went down four steps and into another room. Lucy shivered. It was cold and dank and dimly lit with light filtering through a slit high in the wall.

At first Lucy thought the room was empty,

but then she heard a murmur of low voices from somewhere just ahead of her. She took a few steps forwards and stopped. To her horror, she saw a handful of women moving about in the shadows. They wore cloaks or shawls to guard against the cold of the room. The man who had led them inside pointed towards a low bed, on which a woman lay beneath a grimy blanket.

Lucy hurried to the bed and stared down at the woman she knew as Katherine Tindall, a woman who bore little resemblance to the vibrant, beautiful fair-haired woman she had been. In her place was a stranger, a thin haggard woman with great haunted eyes, who looked as though she had endured torture and famine and suffered a long-term imprisonment, shut away from the sunlight and fresh air. There was something else, too—something less definable. A dreadful sense of loss. A deadness, brought about, Lucy thought, by the death of her husband.

'Katherine,' she murmured.

Katherine's eyes fluttered open. For a moment she stared up at the face hovering over her, unable to believe her eyes, then a smile broke out on her lips. Her face was marked by tiredness and the strain of captivity had deepened the lines either side of her mouth.

'Lucy? Lucy... It can't be!' Her eyes drifted up to the man behind her. 'And Nathan. Oh—thank God.'

Tears blurred Lucy's eyes. Dropping to her knees beside the bed, she took Katherine's hand and placed it against her cheek. 'I'm here, Katherine—with Nathan. We've come to take you home—you and your son. Where is he?'

'With one of the women. They help me to look after him. It's so difficult, you see—never enough to eat...'

Lucy stroked her friend's hair. 'Everything is going to be different now, Katherine, but we must get you out of here.'

Nathan placed a hand firmly on Lucy's shoulder. 'We have to leave.' He glanced around the squalid room. 'How many hostages are there, Katherine?'

'Twelve—excluding me and Charles.'

'Children?'

'No. Only Charles.'

He nodded, grim-faced, wishing he didn't have to leave one hostage behind in this accursed place. But he had no choice. 'Prepare Katherine to leave, Lucy. We can't delay any longer. The sooner we are gone from this place the better.'

Lucy got to her feet. 'Are you able to ride, Katherine? Nathan said you were wounded when you were taken captive.'

'I was shot in the shoulder, but it is healed now. I am still weak, but I will withstand the ride if it means getting out of here. But what about the others? I am not the only hostage. I hate to leave them.'

'I cannot take anyone else, Katherine,' Nathan said. 'I am here to pay your ransom. We can only hope your fellow hostages will be freed very soon.'

'Yes, yes,' Katherine said softly, hurriedly. 'We must get away from here. Quickly. It's a bad place.'

'Where is your son, Katherine?' Lucy asked, looking around for the child.

'Charles—his name is Charles.' Katherine struggled to sit up and called to someone called Kate.

A woman broke away from the others, carrying an infant in her arms. 'Here he is.' She handed him to Katherine.

'Give him to me.' Lucy took him gently from

his mother's unresisting arms, kissing his brown curls, before wrapping a blanket around him.

Nathan was impatient to be away from the castle. His task was to secure Katherine and her child's freedom, to protect them and Lucy, to get them as far away from Gameau before the partisans arrived. He hoped Gameau had too few men to hold them off.

Everything happened quickly. With Lucy's help Katherine collected her few belongings and, after saying a tearful farewell to those who must remain captives of Claude Gameau and his ruthless band of deserters, went outside. Gameau was waiting by the horses.

'You have the woman, now you will give me the money, Rochefort.'

Nathan heaved the heavy saddlebag off the third horse and dropped it on the ground. The coins clinked dully inside the leather. 'There's your gold, Gameau. It's all there.'

Gameau opened the saddlebag and ran his fingers through the coins and looked up at Nathan, his eyes alive with satisfaction.

Without Nathan's assistance Katherine could never have managed to climb on to her mount. Her legs buckled and refused to obey her. Nathan swung her up in his arms and bodily placed her in the saddle on the spare horse. She sat astride, clinging to the reins as if her life depended on it. Lucy climbed into the saddle and took the infant in her arms, balancing him in front of her.

Katherine glanced around, fearful for her son. 'Charles...'

Lucy was quick to reassure her. 'I have him with me, Katherine. Don't worry. He's safe.'

They waited until Gameau was satisfied the ransom money was what he'd demanded before facing Nathan. 'I have counted the money. You can go.'

Nathan's eyes did a quick sweep of the men standing around. 'You have many men, Gameau. How many?'

Gameau held up a hand to stay any more questions, his eyes narrowed. 'You cannot expect me to tell you that. I will just say that there are enough for us to succeed should an army launch an attack.'

Nathan didn't reply immediately. It had been worth a try. 'You have other hostages—all women, I see.'

Gameau shrugged. 'Negotiations are going on for their freedom. They will stay alive as long as your soldiers stay away from here. You understand what I am saying, Rochefort?'

Grim-faced, Nathan nodded. 'You will be caught, Gameau. Our paths will cross again. Be assured of that. I will not show mercy a second time. You are a convicted traitor. You should not be allowed to walk free.'

'But I do, and will continue to do so for a long time yet. Now go, Rochefort, while you can,' he said in the acid tones of an enemy. 'The debt is paid. Whatever happens beyond this point, look to your life.'

The look Nathan gave Gameau before he turned away was a silent promise of future retribution. Deep inside him it galled him to ride away from the deserter. It was like leaving a task half-done. But he was not willing to chance the lives of his charges on wreaking his own vengeance on Gameau.

Chapter Eight

Lucy rode beside Katherine. From time to time she glanced at her, fearing she would fall out of the saddle. But somewhere deep inside her Katherine had found a reserve of strength and she managed to cling to her horse. It wouldn't be nightfall for several hours and Nathan wanted to put as much distance between them and Claude Gameau as possible. They took a different route from the one that had brought them to the castle.

'I don't think Gameau will have a change of heart and come after us, but I can't be certain. It is possible that he and his men will stay where they are, but it would be foolish to tempt fate. Do you see the forest down there? That is the route we will take. As we drop down into the valleys there are villages where we will find shelter for the night.'

Taking Katherine's horse by the bridle, he led it towards the trail which ran deep into the forest. The path wound between thick banks of firs which rose up like walls on either side. The deeper into the forest they went, the narrower the trail became. The trees and chequered shadows closed behind them. They listened to the sound of movement fade and die, and all at once the forest was intolerably quiet. They plodded onwards. A thick layer of fallen needles carpeted the ground, so the shoes of their horses made only the faintest sound. Nothing seemed to stir in that breathless stillness. There seemed to be nothing alive in it but themselves. Lucy knew these woods abounded with wolves, but she tried not to think about that as she held the child close.

As they urged on the flagging horses, Katherine's head fell forwards on to her chest and Lucy knew she wouldn't be able to ride much longer. Through the tops of the trees she could see the sun was going down. They had to find a place to rest soon.

She looked at Nathan, slightly ahead. 'Katherine is exhausted and the child will have to be fed soon. How much longer before we are out of the forest?'

Nathan turned his head and looked at the sleeping child nestled in front of Lucy, then he looked at Katherine. It was clear from the way she slumped in the saddle that she was exhausted, but her eyes were calm and they looked back at him steadily.

'If we can reach one of the villages, we will get some milk.'

'He is nine months old, Nathan. I have no experience of raising babies, but Charles seems to be very small for his age. Milk alone will not suffice. He must have proper food.'

'And I shall see that he gets some. Not long now and we'll be out of the forest.'

After another hour's riding, Lucy breathed a sigh of relief when they emerged into the open. The stars were coming out and Katherine had fallen asleep in the saddle. They headed for a village lying amongst enormous rocks. It was a tolerably good one, with some of the houses built of mud. When Nathan enquired of some locals in Portuguese if there was somewhere they could stay the night, the people were civil and pointed them to what might pass as a hostelry.

They quickened their horses' steps and dismounted outside the low building. Katherine woke when Nathan lifted her from the saddle. He pushed open the door of solid, rough-hewn planks. A young woman who was standing over a cooking pot on the hearth straightened up in surprise at the sight of the travellers. The strange, almost unreal picture they presented was one which would remain for a long time in Lucy's mind.

Without a word the woman beckoned them inside. Nathan spoke quietly to her. She pointed upwards, indicating there were beds, and then at the pot of stew bubbling away. Katherine shook her head and said she wasn't hungry. She was very quiet and seemed to be bewildered by everything that was happening, along with Lucy's presence with Nathan. But she was bone-weary and too exhausted by mental and physical stress to ask questions, nor did she have any desire for food. Lucy urged her to eat, saying that she would need all her strength if they hoped to make good progress the next day.

'You will also sleep all the better for a little food and awake refreshed.'

So they ate what they could, and afterwards Katherine curled up on the bed the young woman had prepared for her and fell asleep almost immediately, her arm wrapped protectively around her sleeping son. His cheeks were flushed and his breathing even, his stomach full of warm goat's milk, which he had swallowed with relish, before being overcome with sleep.

Lucy looked down at them with a heart full of regret. When she thought how she had treated Katherine it wrung her heart, even though an affair between Nathan and Katherine had been a reasonable conclusion for her to jump to at the time. She had committed a terrible injustice to one of the people she most loved in the world.

Nathan stood outside, staring at the shadows of the surrounding hills. There were things he had to think about. Not only did the problem of getting Katherine and her child back to Lisbon safely prey on his mind, he had a rendezvous to keep with the leader of the partisans. They were impatient to attack the deserters' camp and he was grateful they had agreed to wait until he'd got Katherine and her son out. He was concerned for the hostages he'd had to leave behind, but if things went as planned they would all be freed within days and Gameau dead or a prisoner of the British.

Lucy came outside to join him. The glow from the moon caught her in a shaft of light. Nathan turned and surveyed her with faint surprise, as though she were someone he had never seen before. She wore her breeches but had removed her jacket. Her shirt moulded the slender beauty of her upper body with perfection. Her skin glowed in the moonlight and he thought with a complete lack of emotion that she was the most beautiful thing he had ever seen—a stranger. The actress, the Lucy Lane he had once known, the fearful young woman who had embarked on this journey to the unknown, had gone. The wariness had gone, too, and the great dark eyes were no longer unsure, but quiet and untroubled. There was a serenity and a glow about her—and something that was almost happiness.

How can she look like that? Nathan thought, with a faint twinge of irritation, as if she were entirely content and there were no problems that mattered. He had tried to assure her that he knew what he was doing and that everything would be all right. But did she have to be so trusting? Had she no imagination? But of course she had, he reminded himself. She was an actress. Using her imagination was her stock in trade. But didn't the war that was going on around her make her realise that their day-to-day journey was a matter of living from day to day by luck and cunning and the grace of God?

Lucy said, 'I came to say goodnight, Nathan.'

The incongruity of the matter-of-fact statement in that setting and his dark thoughts suddenly struck him, and he laughed for the first time in days.

Surprised, Lucy stared at him. 'Nathan? What is it?'

Nathan saw her teeth gleam and knew that she was smiling. 'Nothing, Lucy. Nothing at all. It's just that you seem—relaxed, more relaxed than you have since leaving England.'

'Perhaps that's because I am. Best of all is the fact of departing, leaving behind that strange and dangerous place which seemed unlikely to free us alive. When I first laid eyes on Claude Gameau, I feared he would not let us go. Now I feel so much better, so much more optimistic.' She gave him a sideways glance. 'I'm sorry about what happened to Harry Connors,' she said quietly. 'How old was he?'

His expression hardened. 'He was a sixteen-year-old ensign, a lad who had dreamed of being a soldier and was desperately eager to please his superiors and make his father proud. He was left to guard Gameau. I let Gameau live and he went on to kill Harry.'

'And you have blamed yourself ever since. I understand now what you meant when you told me Gameau owed you. You let him live.'

Nathan looked down at her and nodded. 'Which I deeply regret. I swore that one day I would avenge Harry's death.'

'Then I can imagine how difficult it must have been for you to ride away from Gameau earlier.' When he remained silent she turned away. 'I'll leave you to your thoughts. Goodnight, Nathan.'

'Lucy,' he said softly, 'I have to thank you.'

'For what?'

'Being here—for Katherine.'

She didn't know what to say. She had embarked on this dangerous journey for him as well as Katherine. Finally, she said, 'I'm just glad I could be.'

'How is Katherine?'

'Sleeping.' Lucy sighed. 'I'm worried about her. She isn't well, I fear. I don't think she's had enough to eat—being wounded hasn't helped her.

Could we not rest here a few days to let her re-gain her strength?'

'There's little enough shelter or comfort for her here. It's not a place I'd choose to linger. I'd like to leave the hills behind. If she's no better when we reach Santarem we'll throw ourselves on the mercy of the nuns. I'm sure they'll let her stay at the convent until she's well enough to complete the journey to Lisbon.'

'I must confess that I'll be glad when we're out of the mountains.' She gave him a teasing smile before turning to leave. 'Goodnight, Na-than. Try to get some sleep. With two women and a child to lead out of these hills, you will need to keep your wits about you.' She was rewarded when she heard him chuckle softly and told her to sleep well.

Having purchased some food and filled some of the canteens with milk and some nourishing soup for Charles, they left the village. Beset by a gnawing tension as they rode south, Nathan wished he could have let Katherine rest a little longer. She looked as though she needed it. But there was no help for it; they would have to press on. He looked up at the gathering clouds, cursing softly. If things weren't bad enough, it looked as though they would have rain to contend with.

It began mid-morning, dark showers that slanted about them before opening directly above them, then a crash of thunder bellowed across the sky growing darker. The hills were steep, the valleys deep, with several feral goats feeding on the sparse grass, goats on which the mountain wolves fed. As they rode along a high ridge, the going was hard and slow. They rested often to give Katherine respite and to feed Charles. Lucy kept him close to her, shielding him from the rain which fell intermittently, thankful that when he wasn't sleeping he would look about him with wide-eyed curiosity.

With Lucy and Katherine wearing heavy coats and wide-brimmed leather hats to shield them from the rain, they rode beside a wide stream, its rain-swollen water tumbling down from the mountains, white and deep and ice-cold over its rocky bed. The rain became relentless and the wind blew straight into their faces.

At dusk, with peals of thunder shaking the rocks and lightning slicing the sky in two and the

rain—a deluge fit to make a man build an ark—
Nathan led them down from the ridge. He pointed
ahead.

'There!' he exclaimed.

His voice broke through Lucy's thoughts and
she followed his gaze, turning slightly to stare
straight ahead into the yawning mouth of a cave.

Cold and wet and conscious of Katherine's
weakened state, Nathan quickly led them inside
and conjured a fire from damp kindling. He then
proceeded to brew tea.

'Making tea is the most essential part of being
a soldier,' he said lightly, when he brought Lucy
and Katherine a mug.

This brought a smile to Lucy's lips. 'And a
good job you've made of it,' she said, warming
her hands on the mug and taking a sip of the hot
liquid, relieved to be out of the rain at last.

Nathan brought the tired horses into the mouth
of the cave and stripped them of their saddles.
Loosely tethered to a post, they nibbled at the
meagre forage just outside and within their reach.
They would need more food before taking up the
journey, but for the present they were happy and
dry. Lucy laid out the bedrolls. Against Katherine's shoulder, Charles stirred and gave a fretful

cry. He had been docile and sleepy for the past three hours, but now he was awake and needed food.

'Give me the baby.' Katherine handed him over. Lucy's heart was curiously stirred by the little boy. 'Hush, now, little love. Soon you shall drink your fill, but first we must make camp.'

She saw Katherine settled before turning her attention to tending Charles, who had begun crying and looked very sorry for himself. Katherine had said little since leaving the deserters' camp, but her concern for her child was evident in the way she watched him and held him to her when they stopped to rest.

While Katherine slept, Lucy sat on the ground with Charles in her arms.

Watching Lucy, Nathan smiled. It never failed to move him when he saw her with the child. She was so gentle and tender with him.

'I have no doubt that one day you will make a wonderful mother,' he murmured, capturing her eyes when she raised them to his.

Sighing wistfully and looking down at Charles, she smiled softly. 'Maybe. Some day.'

Having spooned some thin soup into his mouth followed by more goat's milk, he was content at last, his huge eyes staring unblinkingly into her own. He was always so quiet. Perhaps the world had taught him to be that way. She held him tight, savouring every moment. She had thrown herself happily into taking care of Katherine and Charles. Seeing to their needs and their safety gave her a sense of purpose which not even her success as an actress had achieved.

Rocking him gently in her arms, with the last remaining light disappearing from the sky and the glow of the fire sending flickering shadows around the walls of the cave, she looked across at Nathan. He was seated on the hard floor with his back leaning against the rock. His eyes were closed and he appeared to have drifted off to sleep. Lucy studied his face, the form of the man she loved. His face etched with strain and fatigue, the shadow of a beard gave him an unkempt look. But even now there was a clean, open handsomeness to his face. It was a strong face made for laughing, a man with whom she would like to share her love…

With tears pricking the backs of her eyes, she looked down at Charles who was now asleep. Wrapping him in a warm blanket, she gently placed him next to a sleeping Katherine. Getting to her feet, she went out of the cave to answer a call of nature. Thankfully it had stopped raining. Breathing deeply of the cool mountain air, after seeing to her needs and reluctant to go back inside the cave just yet, she walked towards the rushing stream. Standing on the bank, she wrapped her arms about her waist and looked down. The water seethed white below her, bouncing off the rocks and twisting in pools.

Suddenly, sensing she was not alone and feeling the hairs on the back of her neck bristle, she glanced ahead. From the darkness a shadow took form. It moved with the stealth of a wolf.

Uttering a cry of horror as she was about to head for the cave, her foot slipped and she was unable to save herself from tumbling into a whirlpool of water. The stream was scarcely a dozen paces across, but it was deep and the cold water tugged at her legs. The rocks underfoot were slick and uneven. She struggled to stand, but she was swept a few yards downstream.

When he opened his eyes and immediately saw Lucy missing, Nathan left the cave to look for her, seeing the shape of a wolf slip away into the trees. Hearing her cry, he rushed towards the stream. He saw what he thought was the branch of a tree drifting on the surface. Suddenly an arm flashed in the dim light and he realised it was a person—Lucy. There was a sputtering and thrashing as she struggled for a grip.

His concern and fear for her rampant on his face, quickly he glanced about him. Very shortly she would be moving well beyond his reach and there would be little he could do to save her. She swirled in an eddy and started to roll. Flinging her arm wide, she gave out a weak call before her head went under. The words were lost to him, but the sound of the voice set him to action.

Snatching off his heavy jacket, he ran along the side of the stream until he was ahead of her and splashed into the water. He swam out, fighting the strong current that sought to drag him under as it swept Lucy towards him. Taking a deep breath, he reached out and managed to grasp her arm. He channelled all the strength he could muster into pulling her towards him. His strength was nearly spent and it was all he could do to tug her on to the bank.

Lucy coughed and collapsed to her knees, breathing deeply, a haze in front of her eyes. With an effort she crawled up the bank and got to her feet and looked about her. Then the haze cleared and Nathan was before her. They stood staring at each other for a minute, then Lucy stumbled forwards and as she ran to him she dropped to her knees, aware of her pounding head and thudding heart. He dropped beside her and caught her to him and she felt his arms go about her in a desperate grip.

'Thank God I reached you in time. I thought I'd lost you,' he said, his voice catching in his throat.

Holding her head against him, he rocked her as though she were a child. Her hair clung to her head like a cap and he passed his fingers through it, whispering endearments that she did not hear, for she was shaking with terrible, grinding sobs that seemed to wrench her body to pieces. He could feel the heat of those tears on his neck and he held her tighter, straining her against him until at last they stopped. The racking shudders ceased, and presently she lifted her head and looked up into his face.

Lucy's eyes in the fading light held an odd, beseeching look and Nathan's arms lifted and pulled her down on to the grass. She felt his hands pulling at her clothes, wrenching her shirt away, and he hid his face between her soft breasts. Her skin was cool from the stream, and smooth and sweet, and he kissed it with an open mouth, moving his cheek and his head against it, holding her closer.

There was neither love nor tenderness in Nathan's hands or his kisses. They were deeply and desperately physical. A strange frenzy seemed to have seized him. Wordlessly, roughly, he tore off her breeches, his hands searching greedily for the softness of her skin. With his lips close to her face he was murmuring passionate endearments, only stopping to cover her mouth with kisses. With her eyes closed Lucy allowed herself to be carried away, yielding herself to the slow, overwhelming crescendo of passion which surged through her like a tidal wave.

Half-wild with desire, she clung to him, returning kiss for kiss, and she knew that for the moment her cool body meant no more to him than a balm to his pain—a temporary forgetfulness and release from the intolerable strain and his fear that he might have lost her to the stream. But it was enough that she could give him that.

And then as the world seemed to dwindle to just the two of them, the miracle struck like a spark from two beings created for each other, and all the years they had been apart were swept away as though they had never been. Here in the soft wet grass, with the sound of the stream rushing past, there were only Lucy and Nathan— Nathan's arms and his mouth and his need of her. Lucy gave herself as she never had before and knew a joy which effaced everything.

At long last they lay still. The sky darkened and the stars and the moon appeared above the trees. Far away a wolf howled—maybe the same wolf that had frightened her so much that she had tumbled into the stream—but Nathan slept the sleep of utter mental and physical exhaustion, and Lucy held him in her arms and watched the stars and was not afraid of the rushing stream or the wolves or anything else. They were encapsulated by this moment out of time, a blend of the past and the mystical attraction that still bound them together. She thought of Katherine and Charles sleeping in the cave. They would not know they were temporarily alone.

Nathan's head was heavy on her breast and the weight of the arm that lay across her and pressed her down on the wet grass seemed to increase. But she did not move except to hold him closer. After a while, knowing they should return to the cave, reluctantly she shifted slowly, sliding her body from beneath him and standing up. Pulling on her breeches and her wet shirt, she gently shook his shoulder.

Lying face down, Nathan slowly came awake. He lay still and after a moment slowly opened his eyes, aware of the wet grass beneath him. Rolling on to his back, he looked up at Lucy. He said after a moment or two, 'I'm sorry, Lucy.'

His voice did not express sorrow, or anything else—unless it was, perhaps, regret. Lucy's heart contracted with the familiar ache of pain that she had felt so often when she looked at Nathan. *Are you really sorry?* she thought. *Please don't be, my darling. Anything but that.*

She wanted desperately for him to stand up and put his arms about her and to tell him that she loved him, and nothing in all the things that had happened to them mattered more than that. But she knew that she must not do so. He did not want to hear it and he would not understand it.

'We should go back,' she said, avoiding his eyes. 'Katherine might wake and be afraid to find herself alone.'

Her words brought him to his feet. 'You go. I'll follow in a moment.'

She stared at him, hurt and resentful. How

could he appear so cold, so dispassionate after what they had just done? Her dark green eyes were wide with an effort to hold back tears of angry despair. All that had been beautiful a moment ago now lay in a heap of ashes at her feet.

In a dark corner of the cave she removed her clothes and rubbed herself dry on a blanket before donning fresh clothes and curling up on her bed roll to go to sleep.

Nathan watched her go, finding it hard to come to terms with what had just happened. He had already suffered so much because of her that he could not even bring himself to contemplate the immensity of pain which this new tragedy would inflict upon him. Until now he had managed to convince himself that his memory of the passion that had erupted between them four years ago was faulty, exaggerated. But what he had just experienced surpassed even his imaginings. It surpassed anything he'd ever felt. He stared into the darkness, trying to ignore the way she had felt in his arms.

A slow realisation of what was happening, born on the moment he had taken her in his arms, was moving through him, moving its way from his wounded heart up to his slowly thawing mind. He had become aware that something awe-inspiring had happened to him in that moment it had taken for his heart to acknowledge it. He thanked God Lucy was safe, that he had been in time to save her from being washed away by the stream, but until this assignment was complete and Katherine and her son were delivered into the Newbold family fold, he would not allow himself to consider what the future held for them.

They awoke to find the rain had ceased and the cave was filled with sunlight.

Katherine had taken Charles outside and Nathan was turning away to make the horses ready, but Lucy stopped him, laying a gentle hand on his arm.

'Nathan,' she murmured, gazing at him with eyes shining with tenderness. 'What happened last night… Does that mean you have changed your mind about us?'

His face became frozen, expressionless, as if he had disappeared from her once more. She was on edge with her cravings for things to go back to normal between them, but that was beginning to seem downright unlikely.

Bitter disappointment engulfed her, drowning

out all the wonderful feelings of rediscovering something that had once been so sublime. He looked at her as though nothing important had happened between them.

Nathan turned his head away to escape the soft bewitchment of those lovely imploring eyes. Then gently he detached himself from her. 'I don't know how it happened, Lucy, how I allowed it to happen, how I let my desire for you carry me away.' He sighed, shrugging slightly. 'Perhaps it was old memories...'

She backed away, deeply hurt and disappointed by his casual remark. Old memories! Was that all he felt for her, all that was left? 'Yes—I understand,' she said, unable to conceal the bitterness she felt. 'Old memories. But sometimes old memories are hard to let go of.'

'It was also relief I felt. I was relieved you hadn't been washed away by the current. You could so easily have drowned.'

'But I didn't. I don't understand. Why did you do that if not to take up the thread of our old love again?'

His face hardened. 'Leave it, Lucy. That's enough for now.'

She turned away so he would not see the hurt

in her eyes. What a fool she had been. She had thought she had drawn close to him, that they were as close as a man and woman could be, and yet it would seem that was not so. He had drawn away from her. Nathan was as elusive—perhaps more so—than he had ever been.

What had happened to her? Why had chance, destiny, whatever it was called, turned, so quickly, her supreme resolution not to succumb to this man again, to a painful love that was blurring her mind when she should be thinking not about herself or even Nathan, but about Katherine.

Leaving the cave to join Katherine, she glanced at Nathan. Her green eyes enormous in the paleness of her face, she saw only the small clouds of dust kicked up by his feet as he walked away. As the sun mounted the farthest ridge of hills, silvering the sky for a dazzling day, she felt scalding tears spring under her eyelids so that everything grew indistinct and misty.

Nathan was the last to mount. He wheeled his horse about in time to catch Lucy's eye. There was a sudden duel of glances as his eyes invaded hers, drawing her to him, and she felt again the sudden heat of suppressed passion. They were yards apart, yet in some strange way they seemed joined together. Then his face darkened abruptly and he looked away.

They continued south, towards the Tagus. The rain had passed over and, despite the sun which flared in the bright sky, the entire region through which they rode, arid and wild, had an air of savage melancholy, enhanced by the distant tolling of a solitary church bell.

Lucy's mind dwelt on the previous night and Nathan's reaction to her earlier and her heart ached. No matter how much he tried to show otherwise, she knew he was deeply affected by what had happened between them. She guessed at the distress hidden beneath that inflexible manner of his. Even after they had made love, she was no closer to opening that locked heart. He was keeping tight rein on his emotions, trying to find every reason to hate her from fear of loving her.

They were each sunk in their own private thoughts. Lucy, however, was struggling against an imperious desire to fill the silence which had fallen between them. Her love raged all the fiercer at feeling him to be so near and so distant all at once.

* * *

They were on the outskirts of a small village where they were to rest for the night. A large group of men on horseback were gathered round the gnarled roots of a tall tree. Lucy had the odd impression that they weren't in the least surprised to see them, that they had, in fact, been waiting for them to appear. One man detached himself from the rest and rode towards them. Taut with apprehension, Lucy watched him ride close. She saw he was not a young man, perhaps forty or more. His hair beneath the hat he wore was long and streaked with grey. His expression was sharp, his eyes intelligent. She glanced at Nathan. He didn't appear to be worried.

'Do you know him?' she asked, keeping her voice low.

Nathan nodded. 'His name is Arturo Garcia—the same man you saw me with at the convent.'

Garcia halted in front of them, his gaze resting on Katherine and the child Lucy held in front of her.

'Señor Rochefort! You succeeded,' he said in English.

'We wouldn't be here now if I hadn't.'

The man nodded. 'I congratulate you. No one

rides into Gameau's camp and comes out alive.
But that will end. We are ready. We go in in two
days. But first I will listen to what you have to
tell me. What are your ideas? Can the hostages
be rescued?'

'They can be, as long as you know where they
are.'

'Did you see all of Gameau's men?'

'Most of them. Some will have been on look-
out in various places.'

'What is your opinion? Can we take them?'

'I won't pretend it will be easy. They will be
expecting something of the sort. There will be
sentries. My advice would be for you to go in
at night. Surprise them before they have time
to take their vengeance on the hostages—all
women, a dozen in total.'

'With any luck the rebels will be flat on their
backs with the drink. You are to stay here tonight?' Nathan nodded. 'Then we will talk at the
inn and you can draw me a map of the fortress
and the position of their weaponry.'

When they crossed the threshold of the inn,
they were relieved to find they would have it to
themselves. Leaving Nathan to talk to Garcia,

Lucy went to the room she was to share with Katherine and Charles.

Nathan told Garcia everything he had seen at the castle and Katherine's account concerning the hostages. When he had finished, Garcia left carrying a sheet of paper covered with notes. Night had fallen upon the village. Nathan watched him mount his horse and join the men waiting for him, fully aware of the risks involved in storming the castle and freeing the hostages unharmed.

Lucy came to stand beside him, watching Garcia's departing figure. 'Do you think they will succeed?'

'It won't be easy. There will be losses,' Nathan said, his face grim. 'The rebels who are not killed will be taken prisoner. The British deserters will be returned and dealt with by the army.'

'Would you not like to be involved, Nathan?'

He spoke sharply. 'No. It must be left to the army and the partisans. We came here to save Katherine and her child, and their safety comes first. Our part is done. We cannot afford to take risks with their lives.'

They continued to stand, watching Garcia ride away. The night air was chilly.

'It's a full moon,' Lucy said after several minutes, looking up at the huge yellow orb. When he didn't reply, she cast about for something else to say and inadvertently voiced her own thoughts. 'I can't quite believe we have Katherine and her son safe, and that in a few days we'll be in Lisbon.'

'I am thankful about that. Come, let's walk a while.'

They walked slowly along the street, taking a turn that took them away from the dwellings. The lights from the windows faded and then vanished completely. Suddenly there was nothing in front of them but the darkness of a valley far below and a blanket of stars overhead. Nathan stopped and shoved his hands into his pockets, staring out across the valley. Uncertain of his mood, Lucy wandered a few paces to the end of the path and stopped because there was nowhere else to go. Glancing to her left, she stole a look at his profile. In the moonlight it was harsh and he lifted his hand and rubbed the muscles at the back of his neck.

'I think we should be getting back,' she said when a minute had passed and his silence became unsettling.

In answer Nathan tipped his head back and

closed his eyes, looking like a man struggling with some internal battle. 'Why?'

'Because Katherine will be wondering where we've got to—and there's nowhere else to walk.'

He sighed, opening his eyes, and his relentless gaze locked with hers. 'You're right, there isn't. I just wanted to be alone with you for a while.'

Lucy stared at him, her entire body beginning to vibrate with a mixture of shock, desire and fear. Thankfully her mind remained in control. She had found herself in this situation several times since leaving Lisbon and she was not prepared to let him play with her heart again. Here they were, completely alone. The situation was dangerous. Frightening. And based on her behaviour when he'd pulled her from the stream, she couldn't even blame him for thinking she'd be willing now. Struggling desperately to ignore the sensual pull he was exerting on her, she drew a long, shaky breath.

'Why? Why do you want to be alone with me? Do you want to drag me behind a hedge and repeat what you did to me the last time we were alone together?'

'I didn't have scruples enough to ignore that ignoble impulse. Nor do I regret what we did.'

A treacherous warmth was slowly beginning to seep into Lucy's body and she fought the weakness with all her might. 'It was wrong. Dangerous and foolish.'

'Foolish or not,' he said grimly, 'I wanted you. I want you now.'

Lucy made the mistake of looking at him and his eyes captured hers against her will, holding them imprisoned.

'Neither of us has anything to gain by continuing this pretence that what happened in the past is over and forgotten,' he said bluntly. 'There was too much between us for it to end like that. The night of the storm proved that it's still very much alive, if it proved nothing else, and it's never been forgotten. I've remembered you and everything we had, and I know you've remembered me.'

Lucy wanted to deny it, but she knew that if she did he'd be disgusted with her deceit and she was too affected by what he'd just admitted to lie to him. 'You're right,' she said shakily. 'I've never forgotten you. How could I?' she added defensively.

He smiled at her sharp retort and moved towards her.

'What are you doing?' she whispered when he

reached out and took her hand. She stared at him in paralysed terror mixed with excitement.

'I'm going to take you in my arms and kiss you. I'll not force you. I'll not force you to do anything against your will. When we embarked on this journey to rescue Katherine and her son, neither of us knew what was going to happen.'

'And now we do?'

Raising his hand, he slowly tucked a stray lock of her hair behind her ear. 'I believe we do.' Placing his finger gently beneath her chin, he turned her face up to his and, lowering his head, traced his lips across her cheek to her ear.

Some small insidious voice in Lucy's mind reminded her of his cold rejection of her when she had given herself to him totally after he had pulled her out of the water. But after the misery she had suffered afterwards, was she not entitled to another of his kisses if she wanted it? Another voice warned her not to break the rules again. But his face was touching hers and his breath was warm in her ear. Some inner strength surfaced and she made a move to pull away, but she froze when he murmured, 'You want me, Lucy. Don't deny it.'

As he placed his finger gently beneath her chin,

Lucy raised her eyes to his, the answer written in their depths. It was this that finally crumbled Nathan's resistance that had possessed him since he had weakened and they had made love. Since then, with past experiences still at the forefront of his mind, some protective instinct warned him that he must never again let himself trust her, never again touch her, but just this once…just one more time, to yield to that insistent mouth that was quivering and soft so close to his own.

His smouldering gaze dropped to her lips and Lucy felt her body ignite at the same instant his mouth swooped down, capturing hers in a kiss of demanding hunger. Her lips softened imperceptibly and Nathan claimed his victory with the swiftness of the hunter, except gentleness was his weapon now.

Lucy could feel his hunger, his desperation. His arms held her tighter as she fitted herself to him and he deepened his kiss, crushing her lips, parting them, his tongue driving into her mouth with hungry urgency, and their passion ignited. Heedless of what he was doing, when he felt her arms tentatively reach up to rest on his shoulders, his hands tracing her curves without volition, Nathan urged her to give him back what he was offering her.

His lips were just as warm and exciting as ever, and just as devastating. She opened her mouth fully to him, wanting his kiss, his possession. She was hardly aware that his hand was gliding upwards until she felt his fingers curl around her breast, cupping the swelling fullness and brushing a nipple with one finger.

Her reaction was immediate—she gasped softly. Nathan heard her faint inhalation with satisfaction. Purposefully, he splayed his fingers, covering her breast and moulding it against his palm.

The resultant wave of heat shocked her—it raced through her body to settle as a throbbing ache somewhere between her thighs, in the very core of her womanhood.

Nathan continued kissing her with the same uncontrollable compulsion to have her that had seized him in the past and again when he had rescued her from the stream, and he kissed her until she was moaning and writhing in his arms and desire was pouring through him in hot waves. Tearing his mouth from hers, he slid his lips across her cheek, his tongue seeking her ear while his hand continued to intimately caress her breast.

An eternity later he lifted his head, his blood pounding in his ears, his heart thundering. Lucy stayed in his arms, her cheek resting against his chest, her soft and pliant body pressed to his, seeking the haven of his arms and solace from the turmoil of her emotions. Wind rippled through the long grass, whispering in the trees. Nathan's hand stroked soothingly up and down her spine, his cheek resting against her hair.

Drawing a shattered breath, wanting to understand why this was happening to her, she whispered, 'Why do I always feel this way when you take me in your arms?'

Nathan heard the plea for understanding in her voice and understood what she was asking. It was the same question he had been asking himself. Why did this explosion of passion overwhelm him every time he touched her? Why could this woman always make him lose his mind?

'I can't answer that,' he said, his voice sounding sharp and unnatural to his own ears.

'I feel like we've never been apart.'

'You must be living under some kind of delusion.' He laughed lightly, as if her words had been spoken in jest, having no idea how his reaction wrung her heart. 'Four years, Lucy. It's been four years. That is a long time in anyone's life.'

His arms slackened their hold of her as he recalled how, in the early days of their relationship, he'd been so blindly besotted with the warmly vibrant creature of dancing and laughter, with an aura of hot sensual love about her that he'd lost no time in proposing marriage. He remembered her joy and her acceptance, and how she'd melted in his arms and kissed him with all her passion, exactly as she'd done moments before.

He glanced down at her and saw her watching him, her apprehensive green eyes soft and questioning. As if she saw the answer to some unspoken question she sought, she stepped back, struggling valiantly to make the transition from heated passion to flippancy that he seemed to find so easy. His ability to treat the matter so lightly made her heart squeeze in an awful, inexplicable way.

'You are right. Four years is a long time. A lot has happened to both of us in that time. I am no longer a girl given to foolish dreams and fancies. For the past few weeks we have been too close, alone for most of the time. The past and the present have become so mixed up that I am often confused. It's been difficult for both of us to separate the past from the present.' She managed a tremulous little smile. 'I suppose it's only natural that we would want to know if there was anything left out of what we once had. But I am not a doll, Nathan, to be picked up or dropped at your whim. That night when I fell into the stream...' She swallowed. She could not bring herself to pretend it had never happened. 'That night changed matters between us. Don't you realise that?'

She spoke so calmly that the ironic glint faded from Nathan's eyes. He looked at her pale face and the eyes ringed by deep shadows. Sorrow was etched in their depths and in the lines around her mouth. 'Whatever happened, happened—and no one can change that now,' he answered. 'What you did—when you left me—I realise what made you do it and I understand. Despite everything, what I do know is that I need you, and that is the all of it. But until this is over, until we are back in Lisbon—I can't say what will happen in the future—what I will decide to do.'

Ire sparked in her eyes. 'Until *you* decide? I,

too, have some thinking to do, Nathan—decisions to make.'

His eyes lingered on her for a moment, but the look in them was inscrutable. They both remembered what they had once been to each other, but when Lucy looked into Nathan's eyes, she read nothing in them. He made no effort to touch her again. She remained silent as unbearable relief stirred inside her, seeping back over the terrible suffering and mortification of the past. But he still had not said he loved her. He needed her though, in spite of everything. There was so much damage to repair, it would take time to wash away the hurt. There was still too much between them, too many days of despair. They might never be able to recover the closeness they had once shared, but she owed him this attempt.

She wanted to say all this, but she was afraid to tell him. She felt unfamiliarly nervous as she continued to stare at the strong-boned face she loved so much. She wanted him so much then, wanted to feel his arms about her, feel his thick, strong hair between her fingers—to give him the warmth and love he deserved. But she would wait and see what he decided—and indeed what she decided to do about her future—distanced by what had happened between them four years ago.

With a mighty effort she kept her emotions under control. 'It's as well this assignment is almost over—for both of us. I need you, too.' The words were out, the words she had not said to anyone in a long time, and then only to him. She did need him and now he knew it, too.

His rigidity melted and he allowed the faintest of smiles to shadow his beautiful lips. 'That's a start. If it is possible we will leave the past in the past. The only thing that is important is what's between us, you and me—that we still have something between us to mend. But now is not the time. We are not out of danger. We have still a long way to go before we reach Lisbon.'

'Yes, you are right, which is why I ask that for the time that is left you must learn to keep your desires in check—they *are* inclined to run away with you.' With a toss of her head she looked in the direction of the village. 'We should go back. We've another long ride ahead of us tomorrow and we must make an early start.'

When she began walking away Nathan followed a step behind her, unable to keep his eyes from her swaying hips or to quell the admiration he felt for her. 'I suppose this means that there will not be a repeat of what we just did?'

She turned and looked at him, feeling a little defeated and nonplussed, wondering how he could hold her and kiss her tenderly one moment and then, for no comprehensible reason, treat her like some amusing diversion. It was all too bewildering, too painful, too confusing. He was right. They had been apart a long time and in that time he had become unfailingly heartless.

'No, Nathan, there will not. Enough is enough. I will not dishonour myself any more deeply. I have to draw the line somewhere or I shall lose myself completely.'

Turning away, she walked on. For the time they had left she would see to it that she was never alone with him. That was the only way she would succeed in resisting temptation and keep her feelings in check. She wanted to cry out at the pain of it, but she must not. No matter what might happen from this day, she must suffer her pain in silence.

Chapter Nine

As Lucy walked ahead of Nathan, she had no idea of his inner torment. His expression was grim as a thousand curses poured through his mind. His refusal to commit himself to her had hurt her, *he* had hurt her. He knew that and it preyed heavy on his mind, which felt numb with the realisation. He had hurt that courageous, dear sweet girl. It was the worst feeling he had experienced in a long time and he had no idea what to do about it. Here on the cusp of his mission, just when he most needed to have himself and everything under perfect control, he was utterly routed, completely unsure.

His torment accompanied him to his bed, where he stared out into the dark beyond the window, at the country and the war he had escaped to when Lucy had left him. He had always been the sort of man who, when he made a decision, seldom changed his mind. He had devised this mission entirely by his usual mode of thought—logical, precise, effective.

But he had not bargained on how being close to Lucy once more, how his feelings would alter everything. His whole life had changed after these few weeks of having her close, of having her in his arms again, of loving her, and now the old way of thinking didn't seem to make sense any more. He also knew that when she had left him, young girls like Lucy did not run away and hide without good reason—not when they had Lucy's kind of courage and daring.

He had not anticipated the effect that these weeks with her would have on *him*. He had never meant to hurt her in his desire to protect himself, and now, the deepening of his feelings made it all but impossible for him to leave her when they got back to England. When she had left him four years ago, he had tried to purge her from his mind and tear her from his heart, but without success. He knew he was losing ground in the battle, just as he had been slowly losing it from the moment he'd gone to her house with his proposition that she accompany him to Portugal.

With a sigh, he leaned his head back on the pillow and closed his eyes. No matter what she had done in the past in a moment of anger, loneliness and despair, he would allow her that much—and he accepted that inadvertently he, too, had been to blame—but he could not face living without her now.

Before continuing with their journey the next day, he took her aside and told her how sorry he was for his behaviour of the previous night and stressed that he had no wish to hurt her in any way. Although she accepted his apology and acted as though everything was normal, being pleasant, distant, calm, her trust in him had been shaken and her demeanour towards him had cooled.

The journey to Lisbon lasted another five days in which scarcely anything happened and which proved no less uncomfortable than Lucy had feared now that Katherine was improved and able to ride for longer periods. They were able to buy food in the towns and villages, where they spent the nights.

Since they had left the mountains and their

meeting with the partisans, Lucy knew that the tension in Nathan had relaxed. She was aware, too, that he had developed a habit of watching her under his lashes, especially when she helped Katherine tend Charles. He would sit of an evening while she washed and fed him, and she would look up and find his gaze on her, and feel as always that familiar contraction of the heart. He did not speak of what had occurred between them when he had pulled her from the stream or the kiss they had shared after that, but she knew it was at the forefront of his mind.

Lucy spent most of her time with Katherine and Charles. Until now, each morning when Katherine woke and emerged into the warmth of the day, she was like some crumpled flower on which a cruel foot had trampled. Pale and strange, eyes shielded by her long lashes, head bent, shoulders bowed, silent and blank-faced, not until they had put the place of her incarceration and the brutal treatment of her captors behind her did she begin to lift her head. Then, slowly, the emptiness, the freshness, the beauty of the landscape worked its miracle and she began to stretch and recover.

The last night of their journey found them just fifteen miles from Lisbon. Missing Katherine when she went to the room they were to share, Lucy went outside to look for her. She found her sitting on a grassy bank with Charles lying on his back beside her, happily waving his arms and kicking his legs in the air. With her arms wrapped round her knees, Katherine sat in silent contemplation of the hills along the far horizon.

Lucy sat beside her. 'We'll soon be in Lisbon, Katherine—and after that London.'

'And a new life for me. Nothing can make up for the loss of James or wipe out that picture of him dying cruelly before my eyes. But I am impatient to be back in England.'

'I hope you will be able to put this awful time behind you.'

'I do, too. You don't know what it was like. I had never known fear until that moment I was shot and taken captive. I was more afraid of showing fear than the actual thing I feared, of living through each dragging moment with the uncertainty of what would happen to me. The intolerable heat of the journey into the hills, the pain from my wound and never having enough to eat, of having to look after Charles and fearing he might die—had it not been for the women who were already captives of Claude Gameau,

I would have died. I am sure of it.' Reaching out, she took Lucy's hand and squeezed it. 'Then you came to remind me that the world still contains other things besides terror and violence and wicked people.'

Lucy remained silent, content to let her talk.

Katherine turned her head and looked at Lucy, her eyes calm and serious. 'You and Nathan. I cannot tell you how surprised I was to see you together. I thought… What happened, Lucy? Why did you end your betrothal so suddenly? And why did you leave London without a word to me or anyone else for that matter? You never replied to my letters. I wrote telling you that I was marrying James within days and leaving for Spain with him. What was I to think?'

Lucy remembered the letters, remembered how she had thrown them in the fire unread. Katherine's eyes were gentle with understanding when Lucy confessed what she had done and she didn't blame her. When Katherine was told the facts that had convinced Lucy about the affair, she understood that it was a reasonable conclusion to reach.

'I hurt you, Katherine, and I am sorry for that,

but most of all I lost your friendship and that was the hardest thing of all.'

'You didn't, Lucy. That you would never lose. I am still your friend. Have you not proved it by coming all this way with Nathan to rescue me?'

'I did not know it was you we were coming to rescue until I reached Portugal.'

'Maybe not. But you could have turned back. The fact that you didn't, I consider that a test of true friendship. If I have learned anything over the years, it is that desperate people do desperate things—as I did when I insisted on following James to Spain, fearing he might die like my first husband, denying me the chance to say goodbye. I believe that what you did was done out of desperation.

'Nathan has told me that James's older brother was killed in Spain, which makes Charles the Duke of Londesborough's heir. I didn't know, Lucy.' A deep sadness for the loss of her brother-in-law filled her eyes, but then a smile touched her lips and her eyes brightened a little when she said, 'Imagine that, Lucy. My son will be a duke. There was a time when we would have laughed about such a thing happening.'

Lucy was about to get to her feet when Katherine put a hand on her arm to detain her.

'You still love Nathan, don't you?'

'More than the world. More than my life.'

'Then Nathan is a lucky man—luckier than he knows. Over the years I have come to know him well. He can be obstinate and stubborn, but he has a soft heart beneath that fearsome manner of his. I have seen the way he looks at you, how his eyes warm and light up, how his face kindles with joy. His face cannot lie. If you love him enough and live for the moment, he will come back to you. However obstinate he may be, the day will come when he can no longer struggle against himself and you.'

'Thank you, Katherine, for those kind words. I would like to say they give me hope, but I cannot. Inadvertently I was the one who made his life a nightmare of disappointment and I was the one who wounded him as surely as if I had seared him with his own sword.'

Katherine squeezed her arm gently. Lucy looked at the woman she was glad she could once more call her friend, who was reading her face so clearly. Katherine had an understanding of the situation completely. She seemed to know it all—

Lucy's pain, her grief, her emptiness, her restlessness that was always there at the back of her mind. Katherine never ceased to amaze Lucy, showing aspects of her nature that were admirable. Katherine, soft-spoken and gentle, had a determined will and wisdom far beyond her years. Lucy studied her with the relief of one who does not have to explain anything. The large eyes, edged with thick brown lashes that usually appeared doe-like in the heart-shaped face, now had a certain stubborn glint in them.

Lucy left her then, glad they had talked and made their peace. She felt light-headed, yet strangely resolute, as if a great weight had lifted from her. Katherine's remarks had kindled a little spark of hope, the hope that dies so hard in a loving heart. She knew that deep inside him Nathan cared for her, but she had also learned the price of her weakness for him, her too-willing surrender, and she was beginning to realise what it felt like to be on the receiving end of rejection.

Back in Lisbon at last, the weary travellers were received warmly by Sir Robert and Maria. Such a fuss was made over Katherine and Charles, who was sleeping in his mother's arms, blissfully unaware of the scene swirling around him. Nathan disappeared into Sir Robert's study while tea was prepared and rooms were readied and hot water carried up for baths. Lucy, who was feeling un-usually weary and longed to go to bed and sleep, would have preferred to have been left alone for a while to collect herself, but it was not to be.

'My dear girl, you cannot conceive how happy it makes Robert and I to see you back. I was so afraid that you would get lost in the mountains. But now you are here and everything is all right. But how tired you look—and so very pale. We will soon have some colour back in your cheeks now you are here. You need rest—plenty of rest.'

Lucy smiled in a friendly way at the vivacious Maria. 'What a lot of trouble we are putting you to, Maria. I confess that I do feel tired, but I have no intention of going straight to bed. Tomorrow I'll be better, I'm sure.'

'Your room is ready for you. How was the jour-ney?' Maria asked as she escorted Lucy to the delightful room she had occupied before and to help her become settled. Two servants had taken Katherine upstairs, undressed her and helped her into a hot bath to wash away the weeks of incar-ceration. 'Did you find it very difficult?'

Lucy smiled at her. 'It's been quite an adventure—and not one I would care to repeat.'

'I'm relieved everything went as it should. Robert and I were very worried about you.' She ushered Lucy inside the room. 'You are to stay with us for the time being—which is a not a bad thing.' She smiled. 'I shall enjoy taking you and Katherine and her son under my wing for the time you are here. She has been through a terrible ordeal. It's a wonder she and her son survived it.'

'Yes, it is,' Lucy agreed. 'Gameau's hideout is a terrible place and so isolated in the mountains. I sincerely hope the partisans and the soldiers are successful and the other hostages are rescued safely.'

Maria frowned and averted her eyes. 'I understand the attack has happened, Lucy. Just before you arrived Robert received information about the raid on Gameau's hideout. I do not know the details, but I am sure Nathan will speak of it before he leaves.'

Lucy paused in removing her jacket and stared at her in confusion, wondering if she had heard correctly. 'What did you say, Maria? Nathan isn't staying with us? But—why—where is he going?'

Suddenly an awful thought gripped her. 'Dear Lord, Maria, please don't tell me he's going back?'

Maria bit her lip, wishing she had not mentioned it. She sighed. 'Clearly Nathan hasn't had time to speak to you about going back to rendezvous with the partisans.'

Lucy's heart was beating so painfully, as if it were trying desperately to get out, to escape the bewildering panic it felt. 'He hasn't spoken to me. Why would he want to go back?'

'I cannot say. No doubt it will become clear in time.'

Lucy met Maria's eye and it seemed to her that she read some pity in it. But just at that moment, pity was one thing she could not endure. 'When? When, Maria? When is he leaving?'

'Shortly. Now, I will leave you to bathe and don one of the gowns you will find in your dressing room, then come down and join us on the terrace. You will see Nathan before he leaves.'

'Thank you, Maria. I will.'

When Maria had closed the door Lucy sank down on the bed. A cloud had descended on her, less over this mention of Nathan leaving and the fresh danger that hung over him than because she would miss him dreadfully. The sharpness of her disappointment took her by surprise. God alone knew what she had been hoping for. Perhaps that Nathan's assignment would oblige him to remain with them until they reached England and Katherine and Charles were delivered safely to the Duke of Londesborough. He could not know that, despite everything, how much he still mattered to her, his absence would be a source of grief.

On a sigh she glanced at the bathing tub, which looked inviting. She stood up and began to undress, impatient to rid herself of her travel-stained clothes and to sink into the soapy depths.

When Lucy appeared on the terrace she was surprised to find Nathan alone. Katherine was resting and Charles was being cosseted by one of the servants. Nathan had not heard her silent tread so she paused, taking a moment to study him. He stood with his back to her, looking out at the blue sky and the turquoise sea in the distance, his hands clasped behind his back—Poseidon surveying his realm, she thought.

Forcing herself to ignore the fluttering in her stomach, she walked towards him. He turned to face her, bathed and freshly shaved and having changed his clothes, his dark hair combed smoothly back from his face. Unexpectedly, Lucy found herself the victim of an absurd attack of discomfort. Now his ruggedness seemed more pronounced and the broad expanse of his chest reminded her rather forcefully of how his powerful body had felt pressed against hers. He watched her progress and was observing her with a grim look in his blue eyes.

'So, Nathan,' she said softly, 'no sooner do we reach Lisbon than you are to turn back.'

Nathan was momentarily taken aback by the sight of her. With her glossy chestnut curls falling softly about her head, she looked like a young girl in her high-waisted primrose gown—the girl he had fallen in love with all those years ago. It was a pleasure to see her attired in feminine clothes once more, although already he was mourning the loss of his riding companion in her male attire. He wanted to go to her, take her in his arms, kiss her and soothe her and tell her everything would be all right. Ever since they had become reacquainted he had been plagued with so many conflicting emotions where she was concerned, becoming lost in a turmoil of contradiction and insoluble dilemma. Yet because he was to retrace the journey back to the Sierras, he was resolute in his decision not to further their relationship until this was over.

'I fear I must.'

'Maria told me that Robert has information concerning the attack on Gameau's hideout,' she said. 'What happened? Did it not go to plan?'

'It would appear not—at least not all of it. All the deserters were either killed or captured.'

'And the hostages?'

'Were located and successfully rescued. Unfortunately our troubles are not wholly behind us. A shadow still lurks over us in the shape of Gameau. At some point during the melee, he got away.'

Lucy's face froze with shock. 'It can't be true. How was that possible? And you are going to try to find him? Nathan, do not forget that he no longer owes you a debt. Did he not tell you that should you meet again you should look to your life?'

Nathan nodded, his expression grim. 'The threat is not forgotten. I'm to make contact with Arturo Garcia. He will give me an account of the attack and I will go on from there. I have issues of my own to settle with Gameau. There is also the issue of the gold. Hopefully it will have been recovered—or most of it, which will be returned to the Duke of Londesborough. If all goes well, I shall be gone no longer than two weeks—three at the most. In the meantime Robert and Maria will take good care of you.'

'I know they will. Maria is extremely kind, generous and hospitable. She has made us so welcome—even providing us with the clothes we wear.'

Nathan's expression softened and a slow smile curved his lips as his eyes swept slowly over her. 'I admire her taste. You look lovely, Lucy,' he murmured in an attempt to lessen the fear in her. 'There have been times over the past weeks when the tantalising woman hidden beneath the breeches eluded me.'

A rush of warmth pervaded Lucy's whole being, reawakening the nerve centre which had been numbed by despair. Had his cruel indifference been a pose after all? she asked herself. Hearing his warm words, being here with him now, she felt a sudden, keener awareness of her love for him. The feeling was so strong that for an instant she had a wild impulse to tell him how she felt, but she recollected herself just in time.

The man in front of her had merely complimented her on how she looked and might not wish to listen to a declaration of her love. He wanted only what any woman could give him— the means to slake his physical lust. And he had done just that on the night of the storm. Her mind burned with the memory of the wild abandon with which she had given herself to him. She wouldn't humiliate herself further by letting him know how much she craved his kisses, his touch.

'Is it necessary to put yourself in danger like this?' she asked, unable to conceal her concern. 'Surely Gameau will have been found and taken care of by now?'

'I'd like to think so—and if he has then I will soon return, but I have to make sure. He is just one of the loose ends that have to be tied off.'

Lucy's eyes searched his and for a terrible stabbing moment she knew a squeeze of fear so strong it seemed to take the breath from her body. She strove to control it. 'The ordeal is over for Katherine and me, but the risks are still there for you. At least you'll be able to ride much faster without the encumbrance of two women and a baby.'

There was an unusually brooding expression in his eyes. Then he put his finger under her chin and tilted her distraught face to his. 'You have spirit and courage,' he said, with a serious smile, capturing her lovely green gaze with his own, 'and I commend you for it. But you are right. With just one man for company I'll work much faster.'

'I'm glad you won't be alone, but you will be putting yourself in grave danger.'

'Not for the first time.'

'Don't let anything happen to you. Please be careful.' She wanted to tell him that she couldn't bear to lose him, but held her silence. She wished she could be convinced of his indestructibility, that he had been blessed with some special gift of endurance.

He saw the fear in her face. 'There's no need to concern yourself in this way, Lucy. I don't get killed that easy.'

'I sincerely hope not.'

There was a silence, a silence occupied by Lucy in examining what Nathan had just said. Her joy of a moment before when he had told her how nice she looked evaporated before harsh reality. Her heart heavy with the burden of her love, she was afraid for him. An adventurer Nathan might be, equal to any risks, bold enough for anything, but one thing he would not do, and Lucy knew it, he would never deal dishonestly with himself. There was no arguing with such determination. That strong will of his divided them.

She gritted her teeth and took a deep breath and said at last, 'Well then, what can I say, except goodbye and please take care.'

Nathan looked towards the house where Sir Robert was beckoning him. Taking Lucy's hand, he raised it to his lips, his eyes holding hers for just a moment before he turned and strode across the terrace. Her heart leaden, Lucy's eyes followed his tall figure helplessly.

God keep him safe, she prayed silently.

Five weeks passed and Nathan didn't return. They were weeks in which Katherine grew stronger and healthier and little Charles thrived on wholesome food and hugs by family and servants alike so that he was at serious risk of suffocation.

Lucy worried about Nathan constantly. She tried not to show her concern, but neither Katherine's company nor the respectful and benevolent hospitality of Sir Robert and Maria could dispel her fears. There was only one thing she wanted and that was to remain alone with her thoughts until someone came to her with news of Nathan.

The glow of the few times they had been intimate on the journey had dimmed. She was feeling lost and unusually tired and depressed. Even with all there was to think about and arrange for the final stages of the journey, she could not help wondering what awaited her in England. Would she be able to pick up the threads of her career? Did she want to?

Whatever her intentions, they were thwarted the day she suspected another life grew within her. Assuming the first missed flux the result of the arduous journey, she hadn't worried, but when the time came again and nothing happened, the thought of a child crept in unbidden. It was a thought that could not be shaken. It filtered through her brain like some unwelcome shockwave. It also explained her bouts of nausea and loss of appetite, why she had felt so tired of late and the tenderness in her breasts.

It had happened on the night when she had fallen into the stream, but she knew, no matter how hard she tried to think otherwise, that since then nothing had been the same. The pleasure and intensity she had experienced then was now too painful to contemplate. She knew she was carrying Nathan's child. All those times they had made love in the past nothing had happened. Why now?

Slowly the silent tears began to flow. Pressing her hands lightly together in her lap, she asked herself what was she to do? She had willingly allowed Nathan to take advantage of her, and she had enjoyed it and revelled in it, before she had known he did not intend to take their relationship any further. Now, more than ever, she needed the strength of her forceful personality to keep her sane in the days and weeks to come.

She loved Nathan with all her heart, but she would not tell him. She would keep absolutely silent on the matter. If he would not marry her for herself, then she would not blackmail him into marrying her because it was the right and decent thing to do. She wanted him to want her because he loved her and for no other reason.

She looked into the future with haunted eyes. If Nathan didn't marry her she would go away. The money from the assignment meant she would be able to care for herself and her child. Yet it gave her a strange, rather agonising joy, to know that Nathan's blood was at work somewhere deep inside her. Whatever he did now, he was bound to her by the ties of flesh and blood, so, now that the shock of the revelation of her condition had worn off, nothing could destroy her happiness in the knowledge that she bore his child.

The day was warm. Katherine and Charles were strolling in the garden with Maria and Sir Robert. The chance to recline in one of the chairs in a sheltered part of the terrace was too big a temptation for Lucy to resist and before she knew it she had drifted off to sleep.

This was where Nathan found her. He looked down at her sleeping soundly, her face flushed and the light gleaming on the waves of her glossy chestnut hair, which had grown considerably in his absence. The lovely curves of her body moulded the thin gauzy white folds of her gown. The smooth curve of her arms, the line of the long creamy throat and the black sweep of the lashes that lay against her cheeks were an assurance that she was well rested since her return to Lisbon.

He'd missed her more than he realised.

Reluctant to wake her, aware of his dishevelled

appearance after five weeks of living rough, he went to clean himself up before returning to the terrace.

Coming awake, aware of someone standing next to her chair casting a shadow over her, Lucy stole a furtive glance at Nathan from beneath her lashes. Overwhelmingly relieved that he had come back safe, her heart fluttered foolishly at the sight of him, bathed and barbered and all lordly elegance. He was awe-inspiring in calfskin trousers, the white shirt accenting the sweeping breadth of his shoulders and his trim, flat waist. How well she knew—and had missed—that powerful body beneath that white shirt, that throat enwrapped in a muslin cravat. Ruefully she wanted to say *well done, Nathan*, but despite the splendid way he looked, he was still Nathan, with his air of ruthless danger beneath the polished veneer.

'Nathan!' she breathed. 'At last.' She opened her eyes, but made no attempt to move as she gazed up at him. Everything but the glow of her love had been swept away. Her whole being was irradiated.

'You were asleep,' he said softly. 'I'm sorry if I woke you.'

'I felt unusually tired.'

'Why? Are you feeling unwell?'

'No, merely tired.'

'I've been speaking to Maria. Apparently she is concerned about you. She told me you've been noticeably quiet of late, Lucy.'

Lucy's eyes snapped to his and her brows drew together in a frown. She wished Maria hadn't voiced her concerns to Nathan. Much as she liked Maria and valued her friendship, she also possessed a busy tongue, capable of diffusing an incredible amount of gossip in the shortest possible space of time.

'I have spent a good deal of time resting. I'm just not used to having so much time on my hands with nothing to do.'

'And that's all it is?' he asked quietly, studying her face closely.

Lucy knew him too well not to discern the anxiety underlying his words. She must give him no reason to suspect the truth. 'What else could it be? Shall I be cheerful just to please you? Is that what you want?' she uttered crossly.

Nathan didn't want that. He wanted the young

woman of the past to come back to him, not this distant, reserved creature who for reasons unbeknownst to him kept herself from him.

Lucy sighed. It was not her intention to sound irate. She was genuinely happy to see Nathan after so long an absence. She felt herself being drawn into his gaze, into the vital, rugged aura that was so much a part of him. Being this close to him was having a strange effect on her senses. She was too aware of him as a man, of his power, his strength. Unsettled by his relentless gaze, she couldn't remain reclining in the chair any longer.

Getting to her feet she brushed down her skirts. 'I'm sorry, Nathan. I didn't mean to sound crotchety, but I shall be relieved to be back in England. I'm glad you're back at last. We were beginning to worry when there was no word. Did it go well?'

He nodded. 'Most of the ransom money we took so laboriously to Gameau has been found. Handfuls had been raked off by the deserters, but the bulk of it has been recovered.'

'And Gameau?'

'Still missing. I searched the mountains for him—which is why I have been away so long. There have been sightings of him, but he managed to elude us.'

'I'm sorry, Nathan. I know how frustrating it must be for you.'

Nathan's eyes hardened. She was right. Frustration filled him with anger. He blamed himself for not running Gameau to ground. He should have tried harder, but winter had come to the mountains and it was with reluctance that he had given up the chase to return to Lisbon.

Lucy felt the tension in Nathan and knew how wretched he must be feeling for having failed to locate Gameau. From his tone she could tell the murder of Harry Connors still pained him and she suspected he continued to blame himself for that young man's death by letting Gameau live.

'I know how much you want him caught—what it means to you personally,' she said, pressing her fingertips to her aching temples. 'However, now you are back we can make plans to return to England, where we can put all thought of Gameau behind us.'

'Are you sure you are not feeling unwell, Lucy?' Nathan asked, his voice soft with concern.

Lucy averted her eyes, immediately on the defensive. 'I have a headache, that is all. I must have been out in the sun too long.'

'You were in the shade,' he countered.

'Then it must be something I've eaten.' She moved away from him, for she found his nearness disconcerting. His close scrutiny of her features was making her feel suddenly uncomfortable, as though it might provide an answer to some question he had in mind.

'Perhaps,' he murmured, unconvinced. Stepping close to her, he placed his hand on her arm when he thought she was about to turn away. He was still looking at her in a peculiar way— as though she might be hiding something. 'Can I tempt you to take a walk in the garden before dinner? Some light exercise might relieve your headache.'

Disturbed by his touch, Lucy looked down and found herself staring at his hand—strong, his fingers long, it had the power to tame a spirited horse yet could be gentle and caressing and soothing...

She had a wild desire to hold out her arms to him, but she couldn't. Oh, why didn't he give her the opportunity to tell him how she felt—and that she was going to have his child?

She looked away, pulling herself together, refusing to be seduced any more by him. She didn't mean to pull back from him this way, but she couldn't help it. She was afraid to let herself become open to him again for fear that it would deepen the hurt. Taking a deep breath, she summoned her courage.

'Some other time, Nathan. I really am feeling extremely tired. If you don't mind, I think I'll go to my room and rest before dinner.'

Nathan stepped back. If only she knew how desperately he wanted to take her in his arms. Being away from her had made him realise he could not go on without her. But she had clearly made up her mind to keep him at arm's length. 'Of course. I'll see you at dinner.'

Chapter Ten

Before they knew it, the eve of departure was upon them. The meal that night was over. Katherine was putting Charles to bed and Robert and Maria were chatting over coffee. Nathan had gone to the harbour to make final preparations about boarding the ship and Lucy took a last stroll in the garden.

It had been raining heavily all day. Now that it had ceased and the clouds had passed over, everything was clear and bright and the air fresh and clean. While sad to be leaving Lisbon and the warm hospitality they had received from Sir Robert and Maria, Lucy was glad they were to return to England at last. They had been away longer than she had expected and she worried terribly about Aunt Dora.

It wasn't until she had reached the limits of the

garden that overlooked the road leading down to the harbour that she realised how far she had walked. It was almost dark. Before turning to return to the house, she looked along the road in the hope of seeing Nathan, but it was empty. Suddenly she felt uneasy about being alone. Something in the shadows along the side of the road moved. She was certain of it. Concealing herself behind the stout trunk of a palm tree, she strained her eyes, scrutinising the shadows. Nothing moved, but she continued to stand there.

Suddenly a figure slipped out into the road. It was a man and he was looking in the same direction as she had to look for Nathan. Whoever he was he seemed to be unaware of her watching him. He wore a hat with the brim pulled well down. His clothes were dark, his body language furtive. When he removed his hat to scratch his head, Lucy's mouth went dry and her heart lurched. Although the man was devoid of his black beard she recognised him. Panic gripped her.

It was Claude Gameau and she knew he was waiting for Nathan.

The situation demanded action. Lucy could see

that for herself. Like a shadow she slipped from behind the tree and headed back to the house.

Even now, many weeks later, the memory of the attack and the fact that Rochefort, the English spy in league with the partisans, had outwitted him, filled Claude Gameau with bitter rage. It was only by his own cleverness and cunning he had escaped the partisans and British soldiers, leaving the rest of his band of deserters to their fate. The knowledge was more galling than the attack on his hideout.

He'd escaped into the hills where the terrain was harsh and wild, where he was at one with the brigands and murderers who bowed to no law but the gun and the sword. Having discarded his French uniform and dressed in the clothes of a peasant, his face windburnt and gaunt, he had lost none of his determination. Despite the dangers, he had driven himself relentlessly. He knew where he was bound—to Lisbon and all the way to England if necessary, to revenge himself on Nathan Rochefort.

Rochefort had come after him, this he knew for a fact, having watched him and his companion from the lofty mountain heights of the Sierras. He knew Rochefort would kill him, he had recognised that, so he must kill Rochefort. And if he succeeded in killing the English spy, then there was always hope.

Hearing the sound of a carriage, Gameau slipped back into the shadows.

Nathan stepped down from the carriage at the bottom of the drive leading to the house, waiting in the road until it had gone on its way. In no particular hurry he turned towards the house, skirting the large puddles that had accumulated during the day's rainfall. An almost imperceptible footfall behind him made him look around expectantly, hoping it was Lucy out for a last stroll before bed, which was her usual pattern. But the dark figure that stood there was not Lucy.

Claude Gameau looked straight at him as he aimed a pistol directly at Nathan's chest. 'Now I have you,' Gameau boasted.

Nathan realised he was utterly defenceless. He had no weapon and he cursed himself for his carelessness. He wasn't even close enough to Gameau to launch himself forwards against the man and take him down. All he could hope to do was to gain time until circumstances could be turned in his favour.

'You must be aware that I've just spent the last few weeks searching for you, Gameau, so if you kill me, everyone will have a good idea who did the deed and they will hunt you down.'

'That does not worry me. I should never have let you go. I should have killed you the day you entered the castle. So look now, Rochefort,' he uttered with a terrible triumph. 'See how I will exact my vengeance on you. It was you who brought the forces down on me and I damn you for it.'

'You are wrong, Gameau. The attack on you was planned before I put in an appearance. I merely provided the partisans with necessary information on what I saw in your hideout when I handed over the ransom money.'

'And they acted on that information. You exposed me. I warned you that if we should meet again I would kill you. I always keep my word.'

'So you came all this way to find me. You must want me dead very badly, Gameau.'

Gameau shrugged. 'I had nothing better to do and I knew that, no matter what you do in the future, you will not rest until you have killed me. I have my pride, Rochefort, which you have trampled on for the last time.'

'Pride?' Gameau's mocking tone and easy manner made Nathan angry. 'Is that what you call it? Avarice and lust for power is how I would describe it.'

'I do not deny it. I am all those things you accuse me of.'

Gameau stretched out his arm and levelled the pistol at his foe's head, but Nathan threw himself forwards. Even as he heard the faint rasping of a trigger being squeezed, in the next instant an explosion rent the silence. Nathan looked at Gameau as he tottered stiltedly forwards. A strange gurgling gasp came from his throat and then a heavy trickle of blood spilled down the corner of his mouth. He gaped at Nathan, his astonishment supreme before his knees buckled and he fell forwards on to the ground.

Nathan was equally stunned as he watched the man and saw blood seep through a hole in his chest where the lead shot had passed clear into his lung. In slack-jawed wonder, Gameau lifted his eyes to the slender form standing in the drive, towards which Nathan had directed his gaze a moment earlier.

Lucy lowered the still-smoking pistol to her side. 'You shouldn't have tried to kill Nathan.'

Gritting her teeth together to keep them from chattering, Lucy made a valiant attempt to control her shaking limbs, but her composure was steadily collapsing.

Still clutching his pistol, Gameau turned it awkwardly towards her, but Nathan kicked his foot forwards and knocked it out of his hand. The deafening roar of the exploding weapon seemed to echo across the Tagus below, sending water fowl flying upwards in diverse directions. Gameau attempted to struggle to his knees, but the effort cost him the last of his strength and his breath, for he fell forwards and jerked and then went still. The pool of water in which the deserter's body had fallen was red with his blood, and as the red spilled out farther to the outer edge, it was diluted to pink.

Nathan looked at Lucy. Even in the meagre light he could see that she was shaking uncontrollably, having killed a man. Quickly he covered the distance between them and took her in his arms, dropping a kiss on the top of her head as he tried to quell her trembling.

'Whatever made you come down here with a pistol, Lucy?'

'I—I saw Gameau when I was walking in the

garden,' she uttered brokenly. 'I recognised him even without his beard. I knew he was waiting for you—to kill you. I ran back to the house for my pistol. I had hoped to warn you before you got out of the carriage.'

'Thank God for your quick thinking. I was unarmed and wouldn't have stood a chance. With my experience I should have known better than to leave the house without a weapon, although it worries me to imagine what he might have done to you.'

'I was ready for him. I can't even allow myself to think otherwise.'

Nathan groaned. His heart had already turned cold at the dreadful prospect of her being killed.

Lucy shivered as she stared fixedly at the dead man. 'Why do you think Gameau came to Lisbon to look for you?'

'I suspect he came to kill me because he held me responsible for the attack on his hideout.'

'I doubt he ever considered his hatred of you would cost him his life.'

'Were you not afraid to confront him?'

'I was angry,' she answered quietly, 'the kind of anger that conquers fear.'

As a soldier Nathan knew the kind of anger

she spoke of, having experienced it many times himself. It was a rage that one might regret, when it banishes all humanity and makes a man into a killer, but the rage could keep the man from being dead and so the regret was mixed with relief.

Nathan rubbed her arms vigorously to chase away the cold she was suffering. The shock was settling in. He would have to get her away from the dead man. 'Come, I'll take you to the house and arrange for Gameau to be moved.'

Lucy looked at the lifeless body sprawled out on the road, frightened in the face of death. She had to get away from here, to some place safe away from what she had done. Drawing away from Nathan, she straightened her spine with wilful resolve and, by slow degrees, took hold of herself.

'I'm all right, Nathan, truly. And see, the shot has brought Robert from the house. Here,' she said, thrusting the pistol into his hand. She couldn't wait to be rid of it. 'I'm done with that now. I'll leave you to explain things while I go and find Maria.'

Before she turned and walked away, in the moonlight the anguished eyes and the total despair about the beautiful mouth impressed themselves more vividly on Nathan's mind than anything else.

He had done this to her. He had caused this terrible transformation. It was just as well they were leaving in the morning. He had treated her badly, taking her from a life in which she was happy and secure to a war-torn country to face possible death. There had been many obstacles to overcome and he had nothing but admiration for her. She had not deserved to be treated so badly.

Lucy moaned and opened her eyes, and the sunlight streaming into the room was dazzling, making bright patterns on the polished floor. A bird was singing in the gardens, warbling throatily and lustily. The window was open—the maid must have opened it earlier—and a warm breeze caused the white faille curtains to flutter. Feeling dazed and disorientated, she struggled into a sitting position, resting her shoulders against the pillows. She stared at the room, forcing herself to go through the ritual of waking up. This morning it took more of an effort than ever—her head ached and she had the uneasy feeling that something disturbing had happened.

Then she remembered and her stomach plummeted. Last night she had killed a man. The fact that it had been Claude Gameau and that if she hadn't shot him he would have killed Nathan didn't make it any easier. Last night she had entered the house and informed Maria of what had taken place, but, having no desire to relive what had happened and what she had done further, she had excused herself and gone to her room. Yielding to weariness, she had pulled off her clothes and climbed into bed, where she had fallen into an exhausted and troubled sleep.

She was still caught somewhere between sleep and awareness when Katherine entered the room with a cup of hot chocolate.

'Oh, you are awake,' she said, placing the steaming beverage on the bedside table. 'I was worried that you had taken ill.'

'Why?' Lucy asked, her hands trembling a little as she lifted the cup and saucer and raised it to her lips.

'Because you went to bed without saying goodnight. I came to see you earlier to ask if you would like me to help you prepare for our departure, but you were fast asleep.'

'What time is it?' Lucy asked.

'Nearly nine o'clock. We are to leave in a couple of hours so that doesn't give us much time.' Katherine looked down at her, her expression one of concern. 'I know what happened, Lucy, what you did. It's bound to have upset you.'

'Yes,' Lucy whispered, placing the cup and saucer down. 'I hope I never have to do such a thing again.'

'You saved Nathan's life. Gameau came here to kill him. He would have succeeded but for your quick thinking. Nathan would have liked to speak to you when he returned to the house and was sorry you had gone to bed without waiting for him.'

'I was tired, Katherine. Besides, there was nothing to talk about. The deed is done and that's an end to it.'

'Things are no better between you and Nathan, are they? I—can't help noticing how strained the two of you are when you are together.'

Lucy nodded unhappily. Katherine's eyes were too wise for her age, too knowing. She was, and always had been, in Lucy's opinion, extraordinarily observant. 'You would have to be blind not to. I think he's still trying to punish me and make me suffer for what I did—and I really can't blame him for that. Having jilted him, I can't blame him if he doesn't want anything to do with me. When I think about it all, I feel shattered at the thought of what I might have had—and what I have lost.'

'I don't see how you can be so fair and objective, Lucy.'

'Perhaps that's because I'm beginning to see things from Nathan's viewpoint. I made a terrible and lasting mess of things,' she said, knowing she sounded sorry for herself, but she couldn't help it. 'I doubt he will come near me when we get back to London.'

'Do you truly think that?'

'Yes, I do.'

'And I was hoping that I would be the catalyst for bring you back together. If you and Nathan do part company—and I sincerely hope that does not happen—what will you do when you are back home? Will you return to the stage?'

'I—I thought I might join a travelling theatre company—do the provinces and the like,' Lucy replied, lowering her eyes so Katherine would not see the lie.

'But you've done all that.'

'Then I'll do it again. I doubt Mr Portas would welcome me back.' Tossing back the covers, she swung her legs over the bed. 'I must get dressed if we're to leave soon.'

'I'll send one of the maids to help you,' Katherine said, crossing to the door.

'There's no need, Katherine,' Lucy was quick to say, having no desire to be fussed over, feeling as wretched as she did. 'I intend to wear my breeches for the time we are on board. I can dress myself.' She glanced at her friend as she was about to leave. 'Katherine.' She turned and looked back. Lucy smiled, although she was unable to dispel the strain on her face. 'You and Charles are safe and Gameau is dead. Let us not talk of it any longer. I am impatient to leave Portugal and, like you, I can hardly wait to be back in England with Aunt Dora. Thank you for your concern, but I am all right. Truly.'

Katherine was unconvinced, but she returned her smile. 'I sincerely hope so. I'll leave you to dress.'

Before Lucy knew it, the time of departure was upon them. She was relieved nothing was said about the unpleasant occurrence the night before, although it was on all their minds. Nathan had decided to leave the horses behind, which saddened

Lucy because she had grown extremely fond of Jess, but she could see the sense of it. With the war still being fought and horses in short supply, Sir Robert was grateful to have them. As Nathan loaded the bags into the carriage that would take them to the ship, with tears in her eyes, Lucy said her farewells to Sir Robert and Maria.

'Remember, you will always be welcome here,' Maria said. 'When this wretched war is over, you must come back.'

Even as Maria said the words—and later when Lucy stood on the deck of the ship and there was nothing but the vast expanse of ocean to be seen—she was filled with trepidation about what the future held for her now.

Soon the days became shorter and the temperature dropped. The seas became rougher, too, and the ship was tossed about like a matchstick. Most of those on board suffered from sickness, including Lucy—whether it was the violent motion of the ship or her condition which caused it she was unsure, because her nausea continued when they sailed into the calmer waters of the English Channel.

Most of the time she spent in the small cabin

she shared with Katherine and Charles. Nathan's regular visits broke the days up, but she saw to it that they were never alone, although she was always aware of where he was on the ship, even though they had scarcely spoken since they'd boarded. She managed to distract her thoughts when she was with Katherine and Charles, yet one corner of her mind was always attuned to him.

Nathan made every attempt to approach Lucy, but he was unable to break through her reserve. Her tone when she spoke to him, her very posture, was cool and aloof.

On one occasion after she had been on deck with Katherine, she was returning to the cabin when he caught her arm to delay her, leaving Katherine to go on ahead, releasing it immediately when she flinched at his touch.

He gazed down at her with puzzlement and concern. Her face was drawn by fatigue. Throughout these past weeks she had been courageous in her desire to free Katherine from captivity, to right the wrong between them, and now he could see how the strain of those weeks was showing. Had he asked—expected—too much of her? What had he done to her? And she had killed Gameau, which he had failed to do—a frightened young woman confronting a killer. Lucy's upbringing had never prepared her for such a situation and he should have known it—did, in fact, recognise the fact when he brought her to Portugal. He had wronged her and was too stubborn to admit his error.

'Lucy, would you mind telling me what is wrong? Is there some problem I don't know about?'

Lucy managed to return his gaze briefly. She was glad she was beginning to know how to deal with rejection. She was able to answer Nathan's question with scarcely a pause. 'Problem? I don't know what you mean.'

'The way you are behaving—so cool and formal. I thought we had moved on from all that.'

'Am I being formal? I didn't realise it.' If she sounded cool, perhaps even haughty, then she was glad. Glad that Nathan could not see what an effort it was to be so close to him. She loved him so much. Why else would she be experiencing this painful yearning that was equal parts fear and want? She was finding it harder and harder to retreat into cool reserve when she was near him, especially when memories of his caresses, hot, wild and sweet, kept swirling around in her mind.

He searched her face, hesitating a long moment before he replied, 'Do you have to return to the cabin? Would you care to walk on the deck?'

'Thank you, but I am quite weary after all the turbulence and Katherine needs my assistance with Charles.'

Nathan stepped back. 'Then I will not detain you.'

As he watched her go, Nathan's emotions veered back and forth between hope and despair. There was nothing in Lucy's attitude to give him any encouragement. While she was acting cold, he knew she wasn't cold-blooded, but now he had decided that he must have her in his life for good, that he had come to realise that she was his reason for living each day and he had never stopped loving her despite the years between, she had retreated into a chilly shell of reserve, making it quite clear that she wouldn't accept his attentions.

He wasn't going to try to press the issue, he decided, at least not yet. On board a ship heaving with soldiers and civilians and sickness, this was neither the time nor the place, as he told Katherine when he saw her on deck later.

'I can't tell you how happy I am that you've come to your senses,' she told him. 'Do you have any notion how deeply Lucy is hurting, Nathan? Your indifference to her of late has given her reason to believe you are punishing her for the mistakes she made in the past.'

Naked pain flashed across his handsome face. 'To punish her never entered my head.'

'She is torturing herself about what she did. We have suffered because of it, but I suspect Lucy has suffered more.'

'I couldn't agree more.'

Katherine looked startled. 'You do?'

'Absolutely. Under the circumstances I'm sure I would have acted much as she did. I'll make it up to her,' he replied with a sombre smile. 'I promise.'

'Don't take too long.' Katherine strongly suspected there was something other than seasickness wrong with Lucy and come the summer she would have a child to care for as well as her Aunt Dora. Clearly her friend wanted to keep it to herself so Katherine would not voice her suspicion to Nathan—it was not her place. 'If you delay, you

may find she has left London. She's considering
going on tour with a travelling theatre company,'
she said in answer to Nathan's questioning look,
hoping that would motivate him into asking Lucy
to be his wife.

Nathan hesitated an endless moment, then he
nodded, shoved his hands into his pockets and
stared out to sea. 'Thank you for putting me in
the picture, Katherine.'

'So you see, Nathan,' she said cautiously, 'if
matters are to be set to rights between the two of
you, I very much fear the burden for it will fall
completely on you.'

He nodded. Katherine was right. The melting
away of old barriers had given him back his ability to love, going beyond the boundaries which
for so long had been his defence. His love and devotion to Lucy were laid wide open, so he knew
what he had to do. He could not deny or hide his
emotions any longer.

'Now I have straightened out the confusing
array of emotions beating at me for four years, I
know what I must do. I cannot turn my back on
the woman I have tried so hard to deny, on the
truth my heart has hidden.'

Katherine's eyes warmed at the tenderness in his eyes and voice. 'Don't leave it too long, will you? She adores you.'

On their arrival in Portsmouth, the wharf was bustling with commerce piled with crates and barrels and lined with carriages and wagons. Naval and merchant vessels lay at anchor in the harbour.

It was late afternoon when Lucy accompanied Katherine ashore. Held close in his mother's arms, Charles, who was developing apace, looked about him with interest at the ships and the passengers and soldiers returning home. Nathan had written to the Duke of Londesborough, giving him an approximate date of their arrival. Relief washed over them when they found he had sent a coach for them.

Spending the night in Portsmouth, they began the journey to London the next morning.

Lucy's arrival brought Dora hurrying from her room in her eagerness to be reunited with her niece. Never slackening her pace, she was nearly breathless as she swept into the hall. She was disappointed that Nathan had already left. In his haste to deliver Katherine and a fretful Charles to Lord Londesborough at his London home, he had not stayed long.

'Oh, thank goodness you're safe,' Dora cried in teary relief as she reached out to embrace Lucy, making no effort to halt the profusion of grateful tears coursing down her cheeks as she encompassed her niece within the circle of her arms. 'I was so fearful of what might happen to you!' She wept with joy. 'I've been nearly beside myself, not knowing what Nathan intended to do when you got to Portugal. My greatest fear, of course, with that wretched war raging over there, was that you and Nathan would be killed.'

'We suffered no harm, Aunt Dora,' Lucy assured her aunt as she stood back within the circle of the older woman's arms. 'Now is not the time for discussions. I do not want to think of anything but my relief at being home.' She spoke the truth, for somehow this house where she had lived with her aunt for such a short time before she had left for Portugal had become just that to her. 'I'll tell you everything when I've bathed and changed my clothes.'

Dora clasped her niece's cheeks between her palms and gazed with tear-filled eyes into the face of her only relative before bestowing a fond kiss upon her brow. 'I am so very relieved to have you back, Lucy. I would never have been able to bear your loss if anything had happened to you. But I knew I could count on Nathan to keep you safe. Was it very difficult out there?'

'At times,' Lucy admitted. 'It's strange when I look back on that remarkable journey that it wasn't nearly as punishing as it might have been. I marvel that we came through it so easily. But we did. Our luck held through all of it. Apart from the towns and villages where we stayed the nights, we hardly saw another person the whole way. Of course we were aware there was a war going on and were constantly on our guard, but Nathan assured me the conflict at that time was over the border in Spain. Now, let me go and get cleaned up and I will tell everything.'

The next afternoon Lucy left the house wrapped in a cloak and she needed one. A cold wind blew and the sky was overcast. She felt a curious sense of belonging as she entered Covent Garden. It seemed to welcome her back. Mellowed with age, raffish and not quite respectable, it had its own unique character and colour which she had always loved. This charming neighbourhood, with plump blue-grey pigeons strutting on the stones of the piazza and its bustling market and busy theatres, was, to her, the heart of London and it was good to be back even though she was no longer employed as an actress.

All was total confusion at the Portas Theatre, with stagehands and actors rushing about all over the place. Almost everyone recognised her, calling and waving to her and telling her how good it was to see her back while carrying on with what they were doing. It didn't take long for her to locate Coral. She was on stage and gasped with delight on seeing her friend.

'Lucy! You're back! Lord, love, I'm glad to see you! It hasn't been the same without you.' She hurried towards her, her hazel eyes shining with delight to see her closest friend.

Coral was wearing a pale pink dress and her blond hair spilled over her shoulders in glistening waves. When Lucy hugged her she smelled of scented soap.

'I called on your Aunt Dora and she told me you'd gone away for a while.'

'That's right. I didn't arrive back in London until yesterday. I couldn't wait to come and see you.'

Coral took her hand and together they went to her dressing room where she poured them both a glass of chilled wine. They sank into overstuffed chairs and drank it, talking over old times and the current production.

'Have you seen Jack, Coral?' Lucy asked, keen to know what had become of her former beau.

'Not lately.' A concerned look entered her eyes. 'He's gone to Bath for Christmas. I think he's found someone else, love. Do you mind?'

Lucy shook her head. 'No. He was never known to be faithful to one woman for long. It would never have worked between us. I hope he's happy. And how is Jamie? Still writing his plays?'

Coral nodded, looking awfully pleased. 'He's finally got someone interested in his latest and even got backers to finance it. I've read it and I have to say it's very good—full of wit and verve. He's over the moon about it. We both are.'

'I'm so happy, Coral. Jamie is extremely talented. I had every faith in him.'

'What about you, Lucy? Where have you been?'

'In Portugal—with Nathan.'

Coral's eyes opened wide in amazement. 'Nathan? Nathan Rochefort?'

'Yes. It's all very complicated, Coral.' She had

told Coral the whole story about Nathan and she had been intrigued. She was the only person she had dared confide in after the break up, but she needed to talk to someone about it and knew she could trust Coral completely.

'Are you back together?'

'No,' she answered quietly. 'Four years ago I made a terrible mistake, Coral. I thought Nathan and Katherine...' She bit her lip to stop it trembling. 'Well, you know all about that. It turns out that I was wrong and he finds it difficult to trust me again.' She told her of the assignment and why Nathan had needed her help. What she didn't tell her was about the baby. Giving herself a gentle shake, she smiled. 'But enough of that. I'm back now and I've put all that behind me.'

Coral didn't believe her. 'I think spending all that time with Nathan has reawakened all the old feelings you had for him.'

Lucy sighed, putting her empty glass down. 'I never could hide things from you, Coral. I can't deny it, but it's over. Now,' she said, helping herself to more wine, 'how's the play going? Are you enjoying playing Portia?'

'Oh, yes. Mr Portas is pleased with my performance and the audience appear to be. At least

they didn't throw stones at me on opening night,'
she said, laughing. 'But what of you? Are you returning to the stage?'

'I don't know. I don't know what I'm going
to do. I thought I might go away for a while—
maybe do some travelling with a theatre group,
but I'm in no hurry. I'm just glad to be home
again and spending time with Aunt Dora.'

'Then I see no reason why you can't attend
the party tomorrow night to celebrate Jamie's
good fortune—here at the theatre after the show.
After much persuasion Mr Portas has agreed to
a private party for cast, crew, friends and journalists—the latter never averse to free food and
drink as you know. You will enjoy it, Lucy—
with all your old friends—and maybe a few of
your admirers,' she said with a twinkle in her
eye. 'What do you say?'

Indeed, Lucy thought, what could she say?
She wasn't in any mood for a party, but Coral
wouldn't take no for an answer. With a sigh of
resignation she nodded. Perhaps a party was just
what she needed to take her mind off Nathan.

Chapter Eleven

The noise and chatter grew less as every one of the hundred or more guests—mostly theatrical folk—who crowded on to the stage turned in the direction of Lucy's entrance. There had been much talk when she had disappeared from the London stage and reappeared so suddenly. Now curiosity was matched by envy from the ladies and open admiration from the gentlemen, as Lucy, swathed in a shimmer of crimson satin, the high waist successfully hiding any signs of her pregnancy, stood beside Coral. Her glowing chestnut hair was upswept in an in a delightful elaboration of soft curls.

'How do I look?' Lucy asked, feeling nervous amongst all these people, although why she should be she had no idea. Many of them were friends and acquaintances of long standing.

'Absolutely stunning,' Coral told her. 'Not many women could carry off a gown that bold. You do it with flair, love, so make the most of it. See how pleased everyone is to see you. Enjoy yourself.'

A group of musicians in the pit in front of the stage played a lively country dance and people stepped back as couples took to the floor. There was a crush of people around Lucy and she found herself being vivacious and charming to a coterie of young gentlemen and a pack of journalists from Fleet Street all wanting to know where she had been hiding herself for the past three months.

Without committing herself she moved on, hearing voices telling her it was nice to have her back. She made herself smile back at them, but her heart wasn't in it. She knew she should be pleased that they were glad to see her, yet she did not feel it. Her head ached and the taste of anger was in her mouth, though she could not have said who she was angry with. And yet the candlelit theatre filled her with an admiration which her pride forbade her to show. It was a long way from Portugal and the war.

She was only too aware of herself and the enormous power of her attraction over the men. After all those dangerous weeks in Portugal, coupled with the dreadful experience of killing a man and Nathan's indifference to her, she emerged like some exotically beautiful butterfly, and stood up better than she had expected to the rigours of that night, determined that no one would ever guess at her condition or how unhappy she was.

Oblivious to everything that was going on around him, Nathan watched her from across the crowded stage as she smiled and laughed with a group of admiring swains, all vying for her attention. People gave him curious looks, but his mind was occupied with the proposal he intended to make to Lucy. A breathtaking vision in crimson, she was too exquisite to be flesh and blood—too regal and aloof to have ever let him touch her. He drew a long, strangled breath and realised he hadn't been breathing as he watched her.

They had wanted each other from that first moment they had laid eyes on each other. She was passionate and courageous, quick to anger and forgive. She was serene and regal amongst her friends, jaunty and skilful with a pistol in her hands, passionate and sweet in his arms. She was all of that, and much more.

And he loved her.

As if she sensed his eyes on her, she turned and looked directly at him, their eyes meeting and locking.

Unable to understand what he was doing at the theatre, Lucy watched as a slow, lazy smile crept across his face and he started towards her. Suffused with trepidation and a familiar ache in her breast, she waited for him to reach her. He was taller than any other man present, with powerful shoulders and long, muscular legs. Instead of wearing the bright satin clothes the other men wore he was clad in raven black from head to foot, with the exception of his snowy shirt and neckcloth, which were so white they seemed to gleam against the stark black of his jacket and waistcoat.

Lucy had the thought that he was like a large, predatory hawk in the midst of a gathering of tame, colourful peacocks. Taking her hand, he raised it and touched her fingers with his lips, all the while holding her eyes captive.

'Nathan! Forgive me if I appear surprised. I didn't expect to see you here.' The roguish smile he gave her made her heart somersault with incredulous joy.

'No, of course you didn't. I called at the house, hoping to see you. Your aunt told me where I could find you.'

'I see. I—I didn't expect to see you so soon'— *if at all*, she thought. 'How is Katherine? Have you seen her since she moved into Londesborough House?'

Nathan nodded. Aware that they were attracting curious stares, he drew her into the shadows at the side of the stage. 'She has settled in well— and Charles, too. What she will do eventually I have no idea. I content myself knowing they are both safe. The duke is taking her to the Londesborough ancestral home in Kent for some peace and quiet shortly. She would like you to call on her before she leaves London.'

'I—I will—soon.'

'The duke would also like to express his gratitude to you in person.'

'But—there is no need. I have been paid generously for what I did.'

'He would still like to meet you. Perhaps we could go together?'

He suggested it in a voice which made Lucy think he had already convinced himself that she would accept. Her heart was suddenly uplifted. 'Yes, I would like that.'

'Then that's settled. Now, will you offer me some refreshment, or must I die of thirst?'

Lucy laughed and led him to a long trestle table laden with food and drink. 'I would like to introduce you to my friend Coral. This party is to celebrate her friend's success. He's just had his first play accepted and everyone expects it to do well.'

Nathan smiled, a bit ill at ease, but he soon relaxed. Coral took him under her wing, all friendly warmth. Impressed by his title, Mr Portas was most engaging and chatted about the war in the Peninsula and things in general. Nathan seemed to enjoy himself, but Lucy noticed a certain reserve in his manner and suspected he found the theatre crowd all rather too exuberant and outgoing for his taste.

'He's charming—and devilishly handsome,' Coral told her a while later after talking with him. 'He's also terribly well bred. I can hardly believe you were once betrothed to him.'

Lucy gazed at Nathan, still engaged in conversation with Mr Portas. 'There are times when I can't believe it myself. He's changed—more serious than he used to be. I think I might have had something to do with that—and the war in Spain.'

'I think he's positively divine, love. That voice, those eyes of his—and that scar gives him an air of mystery. He's wonderfully virile—despite that polite reserve.'

'You've noticed,' Lucy said, laughing softly at her friend's outspoken exuberance.

'So have you, love.'

Lucy sighed. 'I am human, Coral. I have noticed.'

'And?'

'And—I don't know, Coral. I have no idea why he sought me out tonight.'

'Then don't you think you should find out?'

With a wink and a smile Coral stepped away when Nathan came back to Lucy.

'I like your friends,' he said.

'Yes. I've been blessed. Everyone has been wonderful, welcoming me back.'

'I can see you've made quite a life for yourself.'

'I've worked very hard.'

'I admire that,' he said quietly.

'Why are you here, Nathan? Have you come to tell me you are going away again?'

A familiar heat flared in his groin. It shocked him to realise just how badly he still wanted her, to make love to her. Imagination only increased desire and heightened arousal. 'That depends.'

'On what?'

'On you.'

There was a moment of silence. Lucy felt ill at ease, wondering what he meant by his remark. She smoothed a lock of hair away from her cheek and asked if he would like another glass of wine, but Nathan shook his head.

'Can I drag you away from all your friends? I want to be alone with you.'

She looked up at him. 'Why?'

'Because what I have to say to you has to be said in private.' When she looked away he reached up and cupped her chin, returning her attention to him. 'You do want to be alone with me, don't you, Lucy?'

'Yes, but—' She pulled free of his grasp and glanced around, as if trying to think how to put what she wanted to say. She was very vulnerable at that moment, remembering how hurt, disillusioned and lonely she had felt when he had stepped back from her in Portugal. It would be so easy to take comfort in what he offered, but she was afraid that that would merely lead to more pain, more disillusionment, far worse than what she had felt before.

'You're afraid,' he said, reading her mind.

'Yes,' she admitted.

'I would never hurt you, Lucy.'

'Not intentionally,' she said.

'I want to give you the world.'

'I don't want the world,' she told him. 'I don't want a title and riches. Those things are not important to me.'

'You're all that matters to me,' he said.

She looked at him and wanted desperately to believe him. 'I once told you that I loved you. Since you came back into my life and the time we have spent together, you must know that my feelings for you have not changed. Yet, you have not spoken to me about how you feel. I am confused, Nathan. I feel I do not know you any more.'

'You know me better than you realise. No one knows me better than you. No one ever will.'

She started to speak, but he forestalled her. 'Listen to me. Words can never be adequate to make you realise how much I desire you.' He put his hands on her waist and drew her close. 'I can say it with my body if you will let me.'

Lucy closed her eyes and something fluttered and softened within her. 'Don't, Nathan. Don't.'

He pushed his advantage. 'You desire me, too. I remember the night we spent in the cave.' He pulled her closer just a little. 'Have you forgotten that?'

'I haven't,' she answered in a fierce whisper.

'Nor have I. On the night of the storm, I saw you only in the dimness of the moonlight. When we make love again I am going to light all the candles I can find. I am going to see you while we make love,' he promised, eager to see the perfect curves of her breasts and hips, to see the tapering length of her legs and the expression on her face as they came together. 'Come with me now, Lucy, away from here. If you want me as much as I want you, spend the remainder of the night with me.' He brushed the backs of his fingers over her flushed cheek. 'I want you more than I have ever wanted anything in my life.'

Taking a deep, shuddering breath she looked into his eyes. 'And you are certain of that, are you, Nathan?'

'Yes.'

That was all she needed to hear. Time enough later to learn why he had changed his mind. Just now, she did not care. He was gazing at her and his face was shadowed. She stared at him in a charmed, relishing silence, then she nodded. 'I'll just say goodnight to Coral and get my cloak.'

He helped her into it and they went outside and climbed into his coach. Seated across from each other, they didn't speak as they left the theatre behind. Moonlight brushed the stones on the road with pale silver and the buildings were a dim mass shrouded with velvety black shadows.

'Where are we going?' Lucy asked as they passed through London's suburbs. 'We appear to be heading out of town.'

'Don't worry. We'll soon be there.'

When the carriage eventually passed through some tall gates and swayed gently along the curving drive bordered with wide sweeping lawns, Lucy recognised the large private residence immediately. An immense expanse of mullioned windows was aglow with lights.

'Why, this is where you brought me when you taught me to ride.' She leaned forward for a better look, straining her eyes in the darkness.

'That's right.'

'I recall you telling me it belonged to a relative of yours.'

'It did. My uncle. Unfortunately he did not enjoy the best of health and died while I was in Portugal. Wilmslow House and his estate now belongs to me—I am his heir, you see, Lucy.'

She stared at him with amazement. 'Goodness! How very grand! Does a title go with it?'

'Indeed it does. Welcome to my home,' he said as the coach halted at the bottom of a wide flight of stone steps leading up to the carved-oak double doors.

Flinging them open, he drew Lucy inside. When the butler came he explained that he would not be needing anything further until morning. The butler departed, with only one quick glance at the hooded woman by his side.

'Come with me.' Taking her hand, Nathan led Lucy across the hall.

Together they ascended the curving marble staircase and he led her to a splendid suite of rooms decorated in subtle shades of green. He turned the key in the lock. At last, he thought, drawing in a deep breath, then letting it out slowly. At last they were alone.

Lucy pushed back the hood of her cloak and

walked to the fire, holding her hands out to its
warmth. Nathan studied her bathed in the soft
light. He was reminded of the first moment he
had ever seen her, for she looked much the same
now as she had then—a little older, of course,
a beautiful, mature and very desirable woman.
Tonight, all he wanted was to show her what he
felt when he looked at her. Arousal was coursing through his body and he longed to take her
to bed, but the next few hours were not for him.
They were for her.

Lucy was aware of him when he stood behind
her. She turned, her breath catching a little as
his gaze bored into her. She was aware of how
warm and close the room had become and she let
her cloak fall. He was still gazing at her, and his
face was shadowed, for he'd turned away from
the fireplace. She took a tentative step forwards.

'Nathan.'

He came quickly to her, taking her into his
arms. She rested her head against his shoulder.
His arms were warm and strong, and she relaxed.

'Lucy,' he murmured and bent his head down.
She raised her face. Their lips met and she caught
her breath sharply. Then her mouth opened under
the pressure of his. His tongue slid in, gently

exploring. Sighing softly, she slipped her arms around his neck and pressed herself closer, feeling the nearness of him. He reached up with one hand to stroke her face, and the fleeting touch sent shivers down her spine.

Nathan looked at her. Her eyes were closed, but he kept his open, for he wanted to see every nuance of feeling he could pull out of her with his hands and his mouth. He slid his hands up into her hair, tangling his hands in the tresses, revelling in the feel of it, warm and satiny between his fingers.

She made a tiny, smothered sound of desire and wrapped her arms around his neck, pressing her body closer to his and igniting his raw hungry need to be inside her, the need he was striving to keep at bay.

'Nathan…' She stopped.

He smiled down at her and ran a fingertip lightly down her cheek, tracing the line of her jaw. 'No words are necessary,' he murmured, his lips against hers. 'Time enough for talking later.'

They kissed again. His kisses were strong and sweet, and she returned them with a fervour she had forgotten she had ever possessed. It was as if they had never been parted, as if they had always been together, sharing their days and nights. His hands slid down to her waist. He wanted her out of all these clothes, but he forced himself to wait, containing his moves until her body told his the next one to make. Thankfully he didn't have long to wait.

When she was quivering in his hold and she could hear the fierce pounding of his heart, she raised her eyes to him. 'Take me to bed, Nathan. I want your love again.'

A slow grin curved his lips and his eyes burned down into hers. 'Anything my lady desires,' he said softly and in one fluid motion picked her up and took her to his bed.

He knelt before her and gently disrobed her, his hands lingering as he removed her chemise, brushing her shoulders and hips, and as each layer of clothing was removed Lucy could feel her skin tingling.

When she was at last naked, his gaze swept over her, absorbing every detail of her body, and he smiled. 'You're still as lovely as ever. More so.'

'You'd best get undressed if you're to make love to me.'

'I suppose I should,' he said, his voice marked

with humour, and he proceeded to remove his clothes.

When he, too, was naked, Lucy gazed at him, at the taut muscles, strong arms and legs, the jutting manhood that bespoke his passion for her.

Pulling her down beside him on the bed, they kissed and clung to one another. His hands, tenderly touching, caressed her body, squeezing, encircling her breasts, then spreading and caressing her thighs, creating a tingle that spread through her, in her blood, in her bones, a delicious, delectable torture that grew and grew until she could feel a warm fountain within, brimming, soon to brim over as she drowned in a flood of pleasure.

Everything about what they were doing felt right. So long they had been apart. So long she had missed him and wanted him. Closing her eyes, she drifted in a blissful void, reeling, drifting, floating far away. His hands were all over her, opening her to incredible pleasure, and then he moved and his weight pinioned her and then slowly, slowly he became a part of her and she felt the joy and wonder of it in her heart.

Nothing she felt was suppressed or hidden from him now. As they twisted and rolled across the sheets, rocking together, locked as one for all time, she clung to him and he to her, and there was exquisite joy in every plane and curve of her face as she let out a soft moan of feminine ecstasy.

Assailed by waves of lust and passion, thrusting her higher and higher to those dizzying heights that made her ache and burn with an ardour she had only ever felt in his arms, Nathan continued to bring her to ecstasy. The feel of her surrounding him was so exquisite that all his good intentions went straight to hell. He heard his own visceral groans as he felt the tension within him rising, thickening until it was unbearable. It was impossible to be gentle now or hold back. His own passion was finally unleashed, the sensations exploding inside him with flash and heat.

Afterwards, breathing heavily, he stilled on top of her, his hands sliding beneath her back. He watched as her breathing returned to normal and she opened her eyes. Smiling, he bent to kiss her swollen lips and she ran her tongue provocatively against his.

'I've missed you, my darling,' he murmured, his fingers stroking the soft planes of her face.

'Have you?'

'These past years have been hellish. I remember how beautiful you were that first time I saw you.'

'You told me. I never believed you. I keep remembering that gawky adolescent girl I was then.'

'You were beautiful back then, Lucy. You were the most captivating young woman I had ever seen, gentle and graceful and totally unaware of your beauty.'

'And now?'

'You're even lovelier than ever,' he said.

'You just want to sleep with me,' she accused.

'You're right about that,' he said and laughed, the sound ringing through the room. He rolled on to his back, taking her with him.

Her face hovered above his and he kissed her, the intensity of their kisses increasing, their passion blossoming once more, and again they were as one.

It was long into the night before their bodies finally succumbed to the dreamy, languid aftermath of complete and repeated consummation. Lucy was the first to wake, and gave a long contented sigh as she watched Nathan sleep beside her. Leaning forwards, she touched his lips with hers. Without opening his eyes he gently kissed her back.

'I'm not asleep,' he said softly, and rolled on to his side to prop his head up with one hand.

'I'm glad. You have made me so happy, but I think we should talk for a while. I—didn't realise you wanted me so much.'

She suddenly found herself in a fierce embrace as Nathan wrapped his arms around her and drew her close. 'Want you! Of course I want you, you wonderful, brave and incredibly beautiful woman.' He breathed against her hair. 'How could you think that?'

Lucy's breath caught in her throat. 'You—never said so.'

'I apologise, my darling.' Sighing, he raised his hand to stroke her hair with a possessive gentleness. 'Do you know how many times throughout the weeks we were together I've thanked God you were there—by my side? Doubtless you saved my life. You kept your head, when other women would have recoiled from doing what you did.'

She shuddered in his embrace. 'I did what I had to do. I couldn't let Gameau kill you.'

'And I thank you for it, Lucy.'

Hearing the sincerity in his voice, Lucy drew back to search his face. Candlelight highlighted his thick hair with gold and increased the sharp clarity of his eyes, making it impossible for her to deny the love she saw there. She took a steadying breath, daring to believe. 'There were times on our journey together when I thought that I had lost you.'

'I'll be honest with you, Lucy. When I embarked on the assignment, it was no different to any other—only I had you by my side. I knew there must be no divided loyalties to weaken my resolve, so I vowed not to touch you, to override any temptation I might have to feel those emotions that had set my blood afire in the past.'

'And you failed,' she said quietly.

'Miserably. It is in my character to be strong, but what is honour compared to a woman's love—to your love, Lucy. I am only human. When Katherine told me you intended to go away when you reached London, I was mortified. I couldn't bear to lose you all over again.'

'Then you shouldn't have held yourself from me.'

'No, I realise that now. I should tell you that the Duke of Londesborough has given an account of what you have done for his family to the newspapers. With your success riding high, there must have been speculation when you disappeared from the theatre scene so suddenly. When they read what you did in Portugal, your popularity will be restored. In fact, I can imagine every theatre manager will be clamouring to have you as their leading lady.'

Speechless, Lucy stared at him. She could hardly think straight for the thoughts tumbling through her mind.

'Of course I hope you will refuse the lot of them,' he went on softly.

'Why, Nathan?' Her tone was suspicious, her eyes wary.

He was smiling now. 'Don't worry. I wasn't thinking of asking you to accompany me on another assignment.'

'Then what?'

'Marry me, Lucy,' he said softly.

She stared at him, unable to believe the words he had spoken. 'You—you want me to be your wife?' she whispered.

'Absolutely. I was mad ever to let you go. For many months I hated you with a bitterness that corroded my life and I was quite determined to put you out of it. I was resolute that when I had done in Spain I would marry and that Lucy Lane would soon become nothing to me.' He smiled as though in disbelief at the very idea, shaking his head at his own foolishness. 'But of course I couldn't forget you. Love is not something that can be turned on and off like a tap.'

'And now?'

'Now I want to talk to you about the future.'

'A future together?'

He nodded. 'You are mine, Lucy,' he said with great gravity. 'Marry me. Be my lady. You won't be sorry, I promise you. I love you—I've never stopped loving you. I want to marry you—and this time there will be no backing out. Come, what do you say?'

'You love me?'

'I do. Very much. And this time I fully intend that we make it to the altar.' He lifted one dark brow, an amused glint in his eye. 'Are you going to argue with me, Lucy?'

She opened her mouth, then shut it, then smiled slowly. 'And if I am?'

'Then for God's sake answer the question first and then kiss me,' he said, dragging her into his arms and tilting her face to his. 'I promise you

I shall banish all thought of argument from your mind.'

There was a glow in his eyes as he looked at her, then they blazed suddenly with their old vivid light. She breathed deeply, then smiled at him, painfully. Feelings rushed to her in a flood. She loved him so much. He was her destiny, her future and she had to make that absolutely clear to him right now.

'Then, yes,' she murmured, 'I will marry you, Nathan. And I love you—with all my heart. I never did stop loving you. Can you ever forgive me for what I did?'

'There's nothing to forgive, my love.'

Holding her close, he kissed her gently on the lips. When they finally drew apart, they regarded one another seriously.

'We will have to set a date for the wedding. When would you like it to be?'

'Soon,' she whispered, her cheeks flushing a becoming pink.

'I'm glad you said that. I have no wish to wait.'

'Neither do I—but there is another reason why...' To her horror, her voice gave way completely.

Nathan looked at her closely, a frown drawing

his brows together. 'You have something to tell me, Lucy? You seem troubled.'

She heard the concern in his voice. Suddenly, looking at him through half-closed lashes, she felt hope dawn inside her. 'I am troubled, Nathan. It's the kind of trouble you landed me in when you took advantage of me on the night I fell into the stream. The result of that madness is—that I am with child.'

Shock registered in his face. 'A child? Good Lord! What are you talking about?'

'It's quite simple. I'm pregnant with your child.'

She heard his quick intake of breath. 'Why did you not tell me before?'

'I didn't tell you because everything was against it.' There was the faintest glimmer of tears in her eyes and all at once it came flooding out, all the fears and the anxieties she had lived with since she had become aware of her condition. 'It was plain to me that you took me in a moment of weakness. I knew if I told you that you would offer marriage only because you would see that honour be satisfied. I wanted to know that it is me you want, Nathan—not for the sake of a child.'

It was quiet and the silence bit keenly into her

nerves. Nathan rolled on to his back and stared into the distance.

'You have suffered all this—alone,' he said at length. 'You should have been honest with me. You should have told me.'

'Please, Nathan, I beg you to understand why I didn't. But I'm glad you know,' Propping herself up on her elbow, she leaned over him. Her eyes found his and she spoke frankly once more, with much relief that someone else knew at last. 'Our child needs a father, a strong man he or she can admire and trust.'

Nathan shoved himself up, his gaze travelling to the gentle swelling becoming visible in her abdomen, his expression holding a rare look of softness and pleasure. Raising his eyes, he looked at her, admiration and respect mirrored in the blueness of his gaze, a look he had never given any other woman.

'You have me, my darling, and pierced me at my weakest spot—you and our unborn child. I am indeed blessed.'

Lucy stared at him, aware of a startling triumph that she had hardly dared to expect, but also aware of how closely it had trembled in the balance. She sighed suddenly as though she had dropped an enormous, invisible load. She saw him through a curtain of unshed tears and felt his warm, strong hands cup her face.

'I don't know what to say,' she said, 'except that you are truly the most remarkable of men—and to make me your wife after all this time, time we have lost because of a terrible misunderstanding, is the most remarkable thing of all.'

'Hush,' he said, smoothing the hair from her brow. 'We are together now. That is what matters.'

Then his lips were on hers. He was wide and solid, with a strength that wrapped her with a satisfying reassurance. All she was aware of was heat, a blaze of power, the pressure of hard muscles in a strong body, a complete blending of passion and tenderness. Then she drew back as a sudden thought occurred to her.

'You never did tell me what you were doing at Katherine's house that day. I saw you embrace on her doorstep. She looked flushed—and you kissed her.'

Nathan stared at her. 'Good Lord, Lucy, you don't still think that Katherine and I...' Suddenly he started laughing and pulled her into his arms. 'You foolish, foolish girl. We were engaged in something far more innocent than an affair. Not only were we to marry, my love, but if you recall you were also approaching your twentieth birthday. We could not let it pass unnoticed and were planning a surprise party to celebrate the event on the river. If our movements appeared suspicious, then I am truly sorry. I never thought you would misunderstand.'

Lucy stared at him in disbelief. Never had she felt so foolish in her life. 'A party? Oh…I should never have jumped to conclusions, I can see that now.'

'No, you shouldn't. Had you given it some thought before disappearing with some travelling theatre company, you would have known Katherine and I were not in the least attracted to one another. Besides, as you know, her affections were directed elsewhere.'

'I didn't realise how much until we spoke recently. Poor Katherine. Two husbands—both killed in war.' She caught back a sob and took a deep breath to hold back her tears. 'Oh, Nathan.' She threw her arms around his neck. 'Will you forgive me for being so blind and so stupid—and so proud?'

'My darling…' he chuckled '…you have added spice to my life that I would have found with no one else. How can I be angry with you for anything? I can only count myself fortunate that you share my life and will continue to do so until we are old and grey.'

'It is my plan, my lord,' she whispered against his lips, 'and my most heartfelt wish, for I do love you. I have always loved you, yet what I feel now is so much stronger and deeper than what I felt before. We will marry soon, won't we? I couldn't bear it if I had to wait.'

'Soon, my love. I promise.'

And they did marry, one week later by special licence, and during the late summer, their son was born.

When he was placed in Nathan's arms, Nathan was speechless. He stared down at his son and could not for the life of him speak the words to express his joy. He looked at his wife who was smiling at him, well content, and his voice was husky with emotion when he spoke.

'This is more than we ever dreamed, Lucy. Who would have thought it?'

'Much my own thoughts, my darling.'
Their eyes met and their love glowed in unspoken communication.

* * * * *